ABDUCTED

Edited by Maddy Leary
Book Design and Layout by Rob Carroll
Cover Design by Rob Carroll

Library of Congress Control Number: 2025944425

ISBN 978-1-958598-37-5 (paperback)
ISBN 978-1-958598-76-4 (ebook)

darkmatter-ink.com

ABDUCTED

PATRICK BARB

ABDUCTED

PATRICK BARB

PRAISE FOR ABDUCTED

"*Abducted* is multifaceted, surreal, and weird in the best way. With hints of an absurdist tone, it explores the desperation of human nature and the way we convince our minds of both dangerous truths and untruths. Barb weaves a tale akin to true crime shows, meditating on the power of grief and loss and the way trauma might change us both physically and psychologically. For fans of *Parasyte: The Grey* and *NOPE*—this unsettling and uncanny story will have readers gasping for breath on every page."

—Ai Jiang, Bram Stoker and Nebula Award-winning
author of *Linghun*

"In *Abducted,* Patrick Barb takes what is best in investigative, conspiracy-riddled science fiction and grabs the reader with a page-turning and dreadful journey deep into the most obnoxious things both humans and non-humans can do. An extremely recommended read for fans of supernatural horror, sci-fi, and the weird mysteries life sometimes throws at us."

—Renan Bernardo, Nebula Award finalist and author of
Disgraced Return of the Kap's Needle

"Compelling mysteries, gritty police detective work, terrifying adversaries, and otherworldly places—*Abducted* has it all. A must-read for fans of alien horror."

—Stephen S. Schreffler, author of *The Bleed*

"Patrick Barb has crafted a deeply unsettling and visceral entry into the alien abduction horror genre. Full of mystery and twists, *Abducted* keeps you guessing and pulls no punches."

—Jendia Gammon, Nebula and BSFA finalist author of
Atacama and *Doomflower*

To Grant and Avery,
Never stop telling your stories.

PROLOGUE

1988

SIBLINGS STACY AND Xavier Keppler are up too late, downing can after can of Milwaukee's Best while watching reruns of the old In Search of... show starring Leonard Nimoy. Or, more precisely, "Leonard Nimoy and his sideburns," as Stacy likes to describe it, teasing her nerdy younger brother while being just as big of a dork herself in her enjoyment of all the pseudoscience and space mysteries and so-called "unexplained phenomena" covered by Mr. Spock on the show. Crushing yet another can under her foot against the linoleum of her parent's kitchen floor and having already lost count of how many cans she's downed, Stacy's finding it funnier and funnier. "It," in this case, being her brother's mild annoyance and the possibility it might escalate to full-blown irritation.

After dropping the crushed can into the garbage, Stacy pulls open the pickle-green fridge that their folks have had since the seventies when they were newlyweds. Swaying on her feet a little, she brushes ringlets of her permed hair behind her ears on either side of her head and then fishes out two more cans of the Beast.

She carries the beers back to the living room and drops one on her brother's lap before settling down at the other end of the couch to pop hers open.

"Mom and Pop are gonna be P.O.ed at you for drinking so many beers," Xavier says, even as he's opening his next beer and taking a deep swig from it afterwards. He's sixteen to his sister's twenty-two, a six-year gap that both siblings have managed to navigate fairly well. They figure one of them has to be the "mistake"—either Stacy, born too early, or Xavier, born too late.

Of course, their parents won't say anything one way or the other.

"What," Stacy asks, reaching across the couch to tousle her baby brother's hair, "are you gonna narc on me?"

The jostling is just hard enough that Xavier's beer-holding hand slips. A bit of foam sloshes from the open mouth of the can and onto his shirt.

"Shit!" he says, leaping up from his seat.

Stacy puts a finger to her lips, shushing in exaggerated fashion.

Seeming to have recovered quickly from the spill, her brother turns to her and rolls his eyes. Flips her the bird with his free hand for good measure.

On TV, they're showing grainy video footage of what's purported to be a Bigfoot sighting. When Xavier's settled back on the couch, Stacy nods to the screen and the blurry apelike (or ape-costume-like) shape there. "You believe in that stuff?"

Xavier shakes his head fast. Not even willing to entertain the notion. "Nah," he says. "There're a lot of monsters out there without us needing to make up boogeymen."

Wise words from a pimply teenager, Stacy thinks. She nods, partially in agreement and partially because she's a little too buzzed to do much more than that.

Finally, words come, and she swings the conversation in a completely different direction. "You think Mom and Pop will be home soon?"

Xavier shrugs.

"Do you think we, uh, we should have gone out there with 'em? To help search for that girl?" Stacy asks.

The girl is Jennifer Ervin, a former high school classmate of Stacy's. Never a friend, maybe a passing acquaintance at best.

This Jennifer had been one of those classic post-high-school failure stories. Teen pregnancy her junior year and then just as suddenly *not* pregnant, with whispers aplenty in the hallways and at the lockers. Then, there was the dropping out—or maybe the dropping out came before the whole not-being-pregnant-anymore thing happened. Then, the usual after-school special of drugs and drinking and homelessness. And then, when she was apparently getting her life back together? *Poof!* No more Jennifer.

Mr. and Mrs. Keppler, or Mom and Pop as they were known to Stacy and Xavier, had been out almost every night helping sweep the parks, the fields, and the sketchier areas of downtown, all in an effort to find this Jennifer Ervin, the girl who'd gone from cautionary tale to redemption story to tragedy-in-the-making.

"Why, Mom? Why do you do it?" Stacy recalls asking.

And there was her mother, bundled up for the snowy, windy weather outside, shaking her head and answering: "Given the choice, what else can you do except try to do the right thing?"

"Why's Bigfoot blue?'

The question from her little brother is the last thing Stacy expected to hear. But what he's asking certainly reflects what they're seeing on the TV screen. Buzzed as they are, it takes the Keppler siblings a moment to realize the swirling, royal blue lights aren't intended to form halos around the heads of Sasquatch and Nimoy alike, but that they're coming from outside. From their driveway.

It's that driveway where their parents are due to return in their minivan any minute now.

Any minute now… Stacy thinks.

Somehow, the noise from outside—the opening and slamming closed of patrol car doors, the slap and crunch of black-leather uniform-grade boots up the walkway, and the single pounding fist against the door—is drawn out to infinite lengths.

Somehow in that brief forever, Stacy's able to see the future. Her dreams of a career in academia cast aside. Her little brother broken, shattered at the moment before adulthood. And Mom and Pop? Their part in this future, or rather, their perceived *lack* of a part, is something that Stacy has no interest in confronting.

Xavier's at the side window in their living room. With the curtain pushed aside, he's got a perfect view of the pitch-black night sky.

He speaks like he's in some sort of dreamspace, like his mind's already doing the heavy lifting, preparing itself for what's coming.

"There's some guy outside," he says. "Big. Bald. He looks like the Moon. Like the Moon bleeding black rivers down its face."

Stacy wants to respond, but can't find the words. Doesn't even know what the right words would be. It's as if she's in one of those nightmares where everyone has their parts and she's forgotten her lines. She wants to tell her baby brother that everything is going to be okay.

Instead, she finally answers the door, and the future barges in, whether she wants it to or not.

SEARCH PARTY FOR MISSING YOUNG WOMAN KILLED IN ANIMAL ATTACK

(Excerpt)

Tragedy compounds on tragedy as the city of Herenton, Virginia, is in a state of shock and mourning following the late-night discovery of the bodies of four volunteers who were taking part in a search for a missing young woman from the area. At approximately midnight, police were alerted to a creek in the wooded area outside Herenton, an area currently being patrolled by police and volunteers as part of the ongoing investigation/search for missing twenty-three-year-old Jennifer Ervin. There, the bodies of four volunteers were found mauled and mutilated in what the authorities are calling "an animal attack."

Among the dead are Kevin and Stephanie Keppler, long-time residents, who leave behind two children...

2005

EVERY TIME STACY Keppler watches the home-video footage provided by the family, the images on the screen remain the same. The only difference, the X factor with each viewing, is her—the watcher. She changes whenever she hits play, every time she rewinds or fast-forwards the tape, when she slows things down to examine the footage frame by frame, or when she speeds it up.

The children appear on-screen, forever six and nine, as captured by their mother and her digital camcorder. Relegated to an off-screen role for the most part, Ruth Freeman still gets the first word with every replay.

"Matt! Matty! Matt! Wanna answer some questions for Mommy, buddy?"

She's talking to her youngest child, Matty Freeman. Six years old. Then, now, and possibly forever. With ruddy-colored kinky hair, deeply tanned skin, and emerald eyes, he's a melting pot in OshKosh B'gosh. He stares into the camera without pretense.

"Okay, Mommy!"

Like it's just that easy.

"Can you tell me how old you are, darlin'?" Ruth asks, her Southern Virginia drawl coming through behind the camera.

"Thix!"

The boy's lisping answer comes right on the heels of his mother's query.

A young girl's laughter follows from off-camera. Young Matty tilts his head to the side, distracted.

Ruth raises her voice, trying to recapture his attention. "No, honey, it's 'six.' S-I... Look at Mommy, honey!"

The footage stops at that point. A break in the recording. It picks up a split second later. The lens dips, revealing what Ruth's carrying in her other hand.

She presents a waffle cone with a big scoop of vanilla ice cream on top. Matty's eyes focus on a bead of melted white cream dripping from the cone and rolling over Ruth's knuckle.

"Here you go, look what Mommy's got for you."

The boy follows this direction well.

Another cut. When the footage resumes, the camera pushes close on Matty's face, which sports a ring of off-white around his pink, full lips that could double for an old man's goatee.

"You really like ice cream. Don't you, Matty?" Ruth's tone is as sugary-sweet as the treat smeared across her boy's face.

He can't verbalize his appreciation, instead settling for lips pressed together and a groan of youthful delight.

Stacy plays that "Mmmmm" back, over and over. She tries to pick apart the layers of sound, hoping to find a clip she can replay to identify a secret message, something trapped between soundwaves.

"Mommy! Mommy! Look what I can do!"

At last, the camera angle changes, and Matty's turned on his side, the grass abutting the right side of the frame and the clouds to the left. Sister Cassie makes her presence known. There's a struggle, the camera shaking, before Ruth regains control. "Mommy! Mommy! You gotta see..."

"Not now, Cass. I'm with your brother."

Stacy doesn't think young Matty appears too bothered by the interruption. Whether on his side or right-side up, he seems content with his ice cream treat. His lips smack. His expression is one of blissful contentment.

Every time she watches the tape, Stacy's overcome by melancholy. A great sadness digs its claws into her shoulders and presses her into her seat.

That's when the tape stops. That's when the static appears.

In the viewing room, Stacy is painfully aware of one fact: She's watched the last available footage of six-year-old Matty Freeman from before his abduction.

CASSIDY FREEMAN, INTERVIEW TRANSCRIPT

(*Excerpt*)

I woke up first and saw the Gray Men standing around my brother's bed, watching him sleep. I think there were three, maybe four, of them, hovering above the carpeted floor and leaning close to Matty's head on his pillow.

I say "maybe," but it was hard to count them. Of course, our room was dark 'cause it was past lights out, but that's not the only reason. Most nights, the only light we get comes from these glow-in-the-dark star and constellation stickers Mom bought and stuck on the ceiling because Matty told her he was afraid of the dark. I'm afraid too, but I never asked for anything. The stickers glow a little, but the Gray Men, they glowed even more. The stickers are neon yellow and green. But a bluish light shone from the Gray Men, falling over my little brother's body while he kept on sleeping.

Not only that, but the glowing insides of the Gray Men made this blurry effect when I tried to look at them straight on. Staring across the room, it felt like I was watching 'em through window glass when there's a thunderstorm outside. Even though it hurt my head to stare too long, I did my best to memorize as much about those…things…as I could. I thought I was dreaming. I did. I thought I was dreaming but awake at the same time, and I wanted to memorize as much of my dream as I could so I could tell Matty about it when we both woke up. I thought it was something he'd think was cool.

Their heads were bare, round, and shiny, then they got smaller toward the bottom, toward where their chins would've been if they were just people. They were shaped like birthday party balloons. Their balloon heads were too big for their bodies. Their bodies were skinny—not like a skinny person's, but like a drawing of a skinny person. Like how some kid Matty's age might draw a person. Big, round heads, with stick-figure bodies stretched out. Long, gray lines extending from the balloon head. A long body, long arms, and long legs.

The arms had hands with three, four, maybe five, fingers on the ends. All colored the same as the rest of their bodies, a bluish glowing gray. Except for the white claws that dangled at the tips of their fingers. Those were sharp—I could tell from across the room—and pointed. Like knives. They clicked and clacked together. Over and over again.

I stayed in bed, trying not to breathe too hard. Trying not to breathe at all. I didn't want them to see me. I know I should've been thinking about Matty and what was happening to him. But I was scared for myself. It took a bit before I could tell there was a pattern to the way the Gray Men clicked and clacked their nails together. I think that's how they talked.

click-clack

click-clack-clack

click-click-clack

Over and over, sometimes slower, sometimes faster.

Matty's usually a light sleeper, always waking up first even before Mommy and Daddy. I thought that the clicking and clacking would've done it. But his eyes stayed closed the whole time they were talking or whatever it is they were doing. The Gray Men heard me whimpering, though. All together, they turned their balloon heads away from Matty and focused their attention on me.

Their eyes were big and black. Not glowing like the rest of their bodies. The darkness in their eyes was deep, so deep. I had to close my own eyes for a bit because I was worried I'd get dragged into the black holes of their eyes and fall through forever and ever. At first, their mouths were just raised bumps in the gray skin below their huge dark eyes. Again, like something a kid might draw.

But when I opened my eyes again, the bottoms of their faces dropped to their chests. They showed their mouths full of teeth. Rows on rows of white, just like their claws. Sharp, pointed, like a shark's. Like some monster shark.

They didn't move toward me. Didn't say anything. Didn't click or clack their claws. When they were looking at me, though, it made me feel sick. Not throw-up, tummy-ache sick, but like I wanted to die. Like that was the best thing in the world I could imagine. To be dead. To...not be.

But before I could do anything else, they looked away and focused on Matty again. That's when I noticed he was floating. A couple inches off his bed, then more. Then, he was wrapped in a blur of too-skinny, bluish-gray, glowing Gray Men parts, and I couldn't tell where they began or he ended.

I couldn't keep quiet. I wanted to, though. I wanted to pull the comforter over my head and fall asleep because I didn't want the Gray Men to look at me again. But it was my brother. My little brother. I yelled, trying to get him to wake him up.

"Matty!"

Then, once more.

"Matty!"

He opened his eyes. I think he opened his eyes. The Gray Men and him moved to the center of the room, heading for our window. The light grew brighter as a result, making it hard to be sure of anything I was seeing. It all came back washed out and blue.

But I want to say Matty saw me. He was being carried away, but he must've seen me. I called to him. I really hope he saw me and knew that I wanted to help him.

It was too late though. Too late to do anything. They moved out the window. Through the window. Not climbed out, nothing where I could tell you how they did it. More like they folded themselves and Matty up and slid out like a piece of paper tucked under a closed door.

Once they left, once the glowing was emptied from the room, I could move again.

I got out of bed as quick as I could. The floor felt cold. Even through our carpet. I ran to the window. It was still closed. I didn't open it. I didn't close it either. I looked through the glass, out into the night.

There was a round, white, light thing above me. Right outside our window. They told me it was the Moon. Later on, when Mommy and Daddy came to our room, that's what they said. They told me it was the Moon. But…it wasn't the Moon. It was someone…something the Gray Men used. I saw it, and then it was gone. And Matty, he was gone.

I was screaming. I didn't remember starting to scream. But there I was, crying. Hitting the glass. Hard as I could with my fists. That was how Mommy and Daddy found me when they came into our room.

"Where's Matty?" they asked. "Where's Matty?"

When I stopped crying, I told them. But they didn't believe me.

No one believes me. They don't believe I saw the Gray Men. I think they're mad that I didn't help him. They look at me now like it's all my fault.

What about you?

Do you believe me?

DAY 3

STACY'S IMPRESSED—WELL, MAYBE impressed isn't quite the right word, but it's the only one she can come up with—with how a crime as heinous as child abduction lights the fires under so many of her colleague's asses. It's day three of the Matty Freeman Abduction Investigation, and the station bullpen's in war-room mode. The briefing room serves as the main hub for this all-hands-on-deck situation.

Everybody's gathered for their daily briefing. Warm, yet *tired*, bodies fill row after row of folding chairs. Uniformed officers, plain-clothes detectives, and even some desk jockeys at the ends of their careers tasked with answering phones—everyone's present. Whoever's come too late to snag a chair must settle for propping up the walls. At the front, someone's pushed two large display boards together. Info about Matty, the Freeman family, and the abduction is captured on both boards. One holds dry-erase-marker theorizing and the other features grainy printouts extracted from the home-video footage Stacy's been studying.

The TV and VCR combo, strapped with bungee cords to a tall, wheeled media tower, gets nudged out of the way. Static roars in everyone's ears. The lieutenant commissioner waits until the cart is pushed far enough to the side for one of his eager-to-please underlings to waddle up and snag it. The LTC (as he insists people in the department refer to him) wears a wrinkled dress shirt with stains from all-nighters at its armpits. His tie hangs loose around his neck. Before clearing his throat to address the gathering, he pats down wild tufts of snow-white hair.

"Alright, listen. Now that we're a few days in, I want to turn the floor over to our newly assigned lead investigator. This is someone I trust—that we should *all* trust. Stacy? Sergeant Keppler? You ready?"

Stacy hurries from the back of the meeting room.

"I'm here! I'm here!"

The LTC smiles, then brings his hands together, leading the others in a quick round of applause.

Stacy blushes at the attention.

"Thanks…LTC," she says.

All eyes are on her. She takes a deep breath and does what her mom always advised whenever she had to give a school presentation: "Just begin at the beginning and tell them everything you know."

"Okay. We all know why we're here, why we've been running twenty-four-hour patrols since we got the call from the Freemans. Matthew, 'Matt' or 'Matty,' Freeman. Son of Malek and Ruth Freeman. They've got that fancy brick house on Bobtail Drive, off Copperwood. Two-car garage with a hoop above the door. Work shed in the backyard."

As her audience's eyes glaze over, Stacy's reminded of her father's additional advice for presenting: "Plus, leave out the boring shit."

Fair point, Dad.

"Two nights ago, while the family was home and both Malek and Ruth were sleeping, Matty was taken from the bedroom he shared…shares…with his older sister, Cassidy. From what we've pieced together, the abduction took place sometime between 2330 hours that evening and 0600 hours the next day. At this point, we only have one witness to the abduction. Matty's sister, Cass. She was in the room when—"

"Excuse me! Excuse me! Missus—I mean *Sergeant* Keppler! Excuse me."

The man with the expensive suit and cheap haircut is FBI. Stacy's heard rumors of someone from the Bureau coming to "assist" with the investigation. But she didn't anticipate them arriving so soon.

But here he is, placing himself at the center of attention. He stretches, fingers interlaced and arms held above his head, before he continues. The stretching gives everyone a good look at the laminate FBI badge hanging from his neck.

"Sergeant Keppler, I don't mean to overstep," he says, with face and body language suggesting that he absolutely *does* mean that. "I've been reviewing the evidence, and the version of events as described by this so-called *witness* is far-fetched at best. Fantastical, even. Despite what you might've seen on *The X-Files*, the Federal Bureau of Investigation does *not* work in fantasy. And I doubt your department wishes to either. We're here to expose the boogeymen, not believe in them. Right?"

The LTC nods. Under her feigned calm demeanor, Stacy's pulse races. She bites her lip.

The agent doesn't notice. "But please, by all means…" He pauses, clearly enjoying the chance to put the detective in her place. "…go on believing the overactive imagination of a nine-year-old *girl*."

Inside, Stacy curses the mansplaining prick and imagines jabbing her finger against his FBI badge, asking just *who the fuck* he thinks he is.

In reality, she shuffles to the side, ceding the floor to the agent.

"You wanna solve this case? You wanna bring that little boy home safe and sound?" he asks the crowd.

Stacy watches him get the rousing moment she imagined for herself. And, worst of all, she hates how good at it he seems, how well-suited for the role. So when the FBI prick says, "It's time we got out there and put in some real work. Shoe-leather work. Investigate. Find the boy," Stacy nods along, same as everyone else.

"You heard the man, folks," the LTC says. "Let's bring the Freemans their son home, safe and sound. Dismissed!"

THE MEETING ROOM'S nearly empty. Its previous occupants are on patrol with flashlights and bloodhounds, questioning persons of interest, applying higher levels scrutiny to anyone who appears shifty, untrustworthy, or otherwise *off* found in the vicinity of the Freeman home. That's all well and good as far as Stacy's concerned. The crowds, the attention—she's decided it's not what she wants from police work. *That's not what matters*, she thinks, repeating the words over and over, like a mantra.

For Stacy, what matters the most is what's queued up on the VCR. She's popped out the ice-cream-eating footage. In its place, a very different recording plays, though one still very much investigation-related.

The black-and-white footage comes from a tiny camera nestled in the upper corner of an interview room at the station. Its bird's-eye view gives Stacy the feeling of looking at the scene through the eyes of God. It's a strange notion, but one she can't shake loose.

On-screen, nine-year-old Cass Freeman sits at a metal table, its surface dulled and dented silver. Her feet *almost* touch the floor. Her eyes are big, even under thick curls that fall across her forehead.

"You comin', Sarge?" the LTC asks, leaning in from the hallway.

"Be there in a minute, LTC. Wanna finish reviewing some stuff first."

The LTC leaves her to it, heading to his office. As he does, he calls to Stacy. "Don't take too long," he says. "Zamuda's riding with you. Think he's almost done on the shitter, too!"

Stacy gives a quick thumbs-up, acknowledging her crudely delivered ride-along assignment. She wrinkles her nose as well, playing the role of the disgusted female officer saddled with a fat, flatulent male counterpart.

But Zamuda's not that bad once you get to know him.

Finally alone, she presses play on the VCR.

The first thing she hears on the playback is her own voice.

"Hello?"

On the screen: Cass Freeman's legs dangle below the hard-backed plastic chair.

"Hi, Cassidy. I'm Detective Keppler. You can call me that, or you can call me Stacy. Whichever you like."

The girl nods, then adds, "I'm Cass. Just Cass."

There's a moment on the tape when Stacy sees herself reflected in the girl's big, wet eyes. With every rewatch, something catches in Stacy's throat, just as it did in the interview room.

"They took my brother," Cass says.

She looks away from the detective who stands with hands folded across her stomach on the other side of the table. Instead of keeping eye contact, Cass tilts her head back to regard the flickering light fixture over their heads. The dim, unreliable lighting is supposed to keep people on edge, make them more likely to slip up and reveal some truth, something they might otherwise keep hidden.

On-screen, Stacy sits down at the other side of the table. "Who did, sweetheart?" she asks. "Who took your brother?"

The answer echoes in both rooms—the interview room on tape and, days later, the meeting room where Stacy watches the replay.

"The Gray Men from the sky. They came down and took him. Up there...with them."

PART 1

RETURNS AND EXCHANGES

CHAPTER 1

STACY RUBS ASPERCREME over her knuckles and flexes her fingers in and out of fists like the nurse demonstrated at her last checkup. She glances around her office, hoping no one passing by wrinkles their noses at the scent of medicinal ointment.

And why do you give a shit? she thinks, chastising herself.

In the last few years, Sergeant Keppler hasn't been one for patrols or "shoe-leather" police work. She's focused on staying cordial with her younger peers whenever they stop by her office to pay respects, chugging reheated bullpen coffee before hopping into their city-issued patrol cars. Just as Stacy did before them.

After flexing her fingers one last time, she grabs her mouse and sweeps the cursor across her screen. The old footage from the Freeman case is digitized now, immortalized electronically for anyone to watch whenever needed. The replay disappears, taking away the nine-year-old girl's face and the fear immortalized in her eyes.

Stacy stares into her blackened monitor. The woman staring back can hardly recall the long-ago version of herself as she appears in the video. For one thing, her hair's much shorter now. Not only that, but she let it take on its natural silvery-white hue.

Lost in the past, Stacy twists her lanyard-covered police ID around and around until the black faux leather cord attached to the ID is a tightly wound ebony ball. It sits almost flush against her neck. Her cell phone pulses on her desk, offering a timely distraction. She releases the string and lets it unspool, lowering the badge down her décolletage. Before the phone buzzes again, she picks it up off her desk, checks the caller ID, and answers.

"Jeff, what is it, hon?" she asks.

Tilting her head to hold the phone between her ear and shoulder, she pushes back from the desk and rises to her feet. A box waits for her on one side of her work area, reinforced with packing tape and containing years and years of on-the-job memories. Case notes with handwriting only she can decipher, awards and commendations, and her personnel files. Her whole career in the department shrunken to fit into a cardboard cube.

Her purse is on the other side of the desk, filled with more ephemeral things. Tic Tacs, a driver's license, a billfold, and the extra phone she saves for family emergencies. Balancing her belongings, she nudges her partially opened office door wider with the toe of her shoe. Then, her fiancé breaks his silence.

"Hey, Stace," he says, his voice coming through the line louder than expected, especially given the shoddy reception inside the building. "I was calling to see how your last day's going."

Stacy smiles, but also rolls her eyes. Jeff tends to have that effect on her. Exhilaration and exasperation all at once. "That's all? You called for that, dummy?"

"Well..."

The pause from the other end strikes Stacy as odd, and unexpected to boot. Trusting her investigator's instincts, she probes further. "Jeff? What is it, hon?"

His continued silence tickles the inside of her ear. "I'm *just* getting out of the office," she says. "Can this, whatever this is, wait 'til I get home?"

Jeff's quicker to answer, coming through crisp, clear, and loud. Maybe louder than last time. "Could you *maybe* hurry up?" he asks.

Who the hell does this guy think he is?

Stacy shoves her office door open and steps into the bullpen. She exits the office with every intention of marching to her car, beelining from there to the house she shares with Jeff, and delivering her wrath upon his head. Or, at the very least, informing him of the fact that he'll be both cooking dinner *and* doing the dishes that evening.

Which is, in her opinion, *the very least he could do.*

But Stacy doesn't have to wait that long or travel that far to see her fiancé.

"Surprise!"

Scanning the overcrowded rows of desks, Stacy thinks she sees the entire precinct, or at the least those officers not on active duty, all gathered in the bullpen, awaiting her arrival. They stand below a banner wishing her "HAPPY RETIREMENT, SARGE!" in a big, black sans serif.

She steps back, contemplating a speedy retreat. The weight of her memory box and purse is suddenly staggering, pulling at her arms. When she hears a soft chuckling under the general crowd noise of the assembled revelers, Stacy knows just where to look to find the man who's exposed her to this emotional reckoning.

Jeff Brayfoyle, Stacy's Jeff, stands under her retirement banner in frayed khaki shorts and a Hawaiian shirt. His phone is still held to his ear. "Babe, do you think you could pick up some ice cream on the way home?" he asks, his voice doubled—in person and through the phone.

The bulky olive-toned mustachioed man, whose pinstriped big-and-tall suit is still too tight even though he's worn it for over a year as the newest lieutenant commissioner, leans in, speaking into Jeff's phone. "Yeah, get me a pint of Chunky Monkey," Zamuda says, sweat dripping from his brow and his hand already loosening his tie. Soon the polyblend silk will sink past his belt line.

Stacy rolls her eyes. She sets her box and purse down on the closest bullpen desk. Free of her burden, she turns two middle fingers up in the direction of her fiancé and her former partner. "Oh, shut the fuck up!" she adds.

But she can't keep up the pissed-off act for long. A smile breaks across her face as the assembled crowd crashes into her like a tsunami wave, drowning her in love and admiration.

She sprints through greetings for the preliminary well-wishers, those folks who require a handshake or even a head nod at most. Making her way through the group, Stacy catches a glimpse of her old boss, the LTC. He towers over everyone else, head and shoulders out of proportion with his dimensions as Stacy remembers them. It takes her a moment to understand she's looking at his portrait, a memento placed in *his* honor when he finally stepped down to spend more time with a growing army of grandchildren.

She doesn't imagine her retirement warrants portraiture. As far as she's concerned, the bullpen gathering is more than enough. Past the initial wave of handshaking, she stops in front of her fiancé and Zamuda. Jeff takes her hand, pulls her close, and kisses her cheek.

"Surprise!" he whispers.

She pulls away and slaps his arm. "Dick," she whispers back.

Then, she jabs a finger at the chest of her former partner. Zamuda cracks, unable to maintain even a modicum of mock shock. A wheezing laugh whistles past his lips.

"And *you*!" Stacy says. "Chunky Monkey? Hasn't the department toilet suffered enough?"

Zamuda's goofy grin is too hard to resist, and Stacy finds herself smiling as well. "I can't believe you—of *all people*—managed to keep this from me!"

He shrugs. "One 'a the advantages of the new gig, Stace. Keeps me busy and outta the office, away from your incisive gaze."

"Yeah, yeah, whatever, ya big lug."

She wraps her arms around her former partner and squeezes tight. She feels the dampness of his sweat-sticky dress shirt against her blouse, but doesn't mind. Zamuda's a sweetheart, the big brother she never had.

"Now, whaddaya say we get this par-tay started!" he bellows, drawing eyes and eventual cheers from the assembled attendees.

He throws in a hip-gyrating dance, rubbing his shirt-covered belly while rotating slowly around Stacy. Jeff pretends to fling dollar bills at the current LTC. Stacy's impressed that Zamuda manages to keep his shirt on. She supposes it's one more sign of things changing, of how everyone—not just her—is getting older, passing torches to the next generation. Or, like Stacy, stepping off the ride for a well-earned rest.

She experiences the rest of her "par-tay," such as it is, as a series of encounters, each falling into one of a few categories. She knows the names of the officers and detectives she came up with, most of them younger than her. After all, policework was a second career, happening after her academic aspirations got placed on permanent hold so she could return home and help her brother. She recalls how one of her academy instructors referred to her as "The Professor," a not-so-subtle jab at her old life. As if the younger folks plucked fresh from high school or undergrad and handed a badge and gun were somehow better than her. Purer, untainted.

Interaction Type One goes like this:

One of her soon-to-be-former colleagues, gripping a red Solo Cup's worth of peach schnapps (apparently the only booze available at the precinct that day), leans in too close, regarding her with pitying eyes. They ask variations on the same question: "Oh, could your brother not make it?"

And Stacy shrugs her shoulders and replies with some version of "Guess not."

Of course, she knows there's an absolutely zero-percent chance that anyone could've gotten Xavier out of their old house to interact with real people in the real world.

But she keeps that to herself.

Interaction Type Two happens with those who know less about Stacy, her background, or her family history. These are the newer hires or transfers from neighboring towns.

"Tell the truth," they say. "Did you have any idea we were gonna do this?"

"No. No, I did not," Stacy answers. Which is true. She hadn't even considered it.

Soon after, she finds herself frozen, struck dumb by the thought of sorting out what the hell she's supposed to do with the rest of her life.

She glances across the room and finds Jeff tracking her, waiting for a moment of mutual eye contact. He smiles and waves when it happens. Goofy and handsome and irresistible all at once, his pseudo-*Magnum, P.I.* getup only adds to his charm. She remembers the plane tickets to Hawaii she found in his sock drawer, one for each of them, and how she tucked them under a pair of argyle knee socks, letting him keep the surprise for himself and whatever moment he'll choose to spring them on her.

"Excuse me," she says to the latest question-asker, extracting herself from further tedium before heading to a more familiar face.

But there's also Interaction Type Three she must watch out for: *Busybodies.* Department gossips. Men and women alike, the folks who want the inside scoop and the juicy details. They smile when asking questions, even while their eyes flash with a ravenous hunger for information.

"So, Stace, what's next?"

Stacy's relieved when Zamuda stands before the partygoers and clears his throat, interrupting her current question-asker. She can ignore the question and no longer has to come up with yet another answer—*knitting, reading, catching up on TV—* that rings false even as it leaves her mouth.

Surprising no one who knows Zamuda well, it isn't long before his cheeks are awash with tears, diamond-tinted dollops glimmering under bullpen fluorescents.

"…and that was my first year sharing a car with Stace. And even back then, I knew, a guy couldn'ta asked for a better partner. And now I'm losing that partner, and this city's losing a hell of a detective sergeant. I hope you realize what a catch you got there, Jeff."

"Oh, I do!" Jeff fires back.

Stacy keeps quiet, but is no less moved by her friend and colleague's emotional speech. Her heart swells in her chest. Suddenly finding standing to be a chore, she sits in one of the bullpen's creaky roller chairs. Jeff moves behind her. His hands massage her shoulders.

As the crowd applauds, Stacy feels her phone—her special *family-only* phone—vibrating through the purse on her lap. She unzips the bag and fetches the device, intending to glance at the message from her baby brother before filing the info away for a later response.

Her plan's quickly thrown out the window.

<MESSAGE | XAVIER | CONTACT>

"Turn on the newz," the text reads.

The next message comes fast on the heels of the first. Even as it appears on Stacy's phone, the devices of the partygoers chirp and beep and buzz to life as well. They're all getting the same news.

But Stacy pays no mind to what the others see. She pays no mind to the concerned looks shared by Jeff and Zamuda, standing in front of and behind her.

At the moment, all that matters is the message from her brother. Three words that change everything:

"They found HIM."

CHAPTER 2

THE XNS SEGMENT begins with a familiar image, that video still close-up of six-year-old Matt Freeman's ice-cream-smeared face. The cable news channel's banner unfurls above the picture, alongside the words "BREAKING NEWS."

"Nineteen years and counting. That's how long one family's waited for the return of their son after his alleged abduction from their home outside Alexandria, Virginia."

The speaker's words over the still image are measured, inoffensively free of accent, polished broadcast-ready perfection.

XNS anchor Debi Megyn sits behind the studio desk and usually delivers sobering news about how the world is falling apart, at home and abroad.

Except this time, the news she gets to share is different.

"Today, for the family of one of this network's own members, everything changes…"

The segment producers know exactly what they're doing as cameras cut to the studio, to Debi Megyn and her designer blouse and somber blue coat, her hair and makeup perfect. After all, this is news that must be delivered face-to-face. The iconic image of Matt Freeman shrinks to a portrait in the upper right corner, floating above the shoulder of the XNS anchor.

Soon, the image fades, replaced by a picture of the other Freemans as they appeared after the boy's disappearance.

First, the father: a tall and muscular Black man, built like a college athlete whose career was cut short due to injury. That's Malek Freeman. His broad shoulders are stooped, his lips set tight. One arm's around his wife, Ruth Freeman. With pale, splotchy skin, unwashed hair, and dark circles under bloodshot eyes, Ruth is heartbreak and agony personified. Finally, off to the side is Cass Freeman. This nine-year-old with the same deep tanned skin as her younger brother. Her chestnut-colored curly hair is pulled into two uneven pigtails.

There's a sadness in her eyes.

In all their eyes.

After all, it's an incomplete family portrait.

"Nineteen years after disappearing from his childhood home, Matt Freeman has been found...alive," Debi Megyn says, leaning into the dramatic pause.

"It's news that must be a relief for Ruth Freeman, the host of *Voice for the Voiceless*—airing every weeknight at 7:30/6:30 Central here on XNS—and for the whole Freeman family. We go live to the scene where Matt Freeman was apparently recovered a few hours ago. Rick?"

The hypothetical XNS watcher is transported via remote footage.

Reporters, correspondents, photographers, and camera operators all congregate with their bulky cameras and microphones showing call letters. They mill around, seeking the perfect angle for their footage.

Through the lens of the XNS camera, fence posts with wood splintering off in chunks and barbed wire wrapped around their tops become visible.

The camera zooms in, hurtling viewers down the road. A farmhouse waits at the end, its exterior dustier than the driveway, paint long since peeled from rotting wood. Color comes from the yellow police tape wrapped around the sagging porch and from the strobing red and blue police and emergency vehicle lights. Someone clears their throat, bringing the foreground back to focus.

Rick, XNS's reporter on-the-scene, enjoys this moment in the spotlight. He stands with microphone in hand and the camera light shining on his face. "Thanks, Debi. We're outside the home of Gordon Patay. According to sources, Patay and his family had been living here, very much off the grid, for years. However, the anonymity they enjoyed has come to an end. If what we're hearing is correct, this house is where Matt Freeman was held captive by the Patays for the last nineteen years."

Rick continues, rattling off facts and statistics that signify next to nothing. The camera operator shifts focus, zooming in on the farmhouse at the end of that long, dusty path. With its busted shutters and cobweb-draped porch eaves, it looks like a house made for haunting.

"There's movement at the house," Rick says.

The front door opens. EMTs wheel out a gurney from the abyssal interior. The black body bag atop it is a sliver of that darkness, a piece cut from the void.

"What the hell do you think you're doin'?"

A new voice.

A new face makes a shocking interruption. Voice and face both belong to a sheriff's deputy with a buzzcut and a low bullshit tolerance. His hand closes over the camera lens, giving the viewers an up-close and personal look at the lines, swirls, and seams of his palm. Then, with a shove, the Patay house goes out of focus.

"Y'all better move," the deputy says. "Stand behind the barricade like we told y'all."

FOR ANYONE WHO remembers the Matt Freeman Abduction, this footage conjures feelings of heartache, fear, and also *relief*. For Stacy, those feelings are amplified times a thousand because she was so close to the investigation.

So close to the truth…

That farm's only, what…a few miles out of town? How'd we never look there?

But Stacy casts that line of thinking to the side. She knows better than to dwell on the past.

What *matters* is that it's over. They've found him. They've found who took Matt Freeman, and where Matt's been for all those years.

Better still—he's alive.

Sitting in the bullpen under a banner congratulating her on retirement, watching the news unfold on a TV set wheeled in from the evidence room, Stacy Keppler experiences all those emotions and so many more. She feels a strange kinship with the Patay house of all things. Like the house, she too feels haunted. Her face grows pale, her once-smiling lips reduced to thin, chapped lines with flaking skin at their edges. She feels those nineteen years of searching, of trying everything she could to get answers for the Freeman family, all come flooding over her.

Jeff's hands remains on her shoulders, keeping her anchored. She looks up at him, her face lined with the pain of every dead-end and false lead from nearly two decades of police work.

"What?" he asks. "What is it?"

"I have to go. I mean, I should see them. Cass, Malek, Ruth. I have to see..." she says, "...I have to see him."

CHAPTER 3

WHEN MAJOR EVENTS take place, unless a person is at the center of them, unless *they're* the ones directly affected, they are more than likely going to live through them at a remove. Cable news and social media networks are, more often than not, the go-betweens, filtering moments and emotions into something that passive media consumers can digest and comprehend.

The family whose photo appears on XNS in a tight close-up is quite different from what's been shown of the Freemans.

"FAMILY OF EVIL?: GORDON PATAY AND FAMILY, PHOTO UNDATED"

The chyron under the black-and-white photograph spoon-feeds the news-devouring audience exactly who they're looking at and how they should feel about them.

The shadowy blend of blacks, whites, and grays is enough to make the depicted family members seem as sinister as the discordant synth track chosen by the segment producer. The image itself is a time warp, like a tintype taken from the turn of the previous century. Faces held in Puritanical grimaces: A man with tight skin, bushy black hair, a long beard flowing down the white of his shirt—this is Gordon Patay. His wife kneels beside him in a black antebellum dress with voluminous shoulders and a hoop skirt that devours the floor below her. And their sons, young men whose ages might fall anywhere between teenagers and thirty-somethings, have dressed and groomed themselves like their father. The background's bare-bones, white walls with slightly darker trim closer to the floor. An end table—with a Bible on top—completes the scene.

XNS's Debi Megyn returns on-screen with more guiding words, helping to shape public opinion further. "It's been three weeks since authorities were brought to the home of Gordon Patay. He, along with his wife Johanna and sons Ezekiel and Moses, is alleged to have kidnapped Matt Freeman, taking him from his nearby home as a young boy of six.

"Since Freeman's recovery, rumors have circulated. The latest reports, still unconfirmed, tell of a Good Samaritan who noticed the now twenty-five-year-old Matt Freeman standing by a window at the Patay house while the stranger was on a nature hike that brought him near the property. The stranger is said to have broken into the residence, dispatched the alleged kidnappers with lethal force, and set Matt free, putting an end to at least part of the long nightmare suffered by the Freeman family."

The flawless transition back to the news desk ends with a close-up of Debi Megyn as she finishes with the word "family."

"Let's go live to City Hall in Alexandria where the Freeman family are set to address the media for the first time since their son's return. Hopefully, we'll soon be able to turn some of the questions and speculations of the last few days into concrete answers."

As though she's snapped her fingers or wiggled her nose, Debi Megyn and her producers make magic happen. Viewers are hurtled miles in milliseconds, taken to City Hall just as their favorite XNS anchor promised.

Under the open rotunda space of City Hall, a makeshift platform has been erected, made of packing flats laid across the floor, then stacked up three, four, five layers tall. A speaker's podium sits atop this construction. A mic stand's silver arm peers from the top with the black microphone cover appearing as a darkened eye, unmoved by the lights surrounding it. A deep crimson curtain hangs behind the temporary stage, cutting off the rest of the Hall from view.

Ruth Freeman stands at the podium. It is her that the black eye of the microphone seeks. She appears different from the old photograph frequently shown on XNS. For one thing, her hair and wardrobe are both perfect, a far cry from the disheveled mess of nineteen years before. Her hair is now dyed a peroxide blonde and cut in a more fashionable, shorter, and angular style. She doesn't wear black, but dark blue. The royal navy pairs well with her red lip and pink cheeks. Her eyebrows are black, and there's not a hair out of place there or anywhere else on her person. Pink and white pearls sit against her skin, catching the camera lights.

Her smile, which she flashes for a brief moment at the gathered crowd jockeying for position around the stage, is even brighter than her jewelry. She's a woman accustomed to the camera and spotlight.

The other two family members—the father and daughter—complete this living portrait. In many ways, the XNS camera operator's framing—Ruth standing tall, Malek with his hand on her shoulder and his belly sinking slightly past his canary yellow polo, and Cass with curly red hair all tangled, her expression dulled—serves to remind loyal XNS viewers of what they've seen in earlier network coverage.

Acting as family spokesperson, Ruth clears her throat, letting the mic pick up the sound. Satisfied that she has the requisite eyes on her, both in person and from everyone tuned in to the news, the Freeman matriarch proceeds.

"It was like…like nothing had changed with our Matty. Nothing at all."

The camera pushes closer. While Ruth's face is brighter, shinier, and fuller than the Ruth seen immediately following her son's abduction, and Malek's face is somewhat ashen and pudgy, both have tears at their corners, spilling past the lower lids. Ruth pulls a tissue from a pack placed discretely on the podium and pats it gently near her eyes.

"Malek and I…we're just…we're so happy to have our family back. Complete once again."

A voice emerges from the crowd of reporters below the stage. It's Rick, XNS's man on-the-scene. There at the Patays' farm and here again at City Hall. "Ms. Freema—"

Ruth catches the reporter's eye, her gaze willing him to silence. As the camera operator pushes in on her face, the tears spotted moments before are already gone. "*Mrs.* Freeman," she says, correcting him.

"Okay. Sure. *Mrs.* Freeman."

Ruth nods, as if to say, *Yes, and…?*

Ever the professional, Rick soldiers on with his question-asking. "When do you think we'll get a chance to see him? To see your son Matt in person?"

Ruth's answer is immediate and on point. Like she's rehearsed it a million times, waiting for this moment to show it off. "At this time, our son's privacy is paramount. We want to ensure he has a chance to readjust to life here in the 'real world' first. When the time comes, we'll let him speak. *If* he chooses to do so."

Rick's not done, though. He's playing his part as smoothly as the woman at the podium. "And what of the police in Alexandria and surrounding towns like Herenton? What about the officers, the detectives, those who *failed* to find your son for all those years when he was apparently being held so close by?"

The XNS camera operator lifts their camera so the line of sight shifts above Rick's head. They zoom in tight on the Freemans. The shot holds as everyone waits for Ruth to answer.

The cheap, stained curtain behind the family moves for a split second. A blink-and-you'll-miss-it moment. But if you're looking in the right spot, there's something to see: an eye peeking from behind the curtain, focused on Ruth standing at the podium. Maybe it's the glare from the camera lights or the klieg lights rigged earlier in the day to illuminate the makeshift stage, or some combination, but the eye appears dark on-screen, a blackened pupil taking up the entirety of this lone, gazing orb. A golden vertical line crosses the blackness, though, giving an insect-like appearance to the eye.

"Believe me, those who failed my son, who failed my family, *will* be held to account," Ruth says. "There are specific individuals who indulged childish fantasies and failed to do the actual police work needed. I intend to hold those individuals to account."

As her words echo through the rotunda, the curtain shifts once more. The eye—what *might have been* an eye—is gone.

FINAL INTERVIEW WITH RUTH FREEMAN:
MAY 8, 2020

SERGEANT KEPPLER (SK): *Ruth.*

RUTH FREEMAN (RF): *Sergeant.*

SK: *C'mon. You know you can call me Stacy.*

RF: *Do I know that? Do I? Seems to me like I don't know what to call you or your partner or anyone else working to find my son. I don't even know if I can call what you've been doing "working." Sixteen years of bumbling around like Barney fucking Fife. And now I hear they're deprioritizing the investigation…*

SK: *I know, believe me, I don't agree with it either.*

RF: *Uh uh, no way. You're not gonna talk me down or shut me up here. My ex isn't here for you two to team up and gaslight me…*

SK: *I'd never do that. Malek wouldn't either. […] Cases like this, there's always fanfare when they start. But if you believe that the vict—the missing individual—is out there, waiting to be found, it's the slow and steady approach that wins the day. But I can't advocate alone for the available resources. Believe me, I've tried. I think the LTC's retiring just to get away from my requests and requisition forms.*

RF: *Still looking for telescopes to spy on little gray men on the Moon or whatever it is my psychotic daughter told you? Or have you realized she's a little lying bitch who can't be trusted?*

SK: *[…]*

RF: *Thought so.*

SK: *There is the anomaly that your neighbor, Mr. Hatton, reported from his time-delayed backyard photography that evening. The white light effect caught on his roll of what were supposed to be blooming orchid photos? The light that came from your side of the fence separating your properties. Now, I've had everyone on staff and even a freelancer look at the images, and nobody can tell me what caused—*

RF: *Shitty equipment used by a paranoid schizophrenic. You know that's what Hatton was diagnosed with, right? Got a restraining order against him to keep his damn photos and theories the hell away from me. Thank the good Lord he got the message and moved. Though now we've got these younger couples on our block, screaming children, yapping dogs, it's a mess. Meanwhile, my experts tell me it's likely just an overloaded camera battery that caused the error.*

SK: *Your experts? For…*

RF: *My show.*

SK: *Oh.*

RF: *What? Got something to say, Sergeant?*

SK: *No, Ruth. I'm happy for you. The show sure sounds like it's getting a lot of interest and coverage. Happy you found a way to help, to get your message out there.*

RF: *It's about keeping my son's memory alive.*

SK: *And finding him.*

RF: *Of course. And finding him. If you all won't do it, I'll find people who will.*

Beto Zamuda (BZ): *So, what'd I miss, ladies?*

RF: *Nothing, Captain Zamuda. I was just leaving. Walk me to my car?*

[STOP]

CHAPTER 4

AFTER THE PRESS conference wraps up, Stacy nods to some members of the City Hall security detail she recognizes. It's a cushy assignment, usually a boring one. She's been to and worked around the Hall enough that it's no problem to get waved through and allowed access to the rest of the building past the staging area in the rotunda. The heels of her flats tap against the polished marble as she rushes through the corridors, moving as fast as she can without breaking into a full-on run.

Reaching the end of one passageway, she spots the Freemans preparing to enter a meeting room. Ruth and Malek walk together, but aren't holding hands. There's enough space between them for two other people to fit. Still, they're together. Their daughter, Cass, curly hair unkempt and slightly nappy, trails behind. Her hands are stuffed into the pockets of her sweatpants and a stretched-out cardigan covers her hunched back. It looks like she's trying to fold herself up and disappear.

Stacy holds out a hand and calls to the family. "Excuse me! Wait! Ruth! Malek! Cass! Please, wait!"

Before she gets a chance to state her case further, the conference room door opens and two beefy bodyguard-types in black suits wearing indoor sunglasses and wired-up earpieces emerge from the other side. Despite their stocky sizes, the bodyguards cover the distance between the somewhat confused Freeman family and the former police sergeant in record time.

Before Stacy knows what's hit her, Beefy Guard #1 and Beefy Guard #2 have their thick mitts around her arms. Their momentum's such that they're already dragging her away from the now half-open conference-room door and the Freemans.

"Whoa there!" says Beefy #1.

"Watch it, lady!" says Beefy #2.

Their twin powers of aggression operate in sync.

Stacy's stunned, but not exactly shocked. She doesn't recognize the Beefy Guards and figures them for private security hired by Ruth. Likely out-of-towners. Whoever they are, Stacy's determined not to let them stand in the way of her mission, her whole reason for leaving the house, ignoring Jeff's insistent reminders that she's officially been retired for almost a month, and coming to the Hall in the first place. "Please, you don't understand…" she says, already confident her excuses will fall on deaf ears based on the two men's confused expressions.

But then, a miracle…

"No, gentlemen, it's okay. Let her through."

It's Ruth who speaks. Certainly, she's the last person Stacy expected to speak up for her. When the guards release her, Stacy rushes to the family. She reaches out with both hands, taking Malek's hand and Ruth's hand in her own. She can feel the dryness of their skin, the extra wrinkles gained in nineteen years.

Stacy presses on, knowing that if she doesn't, then the words might slip away, forever unspoken. "I-I-I needed to come," she says. "I just wanted to say—to you all—that I am so, so happy for you. For your family."

She notes the shimmer of tears in Malek's eyes. But Ruth is stone-faced, not smiling, not frowning. *Neutral* in every respect of the word. But Stacy continues, pushing her luck. Her eyes fall to Cass, the young woman, unkempt, disheveled, pressed against the wall to one side of the conference-room doorway. Despite knowing each other for nineteen years, the young woman won't lift her eyes from the floor to meet Stacy's gaze. "Cass, it's me. Are you okay? You don't look so—"

Before Stacy can finish, Ruth yanks her hand free from the retired sergeant's grasp. A fire blazes out of control in this mother's eyes as she raises her freed hand. Stacy's certain she's about to be struck, slapped hard across the face.

It's only Malek extending his arm, blocking the path of a potential swing, that saves Stacy from the sting of Ruth's palm hitting her cheek. Stacy watches the scene unfold, up close and personal and in the moment. But, at the same time, it's like she's at a remove, considering the events as if they've already occurred. It's a technique she picked up on the job. The ability to take the objective, distanced point of view, even when thrust into the middle of the chaos and violence.

This ability allows her to stand her ground, never trembling, flinching, or retreating. It allows her to notice Malek's left hand as he uses that arm to block his wife's strike. There's no wedding ring on his finger.

And he was *just* wearing one at the press conference.

Guess they're maybe not back together as Ruth wants people to believe...

Ruth Freeman is far from finished with Stacy. "Who do you think you are? *Who?* Did you think we'd just forget...how you *failed* our Matty?"

Malek, perhaps sensing the immediate threat of physical violence passing, lowers his arm. But he's not letting his wife, ex-wife, whatever she is, off so easily. "Whoa, whoa, whoa," he says. "Take it easy, Ruth."

Big mistake.

Ruth redirects her venom, laser-focusing it on Malek. Even though she's a head or two shorter than the former athlete, her presence, her aura, is such that she appears capable of stomping him into submission. "Take it easy? Take it...*easy?*"

Ruth balls her hands into fists, then crosses her arms hard and heavy against her chest. "Oh, that's *just* typical, Malek. All these years and still *never* putting your family first. Not *ever*! Always listening to every woman—whether it's this incompetent bitch or your daughter—except for me. And now look who was right all along. Because it sure as shit wasn't *her*!"

She finishes by hooking a thumb in Stacy's direction. The contempt is evident, almost cartoonishly so, on her face.

Before Malek responds, before Stacy figures out what she could say or do to defuse the situation, a shadow falls across those gathered in the hallway. It's cast by the figure standing in the now fully open meeting-room doorway.

A young man—pale, gaunt, dressed in skinny jeans, an over-sized gray polo shirt, and silver-and-white Adidas sneakers. There's a ruddy coloring atop his head where his hair's been buzzed extra short.

Stacy hasn't seen the young man since he was a boy who existed as flickering images on a TV screen and nothing more than that. But there's no doubt in her mind of who he is.

"Excuse me, is it…is it okay to come out now? I heard voices, but wasn't sure if…"

Stacy interrupts him. She can't help herself. "*Matt*. It's really you."

CHAPTER 5

"HELLO?" MATT FREEMAN says, looking Stacy up and down. There's curiosity to his gaze rather than judgment, so it doesn't exactly make her feel uncomfortable.

But it is still kind of odd.

"Do I know who you are?" the young man asks at last.

Stacy takes a step back away from Matt and his family. Her body moves on pure instinct, a voice in the back of her head insisting: *This isn't the Matty Freeman you know. He's too tall, too strong, too clean. Where's the smile? The twinkle in his eyes? The ice cream around his lips?*

The version of Matty Freeman, forever and always six years old, that she's carried with her overlaps with the present reality. In doing so, the pieces don't align. The child's face on the grown-up's body. The soft-spoken, eerily calm voice of an adult emerging from a kindergartner's lips. Confronting this mix-and-match reality, Stacy's stuck now, lost for words.

And this new incarnation of Matt Freeman that she's standing in front of appears just as lost, just as confused about what to say next.

Thankfully, his father supplies the words.

"Son, you don't know this woman personally, but..." Malek smiles. A calming presence, defusing the tension that's hung heavy in the hallway since Stacy caught up with the family.

"…this is the detective who was helping us look for you for all those years when you were gone."

Tall, lanky, skin and bones where his father is muscle hidden under fat, Matt Freeman leans forward, holding his arms out in an awkward semicircle. Stacy shuffles forward, allowing her body to be drawn into the young man's orbit. Those long arms drop, sudden and sharp against her shoulders. His skin feels cold on the back of her neck.

Stacy scooches into the embrace, not sure what else to do. She presses her face to his chest, letting her tears dampen the fabric of his polo. The rapid-fire beating of his heart makes a chaotic pairing with the pounding rush of blood in her ears.

When the young man speaks, Stacy trembles, hearing the voice emerge from his chest and past his lips. Feeling it. There's a truth present in the hallway, undeniable and unflinching. This really *is* Matt Freeman returned.

"I'm here, Detective," he says. "You can stop looking now."

AS NIGHT SETTLES in after a long and eventful day, the parking lot for employees and elected officials behind City Hall is nearly empty. The media's been kept away by the combined efforts of security and additional local police. They've cordoned off the front of the building and opted for maximum aggression toward anyone who might disobey the rules or so much as look at one of the on-duty officers the wrong way. Stacy recognizes her old partner's policing philosophy in action. She's not surprised to see how easily it's caught on with the other officers.

Or maybe it's just that Zamuda was always more like the others. Not like me…

"Shock and awe," Zamuda used to say, pretending he'd come up with the term and not taken it from the Bush Jr. "War on Terror" years.

Stacy counts herself lucky to be on the lieutenant commissioner's good side. That gets her a pass with all the officers working in and around the hall. In turn, this goodwill allowed her to stay behind, wandering the corridors of City Hall after her encounter with the Freemans. She feels like she needs the time alone to absorb the bizarre, nearly incomprehensible experience of her "reunion" with Matty Freeman.

But can you even be reunited with someone you never met— not really? You have this kinship, but is it with him…or is it with those who were left behind?

Well, some of those left behind…

The look on Ruth Freeman's face when Stacy stepped back from the embrace with her returned son was enough for the former detective sergeant to truly understand how unwelcome her presence was. Even as Malek insisted she "stay and hang out with us" and Cass threw tentative, nervous-looking glances her way, Stacy knew better. She'd pressed her luck by coming, and her encounter with the suddenly returned Matt Freeman only reinforced the notion. She gave her thanks and appreciation for Matty's return, offered another apology to Ruth that fell on deaf ears, and then made her escape.

But she wasn't ready to leave right afterward, not before she got a chance to check on Cass—the young woman who appeared bloated and sweaty, a far cry from the sweet, scared little girl that Stacy interviewed all those years before. She noted the silver gleam of a flask sticking out of Cass's pocket. There were beads of liquid near the closed circular cap, showing clear signs of recent use. Of course, in the intervening years of the investigation, Stacy had gotten wind of personal problems, struggles in and out of school. She'd wanted to do more, to say something. Whatever she had done, whatever she had said, it clearly wasn't enough.

So, Stacy has stuck around because of what she saw in that final moment with the family. With Cass. Curiosity's gotten the better of her, and those detective's instincts aren't fading as fast as she might have hoped.

Though perhaps it's not the instincts she wishes would fade, but the drive that comes once they're triggered. That almost uncanny urge to test her hypotheses, to ask her questions, and to dig as deep into the proverbial dirt as she can.

Which is what has brought her to the parking lot.

She's parked in the back lot as a matter of habit, knowing it's the safest lot and the one most likely to be undisturbed by civilians. The theory holds true as Stacy pushes open the rear exit and steps into a quiet, nearly empty lot. Black asphalt and painted rows of empty parking spots meet the edge of the concrete sidewalk. Skinny, bent-necked light posts situated every five spots or so gaze down from darkness to stare at more darkness. They shine with their singular white eyes.

Stacy heads for her car. But before she makes it, she spots a figure in the parking lot shadows, slumped in a haphazard fashion against one of the posts.

She doesn't have to get closer to know who's waiting for her there. It's Cass.

"I knew you'd be out here," Stacy says, trying to keep her voice steady, even, like she's trying to coax a wounded animal out with treats. "I remember after we met—after, well, you know—you'd tell me how much you liked to be outside. Under the stars. Do you remember that?"

The Cass-shadow shrugs and sways in response. Stacy picks out a few mumbled words, something like "thought I'd find him up there."

Stacy continues forward toward her sedan, moving closer to Cass with slow and steady steps. As she nears the young woman, she can smell booze fumes wafting over. It's like Cass has spilled as much liquor on her clothes as she's imbibed.

"It's not him, Detective. It's not."

Finally able to see the young woman under the lamplight, Stacy regards Cass, trying to reconcile the past with this present version. One of Cass's eyes is open wide and blood-shot, the other's closed. Not wanting to stop, not wanting to get involved, Stacy takes another step toward her old car, keys out.

"I still remember you believed me, ya know?" Cass says. Other than a slurred syllable or two, her words are clear, direct, on-target. "It's not him."

Without really thinking about what she's doing, Stacy's moved to her driver's-side door and has her keys in the lock. She only has to turn and then pull the door open, slide in, close it, and go.

But something keeps her there. Or rather, someone.

"You were the only one who believed my story about who took Matty all those years ago," Cass says. "You were the only one who listened when I talked about the Gray Men. And the Moon…or the man. Nobody else did."

"I know," Stacy says. "I know that sometimes there are things that happen to us…to people we love…that just don't make sense."

She takes a deep breath, as much to prepare herself for what she's about to say as to get the words right for Cass. "But other times, good things can happen to us. To our loved ones. And we…we need to make space for that unexpected good news."

Sensing that her words may not be enough, especially since she's not that sure she believes them herself, Stacy takes her hands off her keys. Too late, though. Cass swings around and throws herself from the light post in a drunken facsimile of a ballet leap. She collides with the sedan's trunk, gasping at the point of impact. When she looks at Stacy again, Cass can barely hold her head up. It rests tilted, her ear touching her shoulder blade.

When she speaks, it's like nothing Stacy said has registered. It's as if she also has words to share, pearls of her own wisdom to impart, and she won't let anything stop them from being spoken. "Nobody else believed me. Not counselors. Not therapists. Not the idiots at rehab. None of 'em listen'd to Crazy Cass. Except you. You listened."

Stacy moves closer to Cass. "Okay," she says, "Let's get you somewhere to sit down, maybe get you some water—"

The drunk and distraught younger woman moves fast, seeming to act on impulse. She grabs Stacy's shirt and pulls her close. The odor of bourbon, sweet but medicinal, assaults Stacy's senses as Cass speaks. Her bloodshot eyes press against her sockets and her words emerge fast, unstoppable.

"He's not my brother. He's…he's different. Whatever they sent back is wrong. A lie."

Cass appears ready to collapse against the former detective, ready to sob into her shirt.

Yet she pulls it together for one final exclamation. "You have to believe me again!"

Her declaration's punctuated by the Hall's rear door slamming open, the fluorescent hallway lights spilling out onto the sidewalk. Stacy looks back at the building. Cass follows, a drunken half-second behind.

Ruth Freeman's silhouette is unmistakable. Her hands are on her hips as she stands in the doorway. She's a presence and a half. Her voice is loud and firm.

"Cassidy Freeman. Come here. *Now!*"

CHAPTER 6

STACY'S SUPPOSED TO go home. She's supposed to order a pizza with Jeff and let him pick the movie. She's sure he'd choose a Will Ferrell comedy, something she'd claim to hate but that'd have her laughing hard enough to cry before it ended. Instead, driving from the City Hall parking lot, all she can think about is what Cass Freeman said to her.

"Whatever they sent back is wrong. A lie."

The words run through Stacy's head once again as she spreads the crime-scene photos from the Patay house across her old desk at the precinct. She's moved some boxes to make room on the wide, flat surface, as her workspace was temporarily converted to extra storage by her former colleagues. But with the slight adjustment made, it's like she never left.

Stacy supposes Matt Freeman's resurfacing and the subsequent blowback on the police force can take most of the credit. Her old ID card still worked to get her in the building, and a nod to Warren at the front desk sealed the deal. She was also pleasantly surprised to find Zamuda's computer passwords had remained unchanged since their time on patrol, granting her access to the cross-departmental evidence database.

Truth be told, Stacy's pretty sure her own old passwords would still work. But she wants to retain *some* level of plausible deniability, *some* coverage for her investigatory extracurriculars.

She takes notes with the voice recorder on the special phone her brother set up for her. The one he crosses his heart and swears on their parents' graves is one-hundred-percent secure. Taking things one step further, the door to her old office is shut, closing her off from the bullpen—sparsely filled at this hour. But it doesn't matter because Stacy's not even there. Not really. Looking at the gruesome collage spread across the scratched and nicked surface of her desk, Stacy is gone—out to the country with Gordon Patay, his wife Johanna, and their adult sons Ezekiel and Moses.

Blood and guts coat peeling wallpaper and stain shag carpeting in the family room.

"According to reports from the Prince William County Sheriff's Office, Matt Freeman has identified the Patay Family as the individuals responsible for his kidnapping and detainment for the past nineteen years."

There's a thickness to the blood captured dripping from a portrait of the crucified Christ hanging askew on the Patays' wall. It's the deep-red hue one might find from vital organs secured deep within the body. Not something found outside the human body—not often, at least.

"The captivity lasted until approximately three weeks ago when, again, according to Freeman..."

Moving from the walls and the floor, here's a look at the Patays themselves. The young man broken in half is one of the sons. It's not that he's been cut or shot in half with a well-swung blade or a powerful enough shotgun gauge—he was *bent* backward until the back of his head touched the soles of his shoes.

"...this 'Some Guy'—yes, Xavier, I *heard* it—used lethal force on the per—the perpetrators after finding the witness, uh, the victim...in the residence."

That's enough.

She switches off the recorder. Reflecting on her words, Stacy stares at the carnage printed from the precinct's laser printer.

"It just doesn't make sense," she says.

"You're telling me. Did you really have to go and print all

them photos in color? I mean, that's a lot of fucking red ink!"

Stacy looks up from her desk, seeking the source of the interruption.

She only has to go as far as the doorway.

Zamuda's standing there. Tie loosened, dress shirt hastily tucked into khakis where he's missed one of the belt loops. Coffee and aftershave waft from him in equal measure. But there's something else there as well—faint and floral. Stacy can only imagine the late nights *he's* had since Matt Freeman's return, running point for the city's response to this latest, most unexpected development in what's been its darkest chapter.

Before Stacy summons any conciliatory or apologizing words, her old partner continues his spiel. His words coming out as a sigh, he says, "C'mon, Stace. Aren't you supposed to be retired or something? Or did I eat all that cake for nothin'?"

Stacy holds a hand up, but not to signal a *mea culpa*. No, that moment's passed them by. Instead, she does it to draw attention to the photo in her hand. Another one fresh from the office printer. Still wet with the red ink.

It's a wide shot. She pictures the photographer on a chair, balancing on tiptoes to get the full capture. The four victims spread across the room. Very much *spread*. Blood, guts, limbs, bones, teeth, and hair—all those physical ingredients that go into making a person. But deconstructed, ruined.

Zamuda doesn't look at that photo. He turns his head to the side. Stacy keeps on him.

"It's just…it makes no sense. Look how these bodies are… the damage here. How could 'Some Guy' do *this* to four adults? How? I mean, maybe wild animals. Wild…wild *something*."

She flashes on a moment from her past—the police officers at their front door, giving Stacy the news about what happened to her parents, and one of them offering her a hug, the other one repeating the news to Xavier, who sat on the couch staring straight ahead, refusing to even look at the officers. It wasn't until the officers were leaving that he'd finally spoken up, saying, "Animal attack? Are we really supposed to believe that bullshit?"

"Let it go, Stace. Please. It's over. Happy-ending time." Zamuda's like Xavier on that couch, still not looking at Stacy. Or the photograph.

Stacy holds it against her chest. She offers an answer she knows her friend wants to hear, but the desperation in her eyes tells another story entirely. "Fine," she says. "Fine, if it's over, then it's over."

She places the photo face down on her old desk. A peace offering. She waits until Zamuda's making a move to enter the room, likely expecting to shoot the proverbial shit about their old times on the beat—

Because that's what us old cops are supposed to do, right? Just talk about the good ol' days...

—but Stacy's not done.

"If it *is* over, then you won't mind me taking the photos and some of the other materials I printed from the files."

Zamuda stops short, throwing his hands up. "Fine, yeah, okay, whatever," he says.

Stacy twirls over to her old partner, elementary-school ballet lessons still paying off years later. She leans over to kiss his cheek.

Of course, she *knew* she'd win. She's known all along. And the grunt Zamuda gives in response to her playful peck suggests he was aware also.

TRANSCRIPT EXCERPT: CALLER "MR. X" TO CLIVE RING'S SPECTACULAR WORLD

CLIVE: *Alrighty, Spectaculators out there, this time we're taking a call from one of our long-time listeners and callers, the gentlemen who uses enough signal blockers that we sure as heck don't know where he's calling from. The one, the only: Mr. X. My friend…what's on your mind tonight?*

X: *Some Guy, Clive.*

CLIVE: *Some Guy, huh? Well, I hate to break it to you, my friend, but this isn't some dating show.*

X: *Ha. Ha. I'm serious.*

[Thirty seconds of dead air]

CLIVE: *You still with us, Mr. X?*

X: *Yeah. Yeah. I'm here. Just, uh, gathering my notes.*

CLIVE: *I see. And I'm sorry for the teasing. We listen and we do not judge here on the Spectacular World. So tell me about this Some Guy, friend.*

X: *That's just the name it—they—I don't know how many were made—was given…is given. Like some cultural, post-hypnotic suggestion meant to downplay the existence of this lifeform. "Some*

Guy," they say. Like the kid who got taken…the one they said was rescued by "Some Guy." Or the Some Guy who finds crop circles, or makes 'em. The Some Guy who calls in hoax sightings to conspiracy radio sho—

CLIVE: *No, hold on, X. Remember, we don't judge.*

X: *You know what I mean. Don't you?*

CLIVE: *I…well, yes, I suppose I do.*

X: *What if visitors from another planet, time, dimension, I dunno which just yet, but my sis…my assistants and I are investigating…what if they're using this Some Guy as cover for their actions?*

CLIVE: *But how—*

X: *I don't know, Clive. I just don't know.*

CLIVE: *And by talking about this Some Guy here on the program, aren't we then playing into their plans, giving this Some Guy, whatever it might be, more real estate in people's minds, so there's less time to think about these—what'd you call 'em? Visitors?*

X: *Oh [EXPLETIVE]. You're right. [EXPLETIVE] me.*

CLIVE: *Well, remember we try not to curse too much on the program…Hello? Mr. X? You there?*

[LINE GOES DEAD. CALL ENDS.]

CHAPTER 7

THE XNS NEWS desk, where anchor Debi Megyn is joined in studio by intrepid reporter of the Matt Freeman beat, Rick, is encased by a glass television screen that's splattered with beer foam. Below, bottles and pint glasses clink and pool balls clack against cues slammed home to corner pockets, drowning out the dialogue of the personalities on the TV set hanging above the full-service bar. It's hard to make out what's being said, especially with Garth Brooks's "The Thunder Rolls" crackling from old sound-system speakers in this country-western honky-tonk. The squat set is bolted to the wall behind a bar, dimly illuminated to aid day drinkers in their bad decisions.

The set's diminutive size makes it hard to tell whether the greenish smudge in the upper right-hand corner behind Debi Megyn's head is supposed to be the Patay house or not. The occupants of the Saddle 'n' Spurs Saloon don't appear to care too much. And the same's true vice versa for Debi and Rick in studio, who continue their banter, oblivious to the goings-on at this particular honky-tonk that reeks of peanut shells and cheap beer.

"So far, authorities still have *not* released a sketch of Matt Freeman's rescuer. This 'Some Guy,' as Freeman is reported to have referred to him, could look like anyone, Debi," Rick says.

"Oh my! I bet Hollywood's hoping for a Brad Pitt–type, or maybe a—"

"Awww, c'mon, shut this crap off! Ain't there a Nats game on?"

It's not even dark outside, and there's already one well-wasted patron at the Saddle 'n' Spurs. This particular wasted patron is the kind of loud, sloppy drunk most people would ignore, not caring to listen to his inebriated ramblings, let alone learn his name.

But Dixon's been bartending for too long, carrying as many pinched nerves as upper-arm tattoos to prove it, and hasn't broken the habit of learning every customer's name yet. The drunk guy's named Joe, but insists everyone call him Shooter. Nobody does.

Dixon rubs his palm across the top of his crew cut, reminding himself that Joe will be passed out before too long, and that he's just got to handle these few blotto outbursts with calm and patience. Though, truth be told, he's feeling his Zen being tested by Joe—the drunk's t-shirt riding up at the armpits and his beer belly smooshing against the bar top as he tries to stretch for the TV set. As if he could reach it and change the channel manually.

"C'mon, Joe," Dixon sighs. The bartender knows he won't get any help from the two good ol' boys playing pool closer to the front. Brock and Schetter aren't the type to help their fellow man. Dixon's just glad one of them hasn't cracked a pool cue across the nose of the other. Still, there's a mop and bucket of sudsy gray water behind the bar, waiting to report for duty if needed.

No, Dixon's sure that handling drunk-ass Joe as he's sprawled across the bar will come down to the day-shift bartender all on his lonesome. There's no one else, except…

Now Dixon notices something in his peripheral. Someone he hadn't clocked yet sits at the opposite end of the bar. Whoever the new guy is, he's a big motherfucker. Massive. A bald—like, totally bald, missing eyebrows and lashes even— big, massive motherfucker. Vague alarm bells ring in Dixon's head, his most primal instincts triggered.

But Joe's nearly belly flopping over the bar and onto the rubber mats under Dixon's feet, so the bartender finds himself with more pressing matters to deal with.

"Hahaha, that's a good one, Debi," Rick says on the TV, still oblivious to the drama at the Saddles 'n' Spurs.

"Change it! Change it!" Joe whines.

Once he sees Dixon's coming his way, the drunk at least has the sense to push himself off the bar and back onto his wobbling stool. But that doesn't stop his complaining.

Dixon's got a rag at the ready, prepared to wipe belly sweat from his bar. "What's so special 'bout that dang kid, anyway…" Joe mumbles, eyelids fluttering and bottom lip quivering.

Dixon sighs, reaching for the remote Velcroed to the side of the TV. "Dammit, Joe, would you wait your fucking patience…" he says under his breath.

His fingertips barely touch the controller. That's how little time it takes before the mysterious figure, the one triggering the lizard-brain parts of Dixon's mind, speaks.

"Do not change that program."

As if he's heard the voice of God, Dixon's hand drops to his side. Suppressing a sudden urge to leap over the bar and sprint for the exit, he instead turns to face the stranger. From his precarious barstool perch, Joe does the same.

The odd-looking giant of a man—or something close enough to a man that no other word comes to mind—leans forward, pressing his bulk against the bar. His bald head is revealed under the lights. Black veins spilling down the side of his skull become visible. Dixon thinks they look like worms, ebony nightcrawlers pulsing under the skin. But the ghoulish head doesn't match the stranger's bodybuilder physique or the outfit he's sporting. His pale but remarkably defined pectorals push against a black tank top and colorful, jungle-print patterned workout pants complete the ensemble.

Zubaz. That's the brand of pants the stranger's wearing. The name emerges from some deep recess of pop-culture knowledge in Dixon's brain.

They're the type of stretchy workout pants that were worn by pro wrestlers in the 1980s, and by that one mullet-headed football-player-turned-B-movie-star. The combo is unsettling. Dixon tries to put a name to this stranger. But he's never seen this guy in the bar before. He's never seen this guy at all.

He's just…Some Guy.

"Leave it," this Some Guy repeats.

"And who the *hell* are you supposed to be, then?" Dixon asks, thinking it's far too early in his shift to deal with such strangeness, and also grateful for the distance between him and the stranger at the other end of the bar.

But before he's even finished his query, the bartender finds the distance between them closing.

Closing fast.

This Some Guy's eyes roll back—not white, but black. Black, like a starless night sky. And even though it's impossible to see anything past or within the ebony orbs, Dixon can't shake the feeling that something else peers at him through those black eyes. A presence not of his world, something staring down at him with the wicked glee of a young boy with a magnifying glass, an anthill, and a sunny day.

CHAPTER 8

THE WOOD-STAINED KITCHEN table at Stacy's house serves as an adequate substitute for her work desk. The table's been in her life since childhood, having served as her parents' kitchen table before their deaths. Stacy enjoys the nicks and dents and scratches in the wood. She appreciates owning furniture that's been lived in.

And through.

She's covered the tabletop's antiqued geography in the crime-scene photos, documents, and other materials taken from the precinct. Everything in hard copies—nothing electronic. A plain black plastic-bodied stopwatch and an extended length of measuring tape are also part of the mix.

Her round-backed wooden chair is pushed to the table, her upper arms pressed against its edge. She scoots back enough to lift her hands. Fingertips hover above the keyboard on her open laptop. A screensaver image of a kitten balanced on an oversized ball of yarn remains on display, however.

Rather than disturb her screensaver-kitten, Stacy runs her fingers through her hair, brushing it back from her forehead.

"There's no way it went down like that. There's just…It doesn't make sense…"

The floor creaks behind her. Before Stacy can turn around, Jeff's at her side. He leans forward, pressing his cheek to hers. Stacy feels his smile radiating even as his eyes look away from the still images of carnage with which she's fouled the dining area. It's clear, before he even opens his mouth, that he's hoping his goofy grin will rub off on her and prove to be a sufficient distraction.

"Boo!" he says. Then adds, "What doesn't make sense?"

Stacy turns her head quickly, letting her lips brush against Jeff's. There's part of her—a part she's growing to hate—that hopes this tiny bit of affection will be enough. Enough to leave him satisfied, enough to grant her a reprieve from socializing, to allow her more time to get lost in contemplation. But when Jeff remains right by her side, Stacy determines a different strategy is needed.

She extends her hand, fingers pointing at the brutal crime scene photos. "It's the Patay house," she says.

One fingertip rests on *that* photo of one of the Patay boys. The young man broken in half. She taps his eternally silent, open-mouthed scream, forever immortalized on the department's printer paper. "Look," she says, hoping this slight exposure to the violence will repel her fiancé and drive him away so that she can continue working. "Look at the way the body's just…severed. Yet the report makes no mention of shell casings or explosive residue on the scene. None of the reports do. And the wounds? There's no evidence of a knife inflicting that damage either. What in the world could've done it, then?"

Jeff now stands directly behind Stacy. He wraps his arms around her shoulders and the back of the chair. He doesn't say anything, letting the embrace speak for him.

"I just…I don't understand how a human being could've been capable of…" Stacy lets the words trail off, the conclusion still out of reach.

"I suppose you could say the same thing about the Patays, though, right?" Jeff asks. "I mean, taking that boy like they…"

Stacy shrugs and Jeff releases his hold. He steps back with a sigh, and Stacy winces ever so slightly.

"I'm gonna order some Chinese," he says.

"Yeah, sure, okay." But Stacy's attention has already returned to the table. This time, she studies her screen. The kitten's gone. Instead, the XNS homepage fills the screen. A page-wide banner headline appears above a smiling professional shot of Ruth Freeman.

NEXT WEEK: RUTH FREEMAN RETURNS TO XNS
HER EXCLUSIVE STATEMENTS ON MATT'S RETURN

Stacy can already imagine the record-breakings ratings and viewership numbers for the event. It makes her stomach ache to think of it. There's Ruth's smiling face, staring from the screen, existing in stark contrast with the flared nostrils, bloodshot eyes, and accusatory words off an acid tongue that Stacy's encountered from her in the intervening years since her son's disappearance.

The *ping* of her messenger app draws Stacy's eyes to her computer tool bar. She expands the incoming message. Sent as an encrypted file, it takes a while for the program her brother installed to translate its gobbledygook into something intelligible. Of course the message is from Xavier. Of course.

"Hey sis"

"Let me know if u need anything."

"About u know what."

Illuminated by the glow of her computer screen, Stacy does indeed know. She knows all too well.

CHAPTER 9

BLOOD PAINTS THE walls, the floor, and the ceiling of the Saddles 'n' Spurs Honky-Tonk Saloon. Limbs and other body parts are strewn about like the detritus from a homeowner desperately seeking a missing set of keys. Intestines, hearts, brains—every surface is covered in organs and flesh.

At least the carnage is poorly lit. Most of the overhead fixtures are smashed, with shards of glass now seasoning the wreckage of bodies. Indeed, the only remaining source of light in the dim establishment comes from above the bar.

The flickering light of the tiny TV set shifts as the broadcast images change. On-screen: There's a still image of Ruth Freeman. Her professional headshot. She's smiling. Her hair is perfect. Blood and guts slalom slow and steady down the glass.

TV-Ruth is unbothered.

Over the bar and down on the floor, the daytime occupants of the Saddle 'n' Spurs are very much dead. The bodies of Dixon the bartender and the two pool-playing shit-kickers lie scattered. Aside from the blood, guts, and so much more blood, there's almost something artistic about the layout of the carnage. Like a Renaissance painting. Like how the Old Masters would paint the same scenes over and over again, refining their craft and techniques. Everything laid out in recognizable patterns—if one knows what to look for.

By the bar, Joe (aka "Shooter") was left bent backwards, his stringy, unwashed hair rubbing the sole of a shoe-clad foot twisted the wrong way.

He's broken in half, yet somehow life remains. He tries to lift a weak, tendon-severed arm and signal for help. His last gasping breaths come via foamy red saliva bubbles. A trail of blood and spittle extends from his gasping mouth and droops to the dingy barroom floor.

No one's there to speak to Joe or the other three dead men. The booming XNS announcer's voice from the tiny TV will have to do.

"From mother to advocate to mother again, next week, XNS's own Ruth Freeman returns to share her family's inspirational story…"

MATT FREEMAN OPENS his eyes, leaving visions of barroom carnage behind. When he speaks, he's direct and curt, but his words are strange. "Thought *you* were watching *me*. Not the other way around. Not me watching your tool, your guard dog. Suppose the lack of control, the need for patterns—those are all the reasons why you changed your plans." After he's spoken, his shoulders go slack, as though he's become untethered from some invisible apparatus.

And after another moment, he sits up, his back straight against the headrest of his old twin bed. The Star Wars sheets, the same ones that were on his bed all those years before when he was taken, come up short and don't entirely cover his body. He's much bigger now than he was then. Wearing a plain white t-shirt and polka dot boxers his mother bought for him, Matt rubs his eyes. His breathing comes as sharp, shallow bursts. His chest pushes forward, then relaxes.

"There, there, Matty. You've just had a bad dream. That's all."

He stops rubbing his eyes and searches for the source of those soothing words. It doesn't take long to find his mother seated in an old wooden rocking chair at the side of his bed.

Ruth rocks slow and steady. She reaches for him. Her hand, with with its well-manicured nails, touches the comforter. Her fingers wriggle over the bedspread, approaching his long, skinny legs.

Matt looks at the woman, his mother. He finds his voice again. "I…I had a bad dream," he says.

His words bring a smile to her face. "Mommy's here, baby."

Matt lets his lips move. The corners curl upward, an imitation of what's displayed before him. He can tell it's the right choice, as Ruth's wide-mouthed grin expands all the more. She stands and reaches into a plastic laundry basket filled with folded clothes next to her chair. Straightening, she holds a hand out, offering Matt a brand-new pair of washed and pressed blue jeans. "I could tell you weren't sleeping well," she says, "but I didn't want to wake you. Thought bad sleep was better than no sleep at all."

Matt doesn't respond. He takes the jeans from his mother, and she continues on with her own diatribe, oblivious to his silence.

"Let's get these jeans on you so we can join your father and sister for supper," she says.

Still not making a sound, Matt throws his legs over the bedside and stands, planting his feet on the freshly vacuumed, carpeted floor. Boxers and t-shirt ride high on his long lanky form. A gasp escapes from his mother's lips like a whisper.

He holds the jeans against his body, the stitched and riveted denim touching his belly and bare legs. "You didn't have to stay while I slept, Ru—uh…" he says.

Ruth stands tall, raising her head to meet the eyes of her returned child. The damp corners of her eyes, marked by crow's feet, reveal deepening tracks from her tears. "Oh, sweetie, you can call me Mom. If…if you're ready to do that again."

Again, his lips curl into a smile, slow and steady. "Okay," he says. "Okay, Mom."

Before another word passes between them, mother and son are interrupted by the cacophony of breaking dinner plates echoing from downstairs.

"Cassidy." Ruth mutters her daughter's name like a curse.

CHAPTER 10

CASS FREEMAN IS fucked up. Drunk enough that even she hears her words slurring. A little stoned too, so everything that's happening in her mother's kitchen feels like a scene from a movie—one she's watching with the reel sped up and the sound dampened. Like she's shoved cotton balls in her ears before the showing.

Never mind that Cass is the one *doing things* in this formerly sparkling, dusted, waxed, and polished kitchen—Ruth's faux Martha Stewart culinary wonderland. Never mind that Cass is the source of calamity. She still gets to enjoy the show. She watches herself pick up another china plate, glistening with disuse, and then bring it down hard against the marble countertop.

Crash!

Smash!

More debris joins the pile she's already created. There's a certain satisfaction Cass feels, destroying her mother's beautiful, precious things. But it's not enough. The booze, the drugs, the property damage at Dear Mother's expense—none of it can shield her from the fear that's taken hold. It's a fear that hasn't left her in nineteen or so years. But it's strengthened these last few weeks. She's certain the Gray Men have returned something that *looks* like it could be her brother, but that the thing they've sent back is more theirs than the Freemans'. Now, the fear is ready to crash down and wash her away.

Her old habits no longer provide the same level of protection as they once did. Her father isn't helping, either. But at least that's not stopping him from trying. He reaches for Cass, but he doesn't touch her. He stops short of that level of direct contact.

It's like she's the one who's got something wrong with her. Something wrong that even her father doesn't want to catch.

"Cassidy, please. Stop it, honey," he says.

She shakes her head, stretching her hands across the countertop in search of more cookware to destroy. "No," she says. "No, I'm not listening to you."

Her tears come unbidden. It's been a long time since Cass has had any left to spare. She used up all the tears for her brother and what happened to him that night in their bedroom long ago. She'd used up her tears for herself, for the feeling that she was well and truly alone without her baby brother. Not believed, not trusted, not loved. These new tears scare her more because she didn't think they were possible.

"You all just…accept. You accept his story. You accept the most…the most…convenient fiction!"

If her father won't believe her, won't even touch her, Cass decides to force his hand. For the moment, she leaves the cookware alone, ignoring the tiny cuts on her hands from ricocheting glass, and grabs her dad's big bear mitts. She holds them to her face, one hand on either side, letting him feel how her tears and blood intermingle. A glance down her nose at his left hand, and there she spies the dull unpolished gold of an old wedding ring.

It's all that's needed to set her off again. She shoves him away, directing her venom at the ring. "Look at that! She's still got you wearing the ring again. God, this is all just her show, isn't it? Mom thinks she's running things and—what? You just let her?"

Her father folds his arms across his chest and his eyes drop, studying the broken dishes on the kitchen floor. It's the smallest this man, her hero once upon a time, has ever looked to Cass.

"I thought so," she says, wiping away those unwanted tears. "But you do know she's not the one in control, right? You know that, Dad?" There's an urgency to her question-asking, a desperate scramble for support.

"Who's that then, Cassidy?" her mother asks

Having spoken of the devils, Cass isn't surprised to see an unwanted pair of them standing in the kitchen entryway. Her mother, Ruth, and the returned being/person/entity—she's not sure what to call him—wearing her brother's skin and new blue jeans. Ruth's face displays outright menace and blatant disgust at the scene they've descended upon.

"You know, young lady, I've had just about enough of your little temper tantrums," she says, every word dosed with spite. "Your brother deserves better from *his* family."

One of the cooking pots hanging from farmhouse-style hooks above the island is the nearest projectile at hand. Cass's own rage is already rising to meet her mother's disgust, and the pot is soon in her grasp. And just as quickly, it's gone.

"He's. Not. My..."

It's something Cass got from her old man and all the hours they spent throwing the football in the backyard because he'd lost his boy and needed *someone* to pass his knowledge on to: She can throw. The silver pot whizzes over the heads of the intruding mother-and-"son" duo. Ruth ducks like there are bullets flying around her house. But the thing in its Matty-suit, to the side, lets the projectile soar past its head.

"...Brother!"

The shattering of the bay window that looks out on the front yard provides final punctuation.

[...]

[Officers departing FREEMAN RESIDENCE, INTERVIEWEE RUTH FREEMAN (RF) speaking at residence door.]

RF: *So, as I'm sure you understand, officers, it was simply a slip of the hand on my daughter's part, and I sincerely wish our neighbors hadn't bothered you with such…trivialities. I mean, you don't hear me complaining about barking dogs, do you?*

OM: *Alright then, Miss…*

RF: *Ruth, please. Ruth is absolutely fine.*

OM: *Okay then, Ruth. Please, um, just keep it down, okay?*

[RF in doorway, hand on curved handle, interior. Smiling, closing the door. Background noise, domestic.]

RF: *Oh, of course. Good night, officers. Thanks so, so much for all you do.*

[Door closes. OM and OR return to vehicle.]

OM: *Whatcha think, kid? She ain't really as hot as she looks on the TV, huh?*

OR: *I, well, I…*

OM: *[Laughter, extended] I'm just fuckin' with ya, rook. […] Still, that daughter of hers, she's got those…crazy eyes…*

[Entering the vehicle]

OR: *Should we call it in? At briefing, they—they said we should call in and share any info about the Freemans. So, should we call?*

OM: *Knock yourself out, kid. […] And hey, you had your cam off for all that stuff I was sayin'…aww man. Sheeeeeit, there's another report I'm gonna have to write.*

CHAPTER 11

STACY KEEPS A police band radio playing on her side of the bathroom counter while she goes through her evening bedtime routine. She used to hate listening to the coded back-and-forth when she was on patrol, cruising the neighborhoods with Zamuda. But now, on the other side of employment, wearing flannel pajamas buttoned to her neck and her silvery gray hair curling after a long humid day, she finds something comforting in the crackle of static, the bulletins cut off mid-word by itchy trigger fingers operating the two-ways.

Embracing this new, strange sense of calm, she uses one hand to run a brush through the sweaty tangles of her hair and turns the volume up on the square, squat radio with her other.

"…checked out a 415 at 1201 Bobtail Drive. They're saying it was an accident."

IN THEIR BEDROOM, Jeff lays on top of the covers in the bed he shares with Stacy. Despite not having pulled the blanket and sheet back, he's already in boxers and a t-shirt, his teeth slightly sparkling and minty fresh from brushing earlier. A worn paperback is open with the cover up for all to see. *Gone Girl*, by Gillian Flynn. It's his third time trying to read it. Maybe his fourth. His eyes are heavy-lidded already. That's not going to work for Stacy though. She's got too much on her mind, too much weighing on her conscience.

She grabs his shoulder and squeezes. Repeats his name. "Jeff!"

"Wuzzat, Stace?"

There he is.

"It's the Freemans," she says. "Two officers from Capaldi's shift took a disturbance call there earlier in the evening."

Jeff doesn't answer. Not at first. He arches his back, keeping a grip on the blankets. Once they're pushed past his ass, he slots himself over the fitted sheet and covers up. He rolls onto his side, facing his nightstand. His book tumbles off the bed and onto the floor. His page is unmarked, likely another aborted attempt at finishing.

He'll be the first to tell anyone that he's never had much of a head for mysteries.

Finally, he speaks. "Uh huh. You can hear more about it tomorrow then. Come to bed, Stace."

A moment passes. A moment in which Stacy wants nothing more than to storm out of their bedroom. To get dressed and ready for work. Gun, badge, sense of purpose. The whole ensemble.

Then, she feels the flannel pajamas against her body and remembers. *It's over. All of that is done.* And like that, the moment's sapped of its power. She pulls back the covers on her side and joins her fiancé.

"Okay," she says.

Jeff's bedside light is already out. "Trust me. You'll hear something if you need to hear something," he says. "Though I can't imagine why you would need to—" He lets those last words get swallowed up by a yawn.

Stacy opts to let it go. She has to believe he's right.

She turns off her lamp and moves to kiss her lover. But she's greeted by snoring. Instead, she scooches up, placing head and shoulders against the headboard. Dim light glows from outside. It's a clear night.

Clear enough so Stacy could even see the stars.

CHAPTER 12

CASS FREEMAN DOESN'T give a fuck what any of them say. Especially not *Mommy Dearest*. Cass knows what's true and what's a pack of lies. She stands on legs that are steady… enough, and reaches behind with her free hand to pull the back door closed. She wishes Ruth could see her there in the backyard. Still standing. Able to grip her half-finished handle of Jack with one hand and close a door with the other.

"I'll show her who has too much to drunk. To drink. Dumb bitch."

She snickers at her curse word. Or maybe it's the use of "dumb" to describe her mother.

As far as Cass cares, everyone always gets her drinking wrong. The drinking, the drugs, her endless flirtations with death and danger. Her mother, the doctors and rehab specialists her mother hires, even her father—they assume it's the substances she imbibes over and over again that put these so-called crazy notions in her head. Like she somehow smoked a joint at nine years old and that made her see the Gray Men, made her watch them take her beloved brother Matty away. Or that a few too many gin and tonics have led to her more recent claims that the person—if that thing in the house can even be called a *person*—who came back using her brother's name is actually…not.

But the substances don't introduce the ideas. No, not at all. She takes them, uses them to try and block them out.

"Think I wanna see Gray Men. Gray-brother-Man? Huh?" she asks the night sky.

She squeezes the neck of her Jack tight to the point where she worries it'll break from her too-strong grip. She recalls her mother's words after the officers left. "I'm going to take a couple Ambien and sleep," Ruth said. "Try not to embarrass me any further until the morning."

"Don't believe me, Mom. Mommy. Don't believe me, huh? Huh?"

Head on a swivel, her eyes scan the expanse of the old backyard. Green and manicured, picture-perfect. She knows Ruth pays for top-of-the-line landscaping work. Anything to keep up her façade of renewed domestic tranquility.

"Izzat so?" Cass asks. A question for no one—or maybe for everyone.

She steps off the brick walkway and on to the grass. A wooden fence, freshly power-washed and free of grass stains and bird shit, encircles the yard. No way for any pesky neighbors to peer over and get a glimpse of Matty Freeman and the rest of the Freeman clan. Cass steps forward, tilting the bottle and letting some of the golden, honey-colored liquor spill on her mother's perfect yard. The full moon and stars shine on the young woman.

Under interstellar illumination, she pivots and finds her destination.

In the far corner of the yard, with a separate brick pathway leading from the gate on the opposite side by the driveway, her father's old work shed beckons. Since he moved out, it's had a few adjustments under Ruth's supervision. A robin's-egg blue paint job and curlycue lattice work give the building a gingerbread-cottage appearance. The updated exterior strikes Cass as odd considering her dad mostly used the one-room shed for storing hammers, saws, and old plywood along with deflated footballs, basketballs, and a hand-me-down set of golf clubs that got used maybe once every three years.

But these outward changes aren't what draw Cass across the yard. She sees something. Something *inside* the shed.

Cass moves closer. A light shines inside, near the window at the side of the shed. It's the sickly pale illumination of a dying uncovered lightbulb.

Before she can decide that she'd maybe have been better off stopping at the window and peering inside first, Cass stands at the door to the shed, her hand on its burnished steel handle. Her Jack's in the grass now, tipped over on its side, drowning an anthill in Tennessee whiskey.

"Wuzz 'is?" Cass asks her audience of no one.

Then, like someone snapped their fingers and said the magic words, the door opens and Cass stares inside. Everything changes. Whatever drunkenness carried her from the house into and across the yard to the shed—it's all sucked right out of her. Fear turns out to be a mighty strong sobering agent. Terror and revulsion twisting her features, Cass brings a hand up to cover her mouth, like she can will the sickness back inside.

But her eyes won't close. Even though she's internally screaming at herself to look away, to run, she cannot move and she cannot look away.

The shed's interior is closer to childhood memories, the changes Ruth made apparently limited to the superficial exterior. The dusty saw bench, last used God knows when, is illuminated by that single bulb spied through the window. But there are no planks or boards or wood scraps spread across the surface.

No, nothing like that.

It's a dog.

It *was* a dog.

Cass experiences a vague sense of familiarity, seeing the lolling black-spotted pink tongue and the glassy eyes. Like she's seen this particular mutt out for a walk or frolicking in its yard, chasing tennis balls, frisbees, or squirrels.

But no more of that now.

Being split down the middle from chin to tail will have that effect. In the wan light, the dead dog's guts pool off the bench, landing in the dirt below. The skin flaps on either side of the carcass are nailed to the wooden bench, keeping the *specimen* in place.

Standing by the table, towering over the dead animal and reaching a hand into the open cavity he's made?

Matt Freeman.

Cass can't look away. Her eyes follow the path of Matt's arm down to his hand inside the dead dog's open chest. His fingers manipulate the animal's deep purple heart tissue, massaging with slow, steady, circular movements.

That's when Cass finally vomits, spewing forth the hot, bloody acidic aftermath of her liquid dinner. She can't bring her hand down in time, so the sick gushes past her fingers. She doubles over and goes again. The strain brings tears to her eyes.

"I found this doggy. I remember we used to have a doggy."

Wiping tears and barf off chin and cheeks, it takes Cass a moment to realize Matt's speaking to her. Or he's just talking, and she happens to be there to serve as his audience.

"I checked. But it's not the same doggy. He's *different.*"

Cass knows she should run. She should sprint for the gate, for their house. She needs to get away. Needs to escape this monster who has her brother's name and face. Flee from the rancid odor of blood and dog filling the shed. But the signals from her brain to the rest of her body are too slow.

Her gaze drifts to the side, and she finds her hands gripping the doorframe. Squeezing tight. Like she's holding herself in place.

Then, Matt's standing right in front of her. Blood covers his front, bits of fur visible in the sticky serum. He reaches out and grabs her wrist. Pulls her inside the shed, inside the abattoir he's made.

"Come here, Cass," he says. "I've wanted to talk to you since I got back."

Snot leaks from Cass's nose, the salty tears and mucus making it hard for her to speak. "Whu-whu-why?" is all she can manage.

She stares past the man claiming to be her brother, focusing instead on the dead dog spread across their father's work bench.

He puts his hands on her shoulders. He's much stronger than outward appearances suggest. He moves her so her back's to the bench. Now, he's standing between her and the open shed door.

"Shh. It's okay," he says. "You don't have to look at it." He nods his chin back behind Cass, acknowledging the carnage.

Then, all of his attention returns to her.

"You were right, you know?"

Cass tries to pull away. She knows she has to try, she has to do *something*, even if the end result is as disappointing as she expects.

"Let me go…" But she can't scream or shout the words, only whisper them.

Matt takes Cass's arm and twists it to her back. Her mouth and eyes both open wide in response to the sudden pain. But again, any potential cry is stifled.

"*They* tell me you call them the Gray Men," he says, like he's talking about some dear old acquaintance. "You and others who they're watching, always watching. But they're not *men*. That's what you all get wrong."

He's closer now. His lips practically brushing against her ear. "You were wrong to say I'm not me though, sister. To say I'm not your brother. I am."

He pauses, holding it a little too long. Holding it so long that Cass grows more and more certain he's not even breathing. Then, finally, he continues. "I'm just different now. Better. Do you understand?"

Even as tears fall and her bottom lip quivers, Cass catches her brother in her peripheral vision. His eyes focus on her. They are, indeed, *different*. Bigger, black and yellow compound structures. Like an insect's eyes magnified a thousandfold.

"Here, let me tell you how I've changed…"

His bug eyes bulge from their humanoid eye sockets. His lower jaw drops and expands past human limits, heading to nightmare territory. His distended mouth and stretched-out skin are held together with something resembling organic wires, hooks, and clasps. A new tongue flicks out from the gaping abyss, long and pink, pointed at the tip. It heads for Cass's ear.

All set to burrow inside and play with her brain.

PART 2

INHOSPITABLE CONDITIONS

CHAPTER 13

MALEK FREEMAN STANDS at the foot of his daughter's hospital bed, unsure of what to do with his hands as he looks down at her. Finding the right words to say is hard enough.

"You know, I kept it all. Everything from when you played ball in high school. Trophies, plaques, news clippings…all of it…"

There's no response coming.

Malek folds his arms across his chest, hands pressing against the layer of fat he's built up, poking his fingers to his ribs.

He keeps on talking.

"I know you thought your Mom, you thought she threw it away, when I moved out, but…it was me. I took them with me."

Here come the tears. But he doesn't feel worthy of them. Doesn't feel he's earned the right to cry. And the antiseptic scent of lemony clean tickles his nostrils and makes it that much worse.

"I guess I wanted to have something of you…with me. I know it was damned selfish."

He knows Cass can't hear him. Can't see his tears or the awkward way he's standing at the end of her bed. When his hands drop to his sides and he brushes fingertips along the end of the baby blue blanket the nurses have covered her with, Malek knows he's the only one in the room actively aware of all that's happening.

As he runs his hands across the blanket, thinking how it can't possibly be soft enough for his little girl, Malek is struck by how small she looks lying there in her hospital bed. Half her hair's been shaved off her head, with monitors attached to the stubbly spot. Tubes run into her nose, down her throat. A drip feed connects a long bag of fluids to her bruised wrist. The many black screens encased in white and gray plastic, with green and blue digital inputs flashing, beep and buzz and chirp before him.

They're the only form of communication he can expect from Cass for the time being. Maybe forever.

"I'm so sorry, Cass," he says.

He steps back from the bed. Reaches into a bag resting on one of the visitor's chairs in the room. Soon, his hands hold a framed photograph. One of his treasures. A memory from long ago. The picture in the silver frame shows a much younger Cass. Eight years old. From before her brother's abduction. Ruth was probably the one who took the photo in the first place.

Their daughter's asleep in her big-girl bed. Curly red hair spreads across her pillow.

"Your mom and I spent so much time worrying about the son we lost. I guess we never realized that we missed the part where we were losing our little girl, too."

He sits, hard and heavy, on the curved, cushioned seat of another visitor's chair in Cass's private recovery room. The picture stays in his hands until he sets the frame down on the cylindrical bedside stand meant for flowers and gifts. The picture's the only thing there.

Malek covers his face with his hands.

RUTH DOESN'T WAIT in the recovery room with her brain-dead daughter or her sobbing mess of an ex-husband. She's got more important business to attend to.

That's why she's set up shop under the awning outside County General Hospital. She can stand there, multi-task, and really feel like she's accomplishing something. In this case, she's tilting her head toward her shoulder to keep her smartphone pinned against her ear. On the other side of her body, her arm's at a near ninety-degree angle with a tablet resting in the crook.

"There's no story, Rick," she says, speaking as calmly as she can into her phone. "I already told you, it's just my daughter, and she's got plenty of probl…"

Ruth trails off. Soon Rick's shouting in her ear or so it sounds like to her. "Ruth! Ruth! I wanted to ask about the police report though. There was…"

Approaching from across the patient drop-off loop before the awning, Stacy Keppler has her hands up in a conciliatory, "I come in peace" fashion. She's talking as well.

Ruth's quite familiar with how much Keppler likes to talk. Talking, talking, talking, but never any *doing*.

"Ruth," Stacy says, then noting the glare her use of the name produces, switches gears to, "Mrs. Freeman. I spoke with your husb…with Malek on the phone. I told him I'd be coming. He told me about what happened with Cass and said it'd be okay if I…"

Ruth's grateful she hasn't hung up on Rick. It's easy enough to turn her back to the former police sergeant and resume the more important business at hand: cutting off any impulse to dig deeper on her XNS colleague's part. "Look," she says to him, "I'll be at the front of the building for the press conference shortly. I figure I'll call on Garrett from the *Times-Dispatch* first. Then, you."

While she covers press conference choreography with Rick, Ruth sends a text with her tablet. Shooting up an emergency flare more like, as the ex-Sergeant Keppler remains standing behind Ruth.

Right away, Ruth's bodyguards Coleman and Lewis materialize next to her, their sleek black suits adorned with hospital visitor badges. The Ray-Bans on their faces add a robotic, unemotional quality to their shared appearance, like something from a cheap sci-fi flick.

Ruth likes it that way.

"I just want you to know how sorry I am," Stacy says, still trying to say her piece. "For Cass..."

As her bodyguards form a beefy wall between her and the ex-cop, Ruth hangs up her phone and tucks her tablet under her arm. She doesn't look back as she turns away and walks down the breezeway, returning to the hospital.

Of course, she can't resist taking one final jab.

"Yes, I'm so sure you are, Ms. Keppler. Very, very sorry. Now, I hope you'll respect my family's privacy at this time and leave us all the hell alone."

CHAPTER 14

RUTH FREEMAN MIGHT be a grade-A bitch, but Stacy appreciates the woman's way with words. Her bodyguards, though? They're not much in the way of conversationalists.

Still, Stacy's years on the force have made it so the big, strong, silent, and tough act doesn't phase her much. Confronted with scowls and frowns, she opts for smiles instead.

"Hey there, fellas!" she says.

One of the thumb-looking bodyguards—the scrawled permanent-marker name on his visitor pass suggests he's Coleman—wrinkles his brow and starts to answer.

"Hey…" he says.

Stacy lets her smile grow. The charm offensive has always worked wonders for her. She never had a "bad cop" routine in her. After all, she always got better results playing hard to the side of the angels.

Being nice helps. But so does paying attention. That's how she notices the other tank of a man—Lewis—giving his buddy an unabashedly incredulous look. "Dude, no," he says, to truly get the message across.

Dissension in the ranks, Stacy thinks. *Could be useful.*

COMING AROUND TO the front of County General Hospital, keeping tabs on Ruth Freeman's bodyguards and their not-so-subtle tailing of her, Stacy finds its easy to get lost in the scrum of journalists gathered before another makeshift platform and mic stand assembled by Ruth's media team. Stacy considers it more than a little gross, the fact that Ruth even has a "team" to begin with, but she's willing to let that slide.

Even after all the grief and anger and rage she's been subjected to via Ruth, Stacy can't entirely fault the other woman. After all, there's no denying the years of separation that kept the Freemans from their baby boy. *Not so much a baby anymore—more of a full-sized adult.*

That said, Stacy isn't one hundred percent certain that the individual who hugged her the other day inside City Hall is anywhere near a grown-up emotionally despite his physical appearance. After all, in that stiff and awkward embrace, Stacy couldn't help but notice a restrained, undernourished development in the young man's bearing. Like there was some essential ingredient missing that would've been useful to take him from "boy with ice cream smeared around his mouth" to "young man hidden and guarded by his family."

There were echoes that Stacy picked up on, traces of similar feelings invoked by her encounters with Cass Freeman over the years. Cass filled her version of that missing "ingredient" with drugs and alcohol. Stacy can't pinpoint what Matt might have used instead.

One thing's for certain: Their mother used the spotlight to ease *her* pain.

Stacy would love to lay all blame at Ruth's feet. She wants nothing more than to give back the scorn as she's received it. But that's not who she is. So, she stands in the crowd, trying to make herself fade into the background, and she listens, watches.

"Ladies and gentlemen," Ruth begins, "I wish I did not have to speak with you all regarding these new, most unfortunate circumstances related to members of my family…my children, even. I know there are many of you who likely have questions about what happened to my dear, sweet daughter Cassidy. In the interest of full disclosure and to combat any rumors or innuendo swirling around, I am here to answer you directly. Honestly."

She takes a moment to scan the audience, then points at one of the reporters.

"So, please, ask me anything. Garrett?"

"Thanks, Ruth. Do you believe the attack on your daughter is in any way related to the abduction and subsequent rescue of your son Ma—"

There's a flash of anger behind the podium, a brief slippage of the media-ready mask Ruth wears. She cuts off the question with a quickness.

"Excuse me, but we aren't here to speak about my son. He was taken as a child. An innocent child. That's completely different. As for calling this an 'attack,' well, my daughter did lead a troubled life."

The Freeman matriarch lets her comment hang in the air, laden with implications about her daughter's "bad seed" status.

Suddenly, Stacy finds the press of cameras and microphones overwhelming, triggering. She flashes to the interview-room footage from years past. Images of her sitting in a room with a little girl whose feet didn't touch the floor. A little girl who was scared.

A little girl who wanted someone to believe her.

Stacy sees red as Ruth continues. "Now, we'll let the police continue their investigation. But the instincts of a mother tell me, well, accidents *do* happen…"

The red is fast becoming all-consuming. Stacy might not have taken to playing "bad cop," but she's never been one to stomach liars. Her eyes dart around the scrum, looking for a stray microphone to grab. For a moment, she entertains the notion of standing up to Ruth, of speaking out.

A hand on her shoulder, a calm voice in her ear, is what Jeff brings to the situation. "She's not worth it, Stace," her fiancé says. "Come on, let's go home."

That's enough. There's genuine concern and care in every syllable uttered. Nothing patronizing. That's never been Jeff's modus operandi. He's the long-time boyfriend of a former detective sergeant. He relishes the role and appreciates his partner's position. He supports more than he protects.

Stacy recalls how tightly he hugged her when she finally shared the news of her retirement. She can still hear the words he whispered to her: "I'm glad you'll be safe now. That's all I've ever wanted."

Following him from the hospital and out to the parking lot, Stacy's anger dissipates and she finds clarity, along with a way to respond.

"Let's take my car," she says. "There's one stop I need to make first."

CHAPTER 15

JEFF BRAYFOYLE SUGGESTED going home, believing it the best thing for his fiancée, Stacy Keppler. Ever since the news broke about the Freeman boy's return right as Stacy was leaving the force, Jeff's had to witness the love of his life unmoored, directionless. He worries that the riptides of current events and resurfaced traumas will sweep her out to sea. So to speak.

But going home? Home's an anchor. Home's safe harbor.

That's not what's happening though. Now, he's in the passenger seat of Stacy's sedan, a raffle prize from a police union benefit dinner years before, peering through the front windshield at the cracked concrete of a long driveway with a thick steel gate around the premises and a state-of-the-art burnished silver callbox on a post by the entrance with cameras above, below, and to the sides. Jeff can't help himself; he has to say something.

"When I suggested we go home," he says, "I meant *our* home."

But Stacy's already leaning out the driver's-side window, extending her hand to the callbox. She enters a long string of numbers, tapping at the silver buttons as fast as she can. When she does provide an answer to Jeff, there's a distracted quality to her speech. "You know his alarms are gonna go off in like twenty seconds if I don't get the code input in time…"

"Well, if he didn't change it every day, it might be easier to figure it out," he mutters under his breath.

If Stacy hears, she doesn't acknowledge the complaint. Instead, her retort comes with the final sequence of *beeps* indicating her successful completion of the entry code. She sits back against the driver's seat. Hands on the steering wheel.

Waiting.

The gears of the electric gate rattle and hum, then slowly push the barricade along its grooved track, providing access to the remaining length of old, busted-up concrete. Rather than put the car in gear and roll forward, Stacy unbuckles her belt and pushes open the driver's-side door. It takes Jeff a moment to figure out her intentions.

"You want me to *go*? Take the car home and…?"

Stacy looks back inside the car, while keeping an eye on the gate. It's open, but perhaps not for very long. "Uh huh," she says. "You know how private he's gotten these last few years… And with the Freeman stuff, he's just…It's better if it's just me."

Jeff sighs and slides over the center console and gear shift, moving into the driver's seat. Stacy's already turning away from the car, making her way through the open gate. She calls back to him, "Thanks again, babe. I appreciate this."

"I know you do," he says, throwing the car in reverse and squealing tires on the pock-marked driveway.

He might hate driving her to this particular house given its connection to what happened to her, her brother, and her parents all those years ago, but Jeff's not worried about Stacy's safety there.

No, he can't imagine a safer, more secure place for her to be than with her paranoid, conspiracy-spouting, shut-in of a little brother.

MATT FREEMAN ABDUCTION THEORIES

Compiled by Xavier Keppler

Okay, sis, I've prepared a general overview for you. I figured you'd come to me with questions eventually. And I do know how much you like lists. Ha. Ha. Some of the info here should be familiar, goes all the way to M & P (maybe, likely beyond).

The Patay Family actually abducted Matt Freeman as a child and he was saved by some unknown Good Samaritan. (Ha. And again, HA!)

The POLICE abducted Matt Freeman and sold him to a child-sex ring run by the Mole People. (Okay, I get it if you don't want to believe this theory. I'm just a messenger here.) Actually traced the IP addresses on some of the earliest postings with this theory. Would you be surprised to find they came from inside the XNS HQ?

Matt Freeman never existed. The Freemans are actually crisis actors. (Though based on what you told me happened at City Hall, you'd think they'd have cast a better "Matt.")

The Gray Men Theory: This one we've been over several times before (even before he came back), and I don't have much new to add. Yet. Plus your star witness just became non compos mentis. (Sorry.)

Have you followed up or asked anything about the Moon-faced Man or "Some Guy"? How many patrons were at the Saddle 'n' Spurs again?

CHAPTER 16

A SECURITY CAMERA rotates on its pedestal hanging under a front-porch eave, directing its attention to Stacy. Nonplussed, she speaks directly into the tiny black eye with its off-centered red-dot pupil that sends its live footage to the house's sole occupant.

From another speaker box by the front door, her brother's voice emerges, hollow and echoing. Devoid of body and form. *The way he'd probably love to be.*

"Okay, step back, sis. Door's opening now."

Stacy wants to say something back to the camera. Something like: "You knew it was me when I entered the driveway gate code. Why go through this extra round of scrutiny?"

But she knows her brother Xavier too well.

Besides, the camera's already rotating to a new position, focusing on the now-open doorway of Stacy's childhood home.

(Though, ever since her parents' deaths and her signing over the house to Xavier in full, both its exterior and interior have moved far from her nostalgic remembrances.)

The front foyer, long ago a place where jackets and bookbags were hung haphazardly and her father's briefcase sat balanced amid the chaos, is now a barren wasteland. No pictures on the walls, no mirrors, no floral bouquets—their mom's specialty— waiting to welcome visitors with a touch of color and beauty.

Focusing only on this space, one might be forgiven for thinking no one lived in the house.

At least, until Xavier's tinny voice emerges from another of the numerous speakers secreted in tiny corners throughout the structure, confirming there is a sort of life within the old house.

"I'm downstairs!" he announces.

"Of course he is," Stacy mumbles. She steps inside and the front door automatically slams shut behind her.

"You know I heard that, right?" her brother asks, forever the petulant younger sibling, even in middle age.

Stacy smiles a big-sister, shit-eating grin, confident her baby brother's watching.

Past the foyer, untouched and unvisited by the home's sole occupant for Stacy can't even guess how long, the presence of someone living there becomes more obvious the deeper one goes. Painfully so.

Making her way to the back of the house, she must tip-toe and turn sideways, squeezing through the narrowed passageway that was once the family's downstairs hallway. It's become a hoarder's paradise of empty(ish) pizza boxes, old magazines and newspapers stolen from the local library before Xavier's reclusiveness fully sunk its teeth into him, and miscellany from their parents, all adding an air of claustrophobia to the immediate surroundings. Stacy's lost count of how many times she's asked her brother if he was going to clean up, or if he needed or wanted her help doing so. At least there's still room to move down the hall. She supposes there's some slight comfort in that.

Soon, she's traversed the obstacle course and made it to another opened doorway. A long set of steps descend from that point, the basement beckoning. Xavier waits for Stacy there.

Now Stacy's closer to the basement than to the chaos of the first floor. There's an electric buzz and hum in the stale air. She fires off another gently teasing comment. "Aren't you gonna ask why I'm here?"

But it's hard to keep up the act when she sees Xavier—his dreadlocks prematurely white, crunchy, and down to his shoulders, and his five-o'clock shadow that's pencil-lead gray—smiling up at his big sister. The sternness she's affecting melts at the sight of his grin.

She takes the final few steps down to the basement level, walks over to Xavier, and wraps her brother's head and shoulders in an embrace. He doesn't rise from his padded and cushioned gaming chair, but that's not unusual. As much time as he spends in that chair, Stacy wouldn't be surprised to find his skin and the chair's leather bonding. She's long ago learned to let it go.

"C'mon, now! Of course I know..." he says.

He pushes back on the edge of his workstation and spins around, the wheels of his chair squeaking on the concrete floor. Stacy already saw the four-monitor setup before she finished her descent, but she lets Xavier indulge in a little dramatic flair. After all, she understands how important it is for him. Information, theories, conspiracies—as Jeff calls them—they're what Xavier's filled his emptiness with. And Stacy's the only one he ever shares them with.

The screens all display the same thing: Matt Freeman's face as a child paired with a blurry video still from a long-distance shot of Matt Freeman as he was recovered from the Patays. The XNS watermark appears behind both images, as if the news network has declared ownership of both these Matts who were separated by time and tragedy.

"You want to know what *really* happened to Matt Freeman," Xavier says. "Well, strap in, sis, 'cause I've got some theories."

CHAPTER 17

MALEK HATES HAVING to chase after his ex-wife like he's one of her lackeys or gofers. He remembers a time when he was the big sports star and she was the girl who caught his eye. The one who wanted to be a part of his world and nothing more than that. Or at least, if she *did* want more, she never mentioned anything to him about it at the time.

Then, of course, their only son went missing for nineteen years, and things…changed.

Now, Malek's the one standing in the middle of the hospital hallway, arms waving, trying to get her attention as she paces back and forth, her cellphone practically plastered to the side of her head. Her heels make a sound halfway between a smear and a squeak as she takes tighter and tighter turns, all her attention directed to her business on the phone.

"Ruth! Hold up," he says, trying to get her attention.

When she does answer, it's to the person on the other end of her call, not Malek. "That's great, hon. Just stay there. I'll be right…"

She pauses to glare at her ex. The expression on her face tells him everything he needs to know about her opinion of his interruption. Then, she finishes the call.

"…there. Don't go anywhere."

Ruth drops the phone in the brown leather handbag dangling off her shoulder and raises her eyes to her former husband's gaze. She takes a second longer before speaking to him. She still knows exactly how to push his buttons.

"Yes, Malek?"

He closes his eyes and tries to find his center, or wherever the hell it is he's supposed find some inner peace. It's hard to do when he can hear Ruth snickering on the other side of his closed eyes.

But he tries.

Finally, Malek opens his eyes and goes for it. "I thought you might want to take a moment—*if* you can spare it—to maybe be with your daughter."

He nods to the closed door of Cass's hospital room. The room he's been in since his daughter got out of surgery early in the morning. Ruth looks at the door, and Malek can't understand the expression on the face of the women he once thought he loved. There's no warmth, no tenderness. None of the care and compassion she'd shown when Cassidy was a newborn, pink and squealing against her breast or cooing in her arms.

He can't figure how the disconnect happened between mother and daughter. But it's there, unmistakable and unavoidable.

"Yes. Always craving Mommy's attention, isn't she?" Ruth says.

Malek's hands come up, balled into fists. He'd never hit Ruth, but he's sorely tempted to punch a wall, maybe knock a hole in the door to Cass's room. He supposes that's one way to ensure his ex looks in on their ailing, comatose daughter. Maybe then she'd understand the horror show that's been playing over and over in his head since he found Cass bleeding from her ears and mouth in his old work shed.

If she only knew the things I've seen, he thinks.

"Ruth, I don't know much about how this world works. But I'd think maybe you'd wanna make sure your *daughter* doesn't die hating you…"

It's saying the word that gets him. He's been as restrained as possible until this point. But "daughter" breaks the floodgates, and the tears come swift and steady. Hands still in fists, Malek wipes his tears away. A blurry image of his ex-wife's face emerges before him.

She looks disgusted.

It hurts Malek that he can't tell who the disgust is aimed at. Their daughter? Him?

Or is it at herself?

LEWIS AND COLEMAN are at their boss's side, ready to act. After all, that's what she pays them for. Acting on her behalf. Keeping her out of dangerous or otherwise unpleasant situations. Making sure the public, her legions of obsessed fans and even more obsessed haters, are kept at bay. Sometimes, the duo understands that the term "haters" refers to her coworkers, authority figures, or even other members of Ms. Freeman's family. Over their years of employment, the duo's become quite efficient at throwing up a shield around their employer or extricating her from messier entanglements.

It's easy to stride over to her side when she's getting into it with her weeping ex-husband. Never mind whatever athletic achievements Malek Freeman might have to his name. Never mind that Coleman had the man's poster on his wall in school, back when Freeman was *Sports Illustrated*'s "College Athlete of the Year."

Malek Freeman doesn't pay their bills.

The one problem though? Protecting Ruth Freeman isn't the pair's only job at the moment. She gave them a different assignment. And now they're standing next to her, ready to deliver news about how they've completely fucked up that particular task.

Towering over their five-foot-nothing employer, the duo recognizes the same emotion on each other's faces.

It's fear.

RUTH'S BODYGUARDS HAVE interrupted the burgeoning argument between her and Malek. It's Malek who catches the terror in the eyes of the twosome. One of the big men finds his voice and speaks at last. "Ma'am, uh, we, uh, we don't wanna panic you, but…"

The stuttering delivery pulls Ruth back from whatever disgust spiral she's traveling down. Her ill temper's suddenly rerouted to her guards. "What?" she says, the word dripping with impatience. "What?"

"Ma'am…"

It's the way the bigger, balder of the two men can't finish his sentence that gets to Ruth at last. Suddenly, she's the one balling up her fists, panic overtaking *her* expression.

"It's Matt," they finally say. "It's probably nothing, but he's no longer in the waiting area in the closed-off wing where we'd stationed him. We've done a sweep, but…"

Malek can't believe what he's hearing. Nostrils flaring, he turns to his ex, ready to unleash hell. "You brought him *here*?"

But Ruth's already on the move. She doesn't look back to acknowledge Malek's comment. Her bodyguards rush after her. She can move pretty damn fast when she wants to. All those days and nights out with the search parties years ago, calling for Matt, trudging across field and forest.

This is familiar territory for Ruth. She's made herself ready for this moment.

"MRS. FREEMAN, PLEASE! Wait!"

Lewis finds his voice and the balls to use it before Coleman beats him to the punch. He calls to their employer, even as his compatriot flashes him a worried grimace. But Ruth isn't stopping for her ex, and she's not stopping for her bodyguards either. She's focused on one person, and one person alone.

"Matt! Matty!" she calls out.

Ahead, a family waits for the elevator, all gathered around a sweet-looking old nana in a wheelchair, her twig of a body swallowed by a hospital gown with a green blanket over her non-existent lap.

Ruth shoves her way in front of the group as the elevator door opens. She's inside the silver box first. She presses the buttons and gives the old woman and her befuddled family members a death stare that says "Stay back. This is mine."

Then, she's gone, leaving Coleman and Lewis to contend with the angry protests of the family and the confused, blank stare of the nana denied her elevator ride.

LOBBY FLOOR: REGISTRATION desk, security, gift shops, cafeteria, the waiting area for non-family members, and…

Ruth.

She's off the elevator, still calling for her son. "Matty! Matty! Where are you, baby?"

A heady, intermingling of sweat and heavy breathing fills the immediate area around her—Coleman and Lewis. The big men are panting, pit stains leaking through their too-tight suit jackets. They've taken the stairs to catch up with their boss and have descended fast enough from the upper floors that it makes a difference for their equilibriums here at the bottom floor.

Ruth's got no time or desire to acknowledge their "sacrifice."

All she's got time for is Matt.

She doesn't care about all the people staring. That novelty wore off years ago. First when she was the mother of the missing boy, and later when she was "that lady from TV."

She doesn't give a damn about whispering nurses. Or a nervous security guard who's almost certainly feeling out of his depth. Or even the sleepy-eyed paparazzi trying to look discreet amid the regular folks despite outnumbering said regular folks by a fair number. It's easy enough to spot the bottom-feeding vultures with their backwards baseball caps and Nikon cameras slung around their necks with cloth straps.

None of it matters. None of *them* matter.

"I swear to God," she says to Coleman and Lewis, finally acknowledging their presence, "if anything—*anything*—has happened..."

But she can't finish the thought. There's just no way.

CHAPTER 18

STACY'S NEVER HAD to knock on the door to Zamuda's fancy lieutenant commissioner's office before, and she feels more than a little weird psyching herself up to do so. After all, he's right there. Door's already open and everything. And the man behind the massive desk—a power-move-style of furniture, as the old LTC described it to her once—is someone she's known for years. Someone she's worked with, spent late nights on the job with, cried with, and laughed with, often all within the same late evening. Only thing is that now he's still serving and protecting, and Stacy is…

Whatever it is she's doing, Stacy's not entirely sure her old partner would sanction it. Hence the hesitation.

Lucky for her, the big man's already well aware of her presence and spares her from having to make the first move. An exaggerated sigh ruffles some of the paperwork on his desk as he looks at her through the open doorway. "What the hell are you doing here, Keppler?" he asks.

Then, knocking those same papers off the desk and onto the floor as he maneuvers up from his chair and around his desk, not seeming to give too much of a damn about the mess, Zamuda makes a beeline for Stacy. She lets the hug come, knowing there's not a chance in hell she could avoid it. It's one of his big patented Zamuda bearhugs, too. The kind you could get only once and never forget.

"Didn't we kick you out of here?" he asks, hands on her shoulders, giving her a sly once-over. "What ya want me to do now? Have 'em lock you up for trespassin'?"

"Yeah, yeah, yeah," she says. "Don't break my ribs and I won't accuse you of police brutality."

His laugh in response is deep and hardy. A gut-busting chuckle Stacy remembers all too well. But as she's crossing the threshold into the office and is already pulling the office door closed, Stacy's got no time for fond remembrances. She's all business.

Still, before she can say anything else, Zamuda catches her by surprise. "You been hanging with that conspiracy nut of a brothers of yours, ain't ya?" he asks, though it's really more of a statement than a question.

Stacy waves off the comment. She can tell Zamuda knows why she's *really* there, and it seems like he's stalling. She's got no time for that.

"Just wondering about those murders over on Landsbury. That's the old honky-tonk, yeah?"

This time, Zamuda's sigh is no act. But Stacy's not having it. She returns his death stare with one of her own. It's a battle of the wills, and it doesn't appear to be one Zamuda's going to win.

He steps aside, giving her access to the open plain of his desk. There's a manila folder with photo printouts waiting on the corner. It's almost like Zamuda's blustery response to the appearance of his old partner pushed that folder right into her line of sight.

Of course, ever the detective, Stacy's searching for the things she's not supposed to see. Like a cocktail napkin, lipstick smear at the edge, taken from a bar near the hospital.

"Go ahead," he tells her, pointing at the folder. At the thing he *wants* her to see.

LOOKING AT THE crime scene photos from the Saddles 'n' Spurs massacre is akin to putting a jigsaw puzzle together—one where the edges are sanded down and the picture overlaps again and again. It's an inefficient system, to say the least. Still, leaning over Zamuda's desk, her former partner at her side like in the old days, Stacy tries her damnedest to do just that.

The black-and-white and color snaps showcase a crime scene reminiscent of *The Wizard of Oz*, moving from gray-scale to Technicolor wonderland. Blood splashes across every surface, and severed limbs arranged just so, look nauseating no matter what their palette may be.

"Oh geez," Stacy says, "those bodies…"

Zamuda nods. "Gnarly, right? Four bodies in all, but damn if the scene doesn't look like it's more…"

Stacy zeroes in on one word from her former partner's statement. She runs that "four" over and over again in her head. Leaning closer, hands moving photographs around on the desk, trying to capture the perfect configuration of death. Once she's satisfied, Stacy steps back and places a hand on Zamuda's arm to move him as well.

When they're at an acceptable distance, she gestures to the spread, hoping Zamuda sees it the way she does, that he too can find the forest for the bloody trees.

"They're laid out in the same pattern as the bodies at the Patay house," she says.

Or like how they found Mom and Dad and the other searchers…
No. You don't know that.

Stacy refuses to spiral, won't let herself get in trapped in a web of theories like Xavier. She just wants to walk a straight line—a straight line to the truth.

"Wait, what?" Zamuda asks, disrupting her train of thought.

He moves to take a closer look and even pulls out the old crime scene photos from the Patay house for comparison. But there's a strange look in his eyes that Stacy catches. A look that makes it clear that he already *knows* she's right. Whatever follows will just be him playing a part. Acting and reacting the way he's supposed to when confronted with a revelation.

She suddenly can't stop thinking about that cocktail napkin, that lipstick. She's certain she's seen that shade before. Could be someone she knows. Could be someone famous.

Maybe even on TV.

CHAPTER 19

MATT FREEMAN STRETCHES, reaching across the holly tree branch studded with shiny, green, jagged leaves. One of his fingers touches the tip of a single leave. There's a quick, sharp pain as it pricks him and cuts open his flesh. He doesn't withdraw his hand though. Doesn't retract the injured finger. When he was a kid, he might've moved the bleeding digit to his mouth. Lips pursed, tongue lapping, he'd suck up the blood. He'd suck harder until the skin around the cut turned white.

But that was a different Matt. A Matt from before.

Now, he lets the blood flow unchecked, unfettered. Even as the scent of hot copper matches the watery serum flowing from the scratch, Matt doesn't flinch. More blood comes, spilling on the holly leaves. Green and red intermingle. His blood's bright red, like holly berries.

Birds, tiny sparrows and a cardinal or two, dash and dart amid the leaves and branches of the tree's mates. The trees planted on this patio are meant for hospital guests. There's a tree nursery to match the newborn nursery on the other side of the building. Beaks snap closed around bloodstained berries. Then, the birds flit away with their prizes while their peers whistle and chirp in appreciation.

But the birds keep their distance from *Matt's* tree.

Finally, Matt withdraws his bleeding hand from the tree and brings it to his face. He studies hand and blood alike. They're both part of him. He knows that. And yet, he also knows that he's much more. He's become much more than flesh and blood.

Someone stands close by, whispering to themself. They're spying on Matt from around a brick-walled corner. This someone doesn't know Matt can hear them. They don't know he's been aware of their presence ever since they snuck outside, holding the heavy glass and metal door while they pulled it closed slowly to dull the sound. Matt's enjoying how these regular people underestimate him.

"Holy shit. What a weirdo. I'm gonna get so much money for a shot of this freak..."

Matt waits for the whispering stranger to make the first move.

And he doesn't have to wait long.

"Matt!" A whispered shout. Like something heard in a dream.

"Matt!" Louder.

"Matt Freeman!"

Whoever it is, their patience seems to have run out. The sweaty, pockmarked face of a paparazzo is visible for a second before his features are covered by a camera he brings to his eyes. "Smile, Matty!" the man says. The camera's aperture narrows like an eye squinting to scrutinize the bleeding young man before it.

The flash goes off in time with the paparazzo's finger pressing the button to take his shot. It's a dying star going supernova, exploding amid the relative calm of the cosmos.

Matt Freeman's seen things that this man and his camera will never understand. There's very little left on this world that can scare or surprise him.

But the reverse?

Oh, there's plenty of scares that Matt Freeman has in store for this presumptuous, unworthy man and the fading light of his camera.

JOEY HAD COME up to the so-called "off-limits" and "under-construction" floor of County General, knowing a bit of bullshit whenever he got a whiff. His contact, a nurse on the night shift, had filled him in on the truth. Turned out the Freemans—Ruth Freeman, at least—brought *him* with her when she came to the hospital after the attack or whatever the hell happened to the daughter. The drunk one. *Him* being the son. The son only very, very few people have even seen since his return.

The returned son—he was the one that mattered and would rope Joey the big bucks as soon as he got a good bidding war going for some snaps.

All the papers, the news networks, and news sites were clamoring for something. For *anything*. Sure, XNS had their exclusive connection through Ruth Freeman, which left everyone else chasing their tails, fighting over table scraps. When he'd overheard the Freeman matriarch herself ranting about *her Matt* being *missing* and having her guards with her, Joey thought he'd hit the jackpot. If he acted fast, played his cards, he'd have the pictures with little to no hassle.

Because if the guards were with Ruth, that meant they weren't with Matt. The math was simple. Joey snagged an old ID that hadn't been deactivated and that worked on the service elevators. Easy enough to take a rickety, bumpy ride to the floor where he suspected he'd find a young man trying to hide from prying eyes.

And then, it was more dumb luck from there. Right place, right time. He thought about being trapped inside, what he might miss if he were in the kid's shoes.

"Kid," like they weren't actually close to the same age...

He stepped around the corner onto the rooftop garden where the tall, skinny young man was bleeding onto one of the trees planted in compacted soil. Joey has seen a lot of weird shit working celebrity and gossip beats. It takes a lot to shake him. But the empty look in the eyes of Matt Freeman, the way he bled without flinching or blinking or wincing, that was enough to knock the paparazzo for a loop. However, the camera hanging around his neck served as a reminder of why he was there in the first place. His purpose was not to wonder why, it was to get the shot and get the fuck out of there.

As his flash fades, Joey lowers the camera.

The face staring back at him should be the same one—the strange young man's—he saw before raising the camera to get his shot.

Except…it's not.

The pale pink and white flesh he glimpsed earlier is gone. It's been replaced by a coloring more cemetery-marker gray, or like the smooth, semi-chalky remnants of a dumped-out ashtray. The eyes staring back, staring holes through the face of the paparazzo, are red, red like the blood from Matt Freeman's wounded hand, red like holly berries. These scarlet orbs press against the gray, fleshy sockets. They bulge forward.

Glittering red eyes slashed by yellow pupils like exclamation marks.

And where before Matt Freeman's mouth was set in an incurious straight-lined deadpan, his new form showcases a distended jaw. Its bottom half hangs low and loose, human teeth and tongue replaced by more predatory features. A twisting pink worm thrashes amid a forest of long, pointed canines.

A nightmare brought to life.

"Jesus Christ!" Joey's a long way and plenty of sins from religious, but figures if there's ever time to call for a savior, it's right then and there.

He blinks. Opens his eyes again, even though part of him wishes he wouldn't. A part wishes he could keep his eyes closed forever.

But when he looks again, Matt Freeman's back. Not the monster seen after the flash, but the unsettling void of a human spied beforehand.

It's hard to say which is worse. Which visage inspires more terror now that they've both been glimpsed? Or is it the combination, the monster and the abyss existing in one being, that disturbs Joey the most?

"Excuse me, *sir*," Matt Freeman says, finally addressing the paparazzo. He holds his hand out, blood still dribbling from his wounded finger. "May I see your camera?"

Joey's already running before the question's finished.

CHAPTER 20

THE DESK SERGEANT wearing pressed dress blues and whispering into the lieutenant commissioner's ear with urgency and not a little bit of panic gave Stacy quite a look when he first entered Zamuda's office. He regarded her with a little shock while somehow also looking past her, like she didn't really matter.

She's used to that kind of reaction. It's not the first time she's gotten it from her fellow officers—most of them men. Old-school, "proper," HR-file-a-mile-long men at that. She's learned to tune it out, to do the work, and to refuse to let others take credit that she deserves.

Except you're not on the job anymore. You don't have anything to prove to this joker or any other sexist machismo-obsessed meathead working here.

What the heck do you have to prove to yourself?

Caught in these resurrected internal debates, she nearly misses when Zamuda's finished listening to the sergeant's news—"Uh huh, uh huh, oh shit,"— and is now clearing his throat, looking her way.

Zamuda stands and makes his way to the door. Stacy knows she'll have to move once he's closer. The doorway's not wide enough for her to keep standing there while her old partner squeezes by. His khakis strain against his belly and the *whick-whick-whick* of fabric against fabric draws attention to the manila folder he holds low against his pants.

As though he's trying to keep the folder out of sight from the desk sergeant.

"Sorry, Stace," he says, "but I gotta tell you to get outta here now. You know how it is."

She steps aside a little late, stepping backward through the open office door with her old partner following a half-second behind. She crouches, fixing some suddenly urgent issue with her handbag. She opens the bag, closes it, opens it once more. The folder's inside, the hand-off complete. She closes the bag again.

No one's going to search her on the way out. After all, she's one of them.

And there's not any chance of any sort of searching happening at the moment anyway. The bullpen's full again. Stacy gives the crowd a once-over. Some familiar faces from her recent retirement party, and some new ones in the mix as well. She supposes that's the way of things. Change, movement, progress.

Making her way to the exit, Stacy takes her time, giving herself a chance to listen, all while appearing as though she's not listening at all—like she doesn't give a damn about what Zamuda's got to say.

"Listen up," Zamuda says, addressing the bullpen assembly. "I need anyone here down at the hospital—County General— like five minutes ago. Anyone on patrol, we radio 'em up, they need to head there too. Unless, of course, they got something going on that's a matter of life or death. In which case—"

"It fuckin' better be!" The other cops in the bullpen finish the speech for their leader, well-versed in his Zamuda-isms.

That's his speech. No frills, nothing fancy. That's Zamuda to a T. An effective approach for this particular cohort, to say the least. Stacy was the one who pushed him to pursue the leadership path when they were partners. She believed he'd thrive.

She's happy to see her prophecy bear fruit.

Of course, for Stacy, the speech is *not* enough. She hangs back, waiting until Zamuda's making an exit of his own. Then, she reaches a hand out, grabs his sleeve.

"What's going on?" she asks, knowing it's not her business, knowing she shouldn't care and should just go home to Jeff.

"Hospital's on lockdown. Apparently Matt Freeman's there. Or *was* there."

Stacy knows her face must reveal the emotional tempest playing out in her mind by the way that Zamuda takes both of her hands in his hefty paws and gives them a teddy-bear-soft squeeze.

"Matt Freeman's missing again," he says.

"I was just there earlier," Stacy says. "I was just there, and I didn't see…"

Right around now is when she starts wondering what else is out there that she isn't noticing. She thinks about what Cass told her and about her brother's theories. A new picture of reality begins developing in her mind's eye.

CHAPTER 21

THE CAMERA HANGS from Joey's neck like an albatross. Like that one in the poem he read in high school.

What was it called? "The Rhyme of the Ancient Mariner"? Except they spelled "Rhyme" weird.

Why the fuck am I even thinking about that?

His frenzied contemplations of Coleridge—*that's the guy's name, yeah*—are the first semi-coherent thoughts the paparazzo's had since he was standing in the rooftop garden of the hospital. Up with the Freeman kid and his fucked-up face.

Except he wasn't a kid. Wasn't a man, either. He was a monster. He was...God, he was awful.

Joey's on the sidewalk now, hands on his knees, watching across the street from the left side of the hospital. His quite recent memories come in flashes of running feet, panicked breaths, nearly tripping down a set of stairs. Blisters formed from holding too tight to the stairwell railing were torn open during his descent. Bruises solidify on his chest, under his sweat-sticky shirt, in spots where his heavy camera equipment slammed against him mid-escape.

The whole way down and then bursting through the emergency exit, Joey was sure the monster-man was behind him. He could feel hot breath steaming in the folds of his ear. The phantom licking of a too-long tongue against the back of his neck.

Now, across the street, the strobing light of the emergency exit produces a miniature lightshow. Not a single person's come to check on the alarm's screeching exclamations.

Probably think they've got better things to worry about!

His eyes now on the roof, Joey's got tunnel-vision. The blue sky and sunshine around him, the treetops and the birds, the traffic rushing here and there—everything's gone except the rooftop's edge.

And Matt Freeman. Who's standing up there, right at the edge. Clear as day.

"I didn't see anything," Joey says, speaking to the man on the roof like he can hear him. "I swear, I didn't see anything."

Those far-off eyes flash red.

A trick of the light? It's gotta be, right? That's gotta be what it was...

Joey's spoken words differ from his thoughts. His words come on instinct, a first reaction to that ruby glow.

"Oh no, no, no..."

Forget the eyes. Now Joey watches the body, the whole of Matt Freeman.

Matt steps off the edge of the rooftop. One foot touching sky. Then, falling. His body stone-stiff and straight. More a descending icicle than a plummeting human being.

No, like a knife, stabbed into the ground.

Joey wants to look away. He *should* look away. But he can't. Because even as Matt Freeman's falling, his eyes—which are most certainly red and glowing now—remain locked on the paparazzo.

Then, Matt hits the ground, and everything that *should* happen—shattered kneecaps, a burst blood-bag of a body, jagged pieces of bone stabbed through skin—*does not*. Feet crunch in concrete, sending up a geyser of gray and white masonry behind the man.

Not a man, though. No man could jump or fall like that. No man could land that way and live.

At least Joey's got the wherewithal to stop staring after the initial impact. He's smart enough to run, to turn tail and let the soles of his shoes slap against the sidewalk. Figuring his invoking the Son of God may have helped him stay alive earlier, the paparazzo doubles down. He shouts his prayers without a care for who else might hear or what they might think of him.

"Heavenly Father, please watch over me. With Your angels and saints and everything and just please help me. *Please!*"

All the praying and running means Joey's not watching where he's going. He misses the large man placed smack-dab in his path. He crashes into the big man's chest. His face aches from the impact, as if he'd smashed into a brick wall. Except this pale-skinned brick wall has the sculpted physique of a body builder with a Gold's Gym tank-top stretched across his pecs like a second skin.

This guy, Joey doesn't know who he is. He doesn't care, either. He's Some Guy.

Shaking the cobwebs from their impact, the paparazzo focuses on the stranger's size, thinking how the big man might protect him, might keep him safe from the monster called Matt Freeman.

"Oh thank God," he says. "You gotta help me, man. He's crazy. He's all fucked up and..."

This is the part where Joey glances at his hands and finds they've gone away. It takes another moment before he realizes they're covered by Some Guy's meaty mitts. The strange strong-man's hands are so big, it's as if Joey's digits are swallowed whole. The paparazzo tries to pull back, to free himself from the giant's grasp. But it's no good. Some Guy squeezes, and Joey's knuckles crack at even this slightest pressure.

"Hey man, let go," he says.

But there's no understanding, no compassion, and certainly no humanity waiting for the paparazzo on the face of this massive stranger. If anything, even though he appears more human than the monstrous form Matt Freeman took earlier, this Some Guy bears a more unnatural and unsettling countenance, as though he exists within the so-called uncanny valley. Like he wears a machine-made approximation of humanity.

"Whoa. Hey! Hey!" Joey struggles to break free. There's little resistance from Some Guy, but only because almost no effort's required for him to keep the much smaller man under his control.

Joey's off the ground, feet pedaling wildly over the sidewalk.

"Please! Stop! Don't!" he begs.

If Some Guy hears these desperate, clichéd pleas, no indication is given. The words bounce off him like they're bullets and he's some kind of cartoon Übermensch.

Then, Joey's flying, thrown away like trash. His body's flung ragdoll-style off the sidewalk and into the path of oncoming traffic.

He doesn't get a chance to land and have his knees strike the charcoal-black asphalt. Instead, a crowded city bus rushes forward to greet him while he's mid-fall. The silver and glass front of the vehicle, the bug-eyed panicked features of a bus driver jerking the steering wheel from side to side as if there's any time to avoid the inevitable collision—these are the next and last things Joey sees.

The last thing he hears? The screeching tires running down the line of the bus's frame, screams from witnesses inside the bus, and the crunch of his camera as it's driven through his sternum. His chest cavity fills with blood, soaking the film, ruining the photographs.

He might've found it funny, if he weren't already dead.

"YOU WERE LUCKY, *Hybrid Freeman-Matt. My proximity will cloud the minds of those who might have witnessed your…display. Remember, you are a test run, not the vanguard.*"

Matt Freeman looks up, down, side to side. Only the slightest hint of a smile shows up at the corners of his mouth as he brushes off a dust of demolished sidewalk and pretends he doesn't know whose thoughts are beaming directly into his skull or where they're coming from.

Finally, he lets his eyes settle on Some Guy, the giant humanoid dressed in overly colorful cotton and spandex. So outrageous, so memorable is the clash of his rainbow ensemble and his white, white skin that looking at him can short-circuit the brain, making him and all events around him seem unreal, impossible.

"Speak for yourself, inferior product," Matt mutters. "Can't even shake your programming enough to stop you from killing some random drunks. What will our Gray Men makers say?"

Unsure if Some Guy has even heard his teasing words, Matt raises his hand, waving to his would-be savior, his would-be protector. For a moment, he considers blowing a kiss. The way he remembers his mother used to do.

But by now, the bus's doors swing open and the passengers spill out. Their mass exodus reminds him of the exploded insides of the paparazzo, the spilled guts of the dog that wasn't the one from his childhood, or his dear sister's brains dumped onto the shed floor.

Another unfortunate "situation" this Some Guy has saved me from.

So, he chooses to stop the teasing. Some Guy was made for him, after all. He supposes that, at the very least, he will be grateful.

THE BUS'S PASSENGERS, shaken, sickened, and delayed en route to their respective destinations by the sudden impact of a human body smacking against their chosen conveyance, line up along the street. Some turn their heads and vomit, some sit in a daze on the gravel-strewn ground, and a select few manage to stand, keeping their wits about them. No one can avoid the smeared red streak across the asphalt, like a giant wiped a bloody booger across the ground.

They all know the smear was once a human being. They saw his face or heard his screams, depending on how close or farther back they were seated on the bus. Then, the heavy-duty bus tires thumped one after the other after the other. The brakes screeched, replacing those all-too-human cries.

None of them notice Some Guy standing in the grass, farther back from the roadside than anyone else on the scene. His smooth, wrinkleless face is splattered with blood. But the dappling is scant compared to the sticky residue of blood and gut juice warming in the sun, producing a coppery odor and a shared feeling like there's peanut butter on the roofs of everyone's mouths, and no one pays any attention to Some Guy as a result.

By the time they remember him, he'll already be gone.

A rough-looking old man, someone who's seen his share of violence in his younger days, comments first. "Saints preserve us, he threw that man right in front of us…"

Then, the floodgates open.

"Who did? Who?" a businessman asks, hoping no one notices the dark spot at the crotch of his gray suit pants.

"Like Some Guy, dude, Some Guy," a skater chick with a stickered-up longboard and dyed green mohawk says, giving an answer that's both accurate *and* insufficient.

A lady in a sweater who's holding a poodle that's scratching at the woolen fabric, both pet and owner reeking of perfume, adds her two cents. "Yeah, he was just here…Where'd he go?"

"Excuse me! Excuse me!" The cries from a familiar voice turn all heads. Someone's coming. Someone they all recognize. A woman from TV.

It's Ruth Freeman. From XNS. Ruth Freeman, who fights for parents who've lost their children. Ruth, who lost…

"I need to find him!" she shouts.

Ruth Freeman bypasses the bloody scene on the road. Accompanied by an entourage of uniformed officers and her two bodyguards, she blows by the bystanders, shoving the slower ones out of the way. "I need to see my son!"

Soon, everyone's nodding, as if to say, *Of course that's what she needs, of course.*

And just like that, any thoughts of Some Guy and the squished body parts blended with camera chunks are all but wiped from their minds.

"Step aside, folks," one of the uniformed police officers commands. The officers' arms are up, elbows bent, forming a human shield around Ruth and her husband. But even the cops can't hold the woman back when her true quarry's spotted.

Ruth pushes aside those walking in front, squeezes herself loose, and sprints for the road. Traffic's held for miles in both directions. And there's someone waiting for her at the end of the bloodred streak. This person becomes the dot to the exclamation mark.

More than a dot, the thin, skinny young man now standing in the middle of the road stares at his sneakers. The toes of his shoes sit inches from the blood smear that used to be a person. He raises a leg, his foot hovering over the steaming remnants, all set to step into the blood.

"MATTY!"

Ruth calls to her son just as he's about to put his foot down in the tomato-chunk wreckage of the human being deconstructed across the blacktop. He stops short after hearing her voice, moving away from the potential ruination of his footwear.

Ruth wraps her arms around her boy. She hugs him as tight as she can. Malek stands there with his hand outstretched, but stops short of touching their son. If Ruth didn't have all her attention focused on the boy, she might take the time to call her ex a coward.

But thinking it is enough for the moment, and Matt's the only one who matters to her anyway.

"Baby, you can't wander off like that. You can't do that to me. I can't lose you again, and now your sister…"

Matt shrugs off her embrace without much effort. Surprisingly strong, that string-bean son of hers. When he speaks, she's reminded of a parent talking to their child. It's a role reversal she's not expecting.

"She's not lost though, Mother. Not yet."

Those last two words stick with Ruth. Those last two words are a revelation.

CHAPTER 22

"OKAY, SO I know you're gonna crap on this. I *know*. But Sis, you gotta believe me, I think there's a connection to the 'Some Guy' stories, the reports, the urban legends, whatever-you-wanna-call-'em, and I believe it's *also* tangentially connected to the Gray Man theories," Xavier says, launching into presentation-mode before Stacy has a chance to finish her descent and take the final step into her brother's hacker paradise.

Stacy can't recall the last time she saw her little brother so excited, so invested in something outside the walls of his home. Of course, she's not stupid, and she sees him forming potential links to their own shared traumas, always trying to make the puzzle pieces fit to produce the picture as he wants it to be. But…at least he cares about something, *anything*, again after years beating his head against dead ends, retreating into fantasies while his sister's been out in the world, facing reality. If there's any silver lining to find here, the little bit of life injected into her sibling must count for something.

But, respecting the boundaries that Xavier's put up over the years, Stacy doesn't press the issue or even try to spotlight it. She proceeds as if their conversation is a mundane, unremarkable one. As if they're discussing the weather and not tap dancing around supernatural conspiracies.

"What do you mean?" she asks.

Xavier's wall of monitors looms behind him. Familiar faces, familiar websites, crime scene photos, and maps of the area searched those years prior, in the early days of the Matt Freeman case. *All that's missing is the red string*, Stacy thinks. And then: *Some of that area's where Mom and Dad were when they were out there looking for Jennifer...*

She cuts that line of thinking right off, though. Too many times in her police work, she would come close to what she hoped or prayed would be answers that victims' families wanted to hear, opportunities for reunion and healing. However, she learned that the answers are very rarely so positive. *They wear on you—death, violence, sadness. You spend so much time thinking they're for old folks, folks who've lived—not me. And then, it is you.*

"Okay, so you know how Matt Freeman claims his rescuer was 'Some Guy?' I mean, pretty vague. Right?" Xavier asks, blowing past his sister's silent reverie, or more likely not even picking up on it at all.

He speaks like he's reading from a script. Living alone since their parents passed, viewing the world filtered through too many screens. Stacy's unsure if her brother's had any genuine human interaction over the years outside of her occasional visits. Not even Jeff's allowed inside the house. "Not until you're married and he's *legally* part of the family," Xavier always tells them.

Her brother leans forward in his gaming chair, elbows on his knees. "But then," he says, "dig deeper. Like into those files your partner—"

"Zamuda," Stacy says, knowing full well the glare she's going to receive for interrupting.

Xavier delivers said glare and keeps going, picking up right where he left off. "—gave you at the station. Those notes about this barroom massacre? There're witness accounts included that say a person was 'maybe' spotted leaving the building shortly after the time the MEs estimate the killings happened, yeah? Guess what these witnesses referred to the 'person of interest' as."

Stacy's stone-faced.

"Come on, guess," he says. "I'll wait."

She's staring blankly, still not giving him anything.

Her brother, nearly as old and grown as Stacy is, juts out his lower lip like a petulant toddler. Pouting. It's all Stacy can do not to burst out laughing.

"Dammit, Stace. You're no fun and never were," he says.

Taking a deep breath, he continues, though the annoyance is clear in his features. "Some Guy walked out that front door. Now, said witnesses *were* hookers working the corner for the daytime crowd. But hey, we all gotta eat, right?"

Stacy rolls her eyes, motions with her hand for Xavier to continue.

He does.

"And I hear ya," he says, "'Some Guy' *is* a pretty nondescript, generic phrase. Could apply to anyone. Men, women. We're all 'some guy' in the end, right?"

He turns to his desk, where keyboards corresponding to the various monitors are spread in a haphazard pattern that Stacy could never hope to decode. He types away, the teletypesetting correspondence lessons he'd mailed away for as a strange youth paying dividends in the here and now, in his time as an equally strange adult. One by one, the displays change. Stacy watches in awe. It's not the first time she's wondered if her little brother wasn't supposed to be the one who became a cop instead of her.

"Look here, I ran a cross-reference search on all unsolved abduction cases—particularly those with circumstances similar to the Freeman abduction. Anything including mentions of 'lights from the sky' or 'Gray Men,' anything slightly X-Files adjacent. The number of hits where 'Some Guy' or a variation of the phrase was used comes out to one hundred percent. Give or take."

"No way," Stacy says.

The phrase "Some Guy" appears on screen after screen as Xavier increases its font size for dramatic effect. In addition to this evidence, he brings up amateur sketches, various depictions of a generic large, bald man with a round face. A child's drawing. A police sketch or two. Grainy convenience-store footage and old 16mm film reel warped by sun exposure and time, video evidence where one can kind of, sort of make Some Guy out if they squint in just the right way.

"One hundred percent," Xavier repeats. "It blows away all statistical probability. Suddenly, we're not just talking about some guy. We're talking about *SOME GUY*. Some Guy, with a face like the Moon."

Stacy's moved closer to the monitors without even noticing she's done so. In a daze, she finds herself putting a hand on her brother's shoulder. "Holy shit," she says.

"You're damn right, holy shit," Xavier answers.

His eyes light up with excitement. He's feeding off the energy Stacy's giving him, she can tell. "And look at this," he adds.

He brings up an open tab on one of his many monitors. Stacy leans closer, so they're cheek to cheek. As she reads, an impatient Xavier jumps ahead, spoiling the surprise. "There's one thing linking all the incidents. Aside from Gray Men or lights or even Some Guy…"

Stacy's a fast reader, though. She's already caught up with what Xavier's going to say. But she doesn't want to spoil the moment, so she stays quiet.

"Look what happens to anyone who's reported it or tried to talk about it to the police, media, anyone with…"

A wall of faces. Black-and-white newsprint, obituary-section visages. The screens fill up with the faces and names of those who came forward to talk about Some Guy and other related elements from these abduction cases.

DEAD.

DEAD.

MISSING / PRESUMED DEAD.

MISSING.

DEAD.

DEAD.

VANISHED WITHOUT A TRACE.

"Which brings me to your star witness, Cass Freeman…"

But Xavier stops, finally noticing his sister's body shaking with the sobs she's been holding in. He's never been one for emotional displays. Stacy's well aware of that. She understands who her brother is—who he became after their own shared tragedy.

It's enough for her when he reaches an arm up and pats her shoulder once, then twice. It's enough that he sees her. It's enough that he lets her cry.

CHAPTER 23

MALEK CATCHES HIS son exiting Cass's hospital room. *His sister's hospital room*, he reminds himself. It's been hard since the boy's return, hard to make the connections between him and the rest of their family. For so long, Malek thought of the boy—his child—as something, someone belonging to the past. A memory instead of a person. Sometimes, he even thought of him as a dream. An ephemeral entity never meant for permanence in the waking world.

But the young man by the doorway to Cass's room is made of flesh and blood, not hopes and dreams. This young man puts a long finger to his thin lips—a feature inherited from his mother, just like his red hair—and shushes his father.

With the closed door shutting off his view of Cass, Malek struggles to find the words to fill the expanding gap between himself and his son. "Listen, uh, Matt," he says, "I'm glad you're okay after what…after everything. From before, and this…what happened outside the hospital…"

Matt Freeman nods, waiting for his father to continue.

Malek's next words come in gulping breaths. "I…I…pray… that Cass…will be…too. We're all praying for her."

"But it's not like we're reading her Last Rites just yet," Matt says.

Malek can hardly believe the words coming from the young man who was, who *is*, his son. There's a familiarity about his tone, almost veering into cruelty.

The older man's sharp intake of breath draws his son's notice. "What's that?" Matt asks.

Malek waves it off, mumbling something about it not being a big deal. Instead, he pivots by asking, "How is she?"

Matt stares ahead. A million light-years away. As if he's moving to catch up with whatever he sees out there, he walks away from the hospital room, turning his back to his old man and ailing older sibling.

After waiting until Matt turns the corner, Malek pushes open the hospital room door. "Cass?" he calls, not expecting an answer but still feeling disappointed when there's no response.

Cass is still there. All the tubes and wires going where they're supposed to. Her chest rises and falls, spurred on by the machinery she's connected to. A patient monitor tracks the slow and steady beating of her heart.

Beep. Beep.

Beep. Beep.

The green line on the monitor shows jagged peaks. No flatline.

ALONE IN THE hospital bathroom, Matt Freeman takes his new face, his true face, out to play. Jaw extended, fangs long and sharp, remade lungs drawing in oxygen and carbon dioxide alike. He enjoys the pain when his sewn-together old flesh divides and his new skin is revealed in the cracks between.

His long-fingered hands direct the stream of water from the spigot onto his face. He splashes himself over and over. The water's so hot that the mirror steams, obscuring his features. Finally, he reaches up to wipe the glass surface clear.

Condensation dripping off his fingertips, Matt Freeman studies the face waiting on the other side. He's reverted to the young man he was supposed to be. From before they came.

Before they changed him.

Before they made him better.

PART 3

LOOKING FOR A SIGN IN THE STARS

CHAPTER 24

[EVIDENCE ITEM #24879013109]

[Letter addressed to home of Keppler, Xavier; Keppler, Samuel and Xenia (deceased) c/o Keppler, Stacy, no postmark]

Dear Sargent [sic],

19 20 years ago when Matt got taken you sent a note that said Cass if you remember anything else or have more to say dont [sic] be afraid. I will believe you. Write to me at this address. You will be safe.

Your words meant a lot. But I wasn't strong enough to take your offer then.

I'm sorry. And sorry for what may hapen [sic] since I kept my mouth shut all this time.

I KNOW Matt wasn't taken by the Patey [sic] family like they say.

I know not only because of what I told you then but also because I'm not the only one in our family who knows the truth [...]

IN THE PAST: The Gray Men come, and one of them wraps a too-thin hand around Matty's skinny arm, bunching up the fabric of his long-sleeved Power Rangers jammies. Skeletal-thin in places, the Gray Man's stronger than he appears, pulling the boy from his bed and lifting him over the carpeted floor. There's no pain on Matt's face, no awkward twisting of his limb as he tries to wriggle free from the Gray Man's grasp. It's like he's floating, like the Darling children in *Peter Pan*.

Cass watches from her hiding place. With covers pulled high so only her eyes and curly red hair are visible. She blinks, stung by the sudden appearance of additional illumination through their bedroom window, targeting her while the rest of the room is shadowed.

When she can see again without spots before her, Cass notices the window's open. The white, lace-trimmed curtains blow back in waves.

[EVIDENCE ITEM #24879013109, CONT'D]

Do you know what it's like to have someone you love ripped away from you?

I do.

When it happens, you want to preytend [sic] what you saw WASN'T what you saw. What you felt wasn't what you felt.

BACK IN HER bedroom, nine-year-old Cass is all alone. The top of her head peeks over the windowsill. She strains on tiptoes to see out the open window.

Her child's body pressing against the wall and sill, Cass finally notices the big, bald head of Some Guy crouching below the window outside the house. Bald and white, a face like the Moon come to life.

Lost for what else to do, Cass screams.

[EVIDENCE ITEM #24879013109, CONT'D]

But you realize it's not just the voice inside your head telling you, "This never happened. Don't say anything about it."

Your version…they convince you the truth is YOUR version…slips away with each denial…

Until your truth is silence.

ON THE NIGHT of Matt's abduction, Some Guy, looking the same nineteen years ago as he does in the present, eye-to-eye with the terrified girl named Cass, holds a fat finger to his colorless lips, shushing her.

SEVEN YEARS WITHOUT Matty later, sixteen-year-old Cass won't brush aside her dyed, jet-black swoop of hair from her forehead or raise her eyes from contemplating strategically placed tears in her fishnets to look at her father as he stands in the doorway to her room. *Her room, her room alone, even if half of it's still filled with a young boy's bed and abandoned belongings.*

When her dad speaks, Cass can practically hear the tears in his eyes. She knows they're genuine, and that's what makes it all hurt so damn much. "I want you to know that whatever happens next, it's *not* your fault."

His car's packed, and the U-Haul trailer's loaded up behind it. He's taking everything. Leaving Cass with nothing but spoiled memories and a mother who doesn't give half a damn whether Cass is alive or dead. A woman focused on only one of her children—the missing one—so that the remaining one is left to wither.

Cass's lip quivers. She takes a hand and wraps it around her midsection, feeling her velvet mesh top press into her belly. With the other hand, she reaches up and touches a stray strand of red hair left on her head. A bit of color in the darkness. When she swallows, her equally black choker bobs up and down.

It's not the most Goth of things of cry. Then again, maybe it is.

[EVIDENCE ITEM #24879013109, CONT'D]

It took 7 years without Matt before we fell apart completely.

We pretended to be okay. But looking back…

We were NOTHING without him.

SIXTEEN-YEAR-OLD, HOT-TOPIC MALL-GOTH Cass finally looks up, but finds her mother in the doorway instead of her dad. Maybe it's the same day as when her father left, maybe not. Time's one more thing she can't keep hold of.

Ruth glares at her daughter. "Of *course* it's your fault," she says.

It's the truest thing Cass has heard her mother say in a long, long time.

She looks up again, and just like that, another twelve years have passed. Cass is in her own apartment now. A shitty run-down rattrap. The worst thing money can buy.

But hey, at least there's money.

She lies on a sorry excuse for a bed with soiled sheets and a pizza-box pillow. There's shag carpeting below her, soaked by the tipped-over bottle of Crown Royal spilling its contents into the fabric.

Her mother's in this new doorway. Wearing the same repulsion she's had for Cass since Matt was taken. "They're *going* to find your brother," she says.

[EVIDENCE ITEM #24879013109, CONT'D]

Here are the facts as I observed since HE/IT came back:

FACT 1: SHE knew where he'd be found before authorities went to Pateys [sic].

A SLIVER OF a doctor's examination room is all Cass can see by peering in from the hallway. She's lucky to have that. *Lucky, yeah, that's the word.*

She tries to stay very still and not knock against the door or breathe too loud. She does her best all while trying to hear what's being said to her mother inside the exam room.

Cass gets a hazy glimpse of Ruth with arms crossed over her chest, listening to a mustachioed doctor with a nasally voice who's showing her X-rays. Giving her a look inside of Cass's supposedly returned brother, Matt.

"Frankly, these X-rays are like nothing I've seen before," the doctor says, unable to contain the excitement under his words.

But Ruth, *Dear Mother*, has no time for games. She's ready to cut through the crap.

"Yes," she says, "but what does it *mean*?"

[EVIDENCE ITEM #24879013109, CONT'D]

FACT 2: The results of Matt's physical following his return were "lost," replaced by forgeries.

FACT 3: The doctor who performed the original physical pulled up stakes and left town one day later.

You've heard me say it before, Stacy. Matt was ABDUCTED by the Gray Men. But I've been thinking more sicne [sic] this new Matt came to our family. Was Matt taken…

or did he go WILLINGLY? Maybe not at first but later on. 19 years is a long time.

BACK AGAIN, NINETEEN years prior, watching six-year-old Matty Freeman with the Gray Men. Light shines on his face. It sure as hell looks like he's smiling.

CHAPTER 25

TIRED FROM TRUDGING upstairs and walking down to the end of the driveway for his once-a-week mail check, but also wired from what he's just read inside the unstamped—meaning someone came to his house to leave it there—letter, Xavier folds up the testimony he's just read and returns it to its envelope.

There's only one thing he can say. Only one thing that feels appropriate.

"Holy fucking shit."

Pieces are falling into place. He knows he should tell Stacy. Or better yet, have her tell someone else, someone still working the case.

But he hesitates.

Like this Cass girl that his sister knew, *knows*, Xavier wants to be believed.

To be believed, he needs more pieces. More connective tissue. There's still more work to be done.

CHAPTER 26

IT'S NEITHER THE time nor the place; Stacy knows this. But she can't help thinking how cute Jeff looks when he's angry. At the very least, she's got enough sense to keep her mouth shut while he holds the folder—with the additional hard-copy evidence Zamuda passed along to her at the station—over the paper shredder in their shared office. The red power light glows on the machine.

"Seriously, Stace, *why* are you doing this? This isn't supposed to be who you are anymore," he asks, forcing the words out.

Stacy's heart aches, hearing the pain in her lover's voice. But there's a deeper ache, a soul-searing pain, driving her at the moment. So, she tries to make him see reason. Her reason, at least.

"Jeff, I get it, trust me. We can talk about it, but first put the file folder down on the desk, okay?"

Christ, she thinks, *I'm talking to him like I'm some hostage negotiator.*

Noting a flash of hesitation in her fiancé's eyes, she pushes. Probably too far.

"It's police property, after all," she adds.

Definitely too far.

Jeff flings the folder at her, sending pages scattering across the floor.

"Then why the *hell* do *you* have it?" he shouts

Partly because she can't face him or the pain she knows will be on his visage, and partly because she wants to make sure to get the pages of evidence back in order, Stacy's on the floor, on hands and knees. She focuses on gathering and sorting the scattered pages.

"Something doesn't add up with what happened," she says. "To Cass. To Matt. None of it made sense nineteen years ago. And it makes less sense today. I owe it to that girl and the promise I made her to figure out why. I know I was on the right track."

Finished collecting the wayward pages and returning them to the folder, Stacy finally looks up. Prepared to face Jeff and continue what feels like a necessary, though quite difficult, conversation.

But she's alone.

"Jeff?"

Stacy remains on the floor of the office for a long time, waiting for an answer that she knows isn't coming.

CHAPTER 27

THE STAFF AND on-air talent of XNS are waiting for something to happen. For someone, anyone, to say something, anything. Gregg Lomax, executive producer of the network's top-rated series *Voice of the Voiceless*, strokes his freshly-trimmed goatee, smiling with the knowledge that he's about to be the *someone* who shares the news and blows the minds of all who're present.

He pulls at the sleeve of his suit, wishing he'd had time to grab a nicer one before the workday. He takes a deep breath in and prepares to shock those in attendance on the exhale. "Okay, guys and gals, thanks for joining us on such short notice. I know that some of you are working on a deadline, so…"

His eyes dance across the conference table, taking in the faces of every executive, producer, anchor, journalist, intern, temp, receptionist, et cetera, all gathered around the table's smooth, flat, shiny surface.

"What's this all about, Gregg?" Debi Megyn asks.

She chews a wad of peppermint bubblegum while talking, an off-air habit that makes her lips smack with every overly enunciated syllable. Gregg does his best to answer.

"Ah yes, well, you see, I'd rather wait until…"

He scans the room again, this time looking past the seated heads around the table. Suddenly, a shadow falls over him and onto the table. Adjusting his tie, loosening it, he turns slowly to find his spotlight already being usurped. After all, *she's* standing right behind him.

Ruth Freeman is there. Ready to speak. Her hair's styled in a severe fashion, not a hair out of place. The pantsuit she wears has a bespoke quality to its tailoring. Her makeup? On-point. She steps to the table, nudging Gregg's chair slightly with the casual swing of a lean, muscular hip, putting a period on the end of his sentence.

Her smile to those assembled is perfection.

Poised and practiced.

"Hello, everyone. I hope you didn't forget about me during my recent…family emergency."

SOAKING UP THE applause from the standing ovation she's just received from her coworkers, Ruth hooks her foot under her producer's conference room chair and pulls it toward her. She'll sit there. Gregg can stand. It only seems fair, as far as she's concerned. She only hopes the fabric seat cushion doesn't smell too much like his farts.

"Oh thank you," she says, "thank you. But I'm not here for all that. I'm here…for the work. The good work that we *can* and *must* do."

She takes Gregg's seat, and everyone else follows. Ruth hands the slideshow clicker to her now-standing producer, arching an eyebrow that says *I hope to God everything was prepared to my specifications.*

Gregg moves fast and snaps his fingers at an intern, urging them to dim the lights in the conference room post-haste. He pulls another underpaid junior staffer from their chair at the table and enlists their help in pulling down the room's projection screen. Ruth smiles when she catches Gregg slipping into the intern's chair.

On-screen, a mocked-up XNS graphic—including channel logo and everything else—appears. The network's call letters overlap a still image of Matt. Chyron text materializes with each click of the device in Gregg's hand.

AN XNS EXCLUSIVE

The first-ever sit-down interview with Matt Freeman

LIVE!

On Ruth Freeman's THE VOICE OF THE VOICELESS

The lights come back up, and Ruth's smile has grown even bigger. But there's no applause coming. Only silence.

She feels her lipstick cracking at the corners of her smile. Suddenly, she's uncertain how long she'll be able to hold her carefully constructed, carefree grin.

At least Gregg has the sense to pick up the baton and move things forward. "So, how soon until we can get this to air?" he asks the room. Ever the producer, ever the problem-solver, he's always been a good fit for Ruth, helping her build her very own tiny TV empire. She supposes the loyalty's why she's kept him around.

But he's thinking too small. Being too cautious.

Ruth slams a fist against the tabletop, bringing all eyes back to her.

"We're doing it in one month."

Ruth Freeman has spoken. There will be no further discussion.

CHAPTER 28

AN XNS EXCLUSIVE

The first-ever sit-down interview with Matt Freeman

LIVE!

On Ruth Freeman's THE VOICE OF THE VOICELESS

"YOU SEE THIS, sis?" Xavier asks, gesturing to the screen where he's played the commercial for the upcoming Ruth and Matt Freeman interview special. "Already starting the hype train for this thing. Can you believe it?"

He's messing with Stacy, of course. He's still her annoying little brother even as their many shared decades of existence have accumulated. After all, there's been no escaping XNS's promotional blitz of Ruth's interview with her returned son.

With a long, drawn-out sigh, Stacy reaches past Xavier toward his wall of monitors, flicking off the power button for the screen displaying XNS's ubiquitous interview advertising.

"Ugh, turn it off," she says. Having already switched off said programming for him, Stacy's words are more of a warning to Xavier, with the clear implication that he'd better not turn that channel's programming *back* on, at least if he values his life.

Xavier's hands stay clear of his monitors and keyboards. Instead, he gives Stacy a big shit-eating grin. "What can I say? Know thy enemy, right?"

Stacy backs away, folding her arms across her chest and rolling her eyes at her brother's comment. If not for the bags under their eyes, the liver spots on her legs, and the gray and white hairs on both of their heads, this could be a scene from their childhood.

"Ruth Freeman is *many* things," she says, "but she is *not* my enemy."

Scanning her brother's wall of monitors, something more interesting catches Stacy's eye. She leans forward to tap at the new screen. There's a file folder open, one Xavier's labeled "SOME GUY SIGHTINGS."

"But whoever *this is*, or whomever they're working with," Stacy says, "they just might be worth considering."

Xavier's dragging more files to that folder by way of the wireless mouse in his hand. The display of dates listed by the file names contains uploads from well before Matt Freeman's return. Xavier clears his throat, getting Stacy's attention. He nods toward the files, indicating that he knows she's seen it too. He lifts his eyebrows in an exaggerated fashion, as if to say: *I know, right?* The switch from teasing to getting down to brass tacks is so smooth as to almost be imperceptible.

"I've also run multiple alerts for the last few days. Do you *know* how many hits come up daily for the phrase 'Some Guy'?" he asks.

"Too many. That's how many," he answers before Stacy can.

He turns his chair around, putting the monitors to his back. "So, is this what all your police work was like, or what?"

Now, it's Stacy's turn to give back a little of the smart-ass that her brother's been giving her all afternoon.

"Well, I mean it *is* work. It's not like evidence just falls into your—"

doot-doot-doot-doot-doot

As though the gods themselves saw fit to put the lie to Stacy's statement, her cellphone rings loud and clear in her brother's basement sanctorum. She checks the ID, then puts the phone to her ear. It's Zamuda, calling from the office.

"Zee, what's up? Sorry, reception's bad down in—"

"You over at Xavier's?" Zamuda asks through some crackling static on the line.

"Yeah, he makes it that way on purpose. I told him—"

But Zamuda cuts Stacy off, seemingly not in the mood for his usual chitchat. "Look, Stace, I don't want you to find out about this from some jerk-off process server. But it just got approved—fast-tracked for approval, actually—in the court and, well…"

"What, Zee? Can barely hear you," Stacy says.

Then, the hammer falls. "It's Ruth…Ruth Freeman. She, uh, she filed a restraining order against you. Part of some case she's spearheading, blaming you for…ummmm…for how long it took to find Matt."

"Wait…*what?*"

IF SOMEONE WANTED to see a pissed-off Stacy Keppler, they could do worse than to watch her at this exact moment inside the office of Lieutenant Commissioner Zamuda, her old partner and someone she *thought* was a trusted friend.

"A restraining order? *Really?*"

Zamuda sits behind his desk, shrugging his shoulders. The gesture only serves to deepen the divide between the pair. "Stacy, come on. What can I do here?"

Stacy leans forward, her finger poking close to Zamuda's left nostril. "This is…this is *bullshit* and you know it, Zee!"

Zamuda's nostrils scrunch as he pushes his chair away from the desk and his former partner's accusatory pointing. "Awww, c'mon, Stace…"

He grabs the top of the desktop monitor sitting on one corner of his desk, swinging it around and knocking a few stray pens to the floor in the process. He's got the XNS website open. Now it's Zamuda's finger that does the pointing. He underlines the headline with his fingertip, reading it out loud:

"HEIGHTENED SECURITY PLANNED FOR LIVE FREEMAN INTERVIEW."

"You get it now?" he asks. "There's a lot riding on this for the department since we'll be running the show security-wise… Ruth's got the network to entrust us with the protection detail. It's lucky she's not going after all of us who were involved in the case back in the day."

After rising from his chair, Zamuda marches past Stacy and parks himself by his soon-to-be-opened door. He taps at the frame, nodding to the bullpen beyond. The implication—that the time for discussion or debate has ended—comes across painfully clear for Stacy. She glares at her old partner. The feeling of betrayal is palpable inside the office. Zamuda's at least perceptive enough to pick up on that fact.

"I'm sorry, Stace. I really am," he says.

She steps through the open doorway and doesn't look back.

"Yeah…I bet you are," she says.

THE THICK-PANED, REINFORCED glass doors of the police station open to concrete steps framed by black-painted handrails on either side. Sunlight reflects off the glass, warming the rails as well. The sky is blue, the scent of freshly cut grass is in the air, and city birds coo from rooftop perches.

Stacy shoves open the double doors and brings her personal storm clouds to this otherwise lovely day. She stomps down the steps with focus and determination, pissed off and ready to take on all challengers.

But her legs buckle when she reaches the bottom step. She collapses to the walkway, hands covering her face. All she can do is allow herself to be overwhelmed by the moment.

When she finally feels a hand on the top of her head, she doesn't flinch or strike out. She knows who it is that's come for her. She's felt his touch plenty of times before.

"Well, hey there," her fiancé says. "Come to this station often?"

Stacy looks up into Jeff's gentle, smiling face. She uses the backs of her hands to wipe away wayward tears. When she's done, she's able to smile in return. "Jeff. Where'd you come from?" she asks.

Even as Jeff holds a hand out to her, Stacy reaches for the railing, using its support to pull herself up instead. There's no offense registered on her beloved's face, however. If anything, she catches a hint of pride. It's probably why she loves him the way she does. He's the rare type of man who understands her need to do things for herself and doesn't see it as a strike against his own ego or masculinity. He waits until she's fully upright before getting his next quip in.

"Ah, ya know, I can't stay mad at you," he says.

"Plus Zamuda called while I was on the way over here and let you know about Ruth Freeman's restraining order against me?"

Jeff puts his hands up in mock surprise as Stacy nestles herself against him, leaning her body into his. She doesn't have to say anything; soon they're already walking to his car, parked next to hers in the visitor's parking lot.

"Welllllll, yeah," he says, coming clean.

Stacy delivers a gentle elbow to her fiancé's ribs. "Sheesh!" she says. "Good thing I never had *you* in my interrogation room. You'd have confessed to being the Zodiac or something in no time."

"Yeah, yeah, yeah…" Jeff says, pulling free from Stacy so they can climb into their separate vehicles.

Before he ducks into his car, Jeff calls over to Stacy. "We've got a backlog of *Jeopardy!*s on the DVR. You game?"

Stacy's in her driver's seat with the window rolled down and the engine running. But she's quick with her answer.

"Uh, what is…yes!"

They both laugh at her terrible joke. And, for a moment, Stacy able to trick Jeff and herself into thinking she's forgotten about everything else.

CHAPTER 29

THE LAST PAGE of Cass Freeman's letter sits face down on Xavier's flatbed scanner. He brings the lid down and presses the scan button, waiting for the white lights beneath the cover to flash in their sequential pattern.

"Alright," he says, "let's do this."

The rest of the pages sit next to the scanner, having already been fed one by one into the machine. To smooth them as much as possible, Xavier's had the thrice-folded, slightly crinkled pieces of paper pressed between some of the programming manuals he bought after his parents were killed when he elected to forego college, pursuing instead what he'd described to his sister as an "independent course of study."

In his machine-filled basement, the chime of the finished scan rings out. On one of Xavier's monitors, a crystal-clear image of the tear-stained paper he's just finished scanning emerges.

Then, a pop-up appears, overlapping with the scanned page.

Attaching PDF...

Below that, the long rectangle of a progress bar, filling in its light gray space with a slightly darker gray.

Uploading...

Finally, a new pop-up materializes, square and definitive. The arrow cursor hovers over it.

Upload Complete.

Post?
Y | N

Xavier clicks the affirmative. On another screen, a website unavailable via the usual browsers and networks has the spotlight. He's in a digital gathering place, one very much off the grid. It's the type of space accessed exclusively by crypto bros, drug dealers, and much seedier characters—the real scumbags. Xavier's posting in the electronic boogeyman farm known as the Dark Web.

He logs on to a message board. After doing so, a new pop-up appears on the screen, announcing his arrival.

NEWB POST. I HAVE LETTER FROM CASS FREEMAN.

The pop-up's temporary, disappearing in the ether soon after its birth. The TOR browser reloads, and Xavier's first post is already up on the board.

SUBJECT: I HAVE LETTER FROM CASS FREEMAN

MAJOR ALLEGATIONS AGAINST MOTHER RUTH. SUGGESTING COVER-UP RE: FREEMAN ABDUCTION AND "RESCUE." DEFINITE EXTRATERRESTRIAL INVOLVMT.

Reading his own post, mouthing along to the words, Xavier rubs his hands together with a certain gleefulness. When he's finished and there's no other sound but his own breathing, he lets out a long, low whistle. And then, unsure of what exactly will happen next, he tells his empty basement, "Okay, now the fun begins…"

ANIMELOVER69420 IS THE first commenter on the newb's post about Cass Freeman and aliens and that MILF host from *Voice of the Voiceless*. Their *Bleach* anime avi, testifying to the truth behind their screenname, shouts out a quick line of inquiry commentary.

"IS THIS LEGIT D00D? LOOKS LIKE IT. SICK."

ANIMEL0VER69420 lives up to every cliché their chosen screenname invokes. His heavy mouth-breathing causes the lightly tinted mustache hairs on his upper lip to flutter as he sits back in his gaming chair, awaiting a reply.

BUT XAVIER ALREADY knows what to expect from his nerd brethren. So, he's already one or two steps ahead of the posting hoi polloi. His follow-up message comes fast, showcasing a different scanned document.

[CASS FREEMAN WITNESS STATEMENT AGE 9-DOT-PDF]

"CHECK THE HANDWRITING ON WITNESS STATEMENT VS LETTER…D00D."

While his sister has kept her post-retirement investigation quiet by working offline, not wanting to rock the boat and cause trouble, Xavier's ready to rock a whole marina's worth of boats. He feels himself balanced precariously on the edge of truth, and he refuses to look away.

Deep down, he wishes his mom and dad were still alive to tell him what he's doing is the right thing. Or to tell him it's stupid.

Either way, he just misses them too damn much.

SOON, XAVIER'S NEWS breaks free from the constraints of the Dark Web and makes its way into the light. A new post on one of the seemingly endless number of social media sites where people virtually yell and scream at each other contains a summary of what he's already shared.

"Okay, normally I find conspiracy messageboards gross (4 real). But look what I found re: CASS FREEMAN. Definitely wasn't an accident YALL."

This poster, with her mountainous dreadlocks and a snake tattoo coming up from her chest to her cheek with venomous fangs stopping short of her lips, leans back in her office chair, feeling as though she's done something important.

"WHOA."

In a rare lonely corner of XNS's headquarters, a fresh-out-of-high-school intern wearing his XNS Internship Program badge around his neck with pride manages to connect to the office's nearest available, still-functioning printer. He hits CTRL-P on his laptop, which he's logged on to the network's server.

The "Cass Freeman letter," as it's become known rather rapidly in online circles, appears on his screen and will soon be spat out in its entirety from the fax machine/copier/printer that many of his fellow interns have no clue how to even work.

Soon, he's navigating XNS's crowded hallways with the printed-out letter held tight to his chest by one hand. His other hand holds a smartphone to his ear. He's trying to whisper, but it's hard to be heard over the raging ambient noise of the workplace.

"I dunno, Karla," he says. "I mean what *should* I do with it? This stuff about Ruth…Ms. Freeman, it's—"

"What is it?"

The speaker addresses the intern in a monotone voice that takes a moment to register. The young man finds his progress halted by a most unexpected source—Matt Freeman himself. Or at least someone who appears a hell of a lot like how he's been rumored to look. Even though there's no one else but the two young men standing face-to-face in the hallway, the walls suddenly feel like they're closing in for the intern.

Realizing he was just asked a question by one of the most important figures in the current media cycle, the intern hangs up on whoever Karla might be as he scrambles to answer Matt's question.

"Oh, sorry, um, Mister, Mister Freeman, sir. It's just some… they asked me to pull some…research for that interview your mom, I mean, your mother is doing…with you."

"I see," Matt says, before holding his hand out.

The intern isn't stupid or clueless. XNS doesn't give internships to dummies, after all. He hands the pages to Matt, even before he can ask for them.

Once they're in his possession, Matt's blank-faced again, rifling through the pages. Giving nothing away as he scans their content.

"Interesting reading," he says. "Very interesting."

MATT FREEMAN SITS alone in a dark room. Naked and alone in this dark room. It's a space so pitch black that it's impossible to tell floor from ceiling from walls. It's against this impenetrable shade that his thin, pale, and scarred shell of a human body appears to float.

His eyes are closed.

He brought the pages to his mother. He showed her the things that were said about her, about him. She tried to laugh it all off.

"This is nonsense. Crackpot, hysterical nonsense," she said.

But, as she stood there in her private office, flipping through the printed pages, rifling through them front to back and back to front, her nostrils flared and one eye started to twitch. Matt saw the anger, the rage growing inside of his mother.

"This is…this is…God, these people sharing this…this… crap, they're not human. They're subhuman. They don't even deserve to live on the same planet."

That single outburst was all the inspiration, all the permission that Matt needed.

Now he sits naked and alone with his eyes closed in this dark room. Beneath wafer-thin eyelids, both sets of his eyeballs— human and *more than human*—jerk and twitch. He places the palms of his hands against the hairless plane of his chest. He presses on his pectoral muscles.

A light appears in the dark room where Matt Freeman sits naked and alone with his eyes closed. The bright white illumination radiates from his chest—from inside his transformed body. It grows in intensity. Shining brighter. Brighter.

Brighter still.

His inner light envelopes the darkness until his features are washed out. It's so bright that if one looked directly into its source, they'd go blind. As if they'd stared into the heart of the sun.

THE PSYCHIC SIGNAL embedded in the light travels from Matt Freeman and escapes the dark room. It leaves Virginia, leaves the Earth itself. It bounces off that pockmarked, natural satellite the people of Earth call the Moon. Ping-ponging off man-made satellites that watch the people below. Moving unnaturally, nothing like the way *true* light travels.

Finally, it reaches its destination. A shimmering metallic object. Liquid and solid in equal measure. Nothing of humanity in its construction, but nothing of the natural world either. Nothing of Earth about its makeup.

The craft sits beyond the range of satellites and telescopes, orbiting Earth. Technology beyond humanity's capacity keeps it invisible to their gaze.

A message is received.

CHAPTER 30

BACK AT THEIR home, all is forgiven and seemingly forgotten as Stacy snuggles against Jeff on their living room couch, both slotting themselves into the grooves their bodies have made in the cushions. The lights are off and the only illumination comes from the TV. "Oh sorry," Ken Jennings says to one of the Jeopardy contestants, "but we were looking for René Descartes."

Stacy still misses Alex Trebek. But she's learning more and more how inevitable change can be.

Doesn't mean I have to like it, though.

"I love you," Jeff says.

She turns to him and smiles. "Oh, sorry," she says, mimicking the blond gameshow host on TV, "but I'm afraid you didn't phrase that in the form of a question. Though I suppose I can let it slide. This time."

She wraps her arms around the back of Jeff's head, fingers running through the salt-and-pepper of his hair. They kiss.

It's been a good night.

LATER IN THE evening, they brush their teeth, standing side by side at the bathroom sink. They haven't said anything to each other for an hour or more. But there's been no need. It's enough to be in the same space, to breathe the same air. Stacy finds herself appreciating this moment. Here's the life she left police work for, a promise for a calm and peaceful future.

Then, her phone comes to life, buzzing on their bathroom countertop.

Acting on instinct, unable to resist the urge to know more and dig deeper, Stacy's free hand reaches for the phone. But her efforts are halted by Jeff, his hand spread wide to block hers. He spits toothpaste into the sink and wipes the side of his hand across the white foam on his lips.

"C'mon, Stace," he says, "you promised you'd leave it for tonight."

"I know, I know," she says, watching the call stop abruptly and switch to voicemail, only to resume ringing once again. The staccato beeps from simultaneous text messages fill in the gaps of silence.

"But…you also know me," Stacy says to Jeff. She can't meet his gaze. Her eyes stay on the ringing, buzzing phone.

"Yeah," Jeff says, "I do. I *really* do."

He holds his hand away from Stacy, away from her phone, conceding to what he must know is an inevitable conclusion.

Stacy's fast. She snatches up the device. First, she scrolls through a wall of texts.

"No friggin' way…" she mutters.

XAVIER KEPPLER WORKS down in his basement. Where else would he be?

Eyes somewhat bloodshot from staring at screens too long, *no surprise there*. He's been reading, watching, studying. On the flat surface of his workspace, he's got a cellphone matching his sister's—though his has been further retrofitted and modified to remove any spyware or other tracking devices implanted by the government, corporations, or whomever else might be so bold as to inquire about his goings-on.

He's in no rush to answer the incoming call though. Instead, he's content to let the phone buzz away, adding ambient noise to his immersive research efforts.

MEANWHILE, STACY LEANS against the open doorway at the front of her house. She's switched to the phone she uses exclusively for communicating with Xavier. She keeps it pressed to her ear as she waits for her brother to pick up.

Finally, there's a single *click* on the line.

"Well, it's about time you picked up," she says.

"Yeah, yeah," Xavier answers from across town, "whatever."

"I didn't catch you at a bad time, did I? Not getting ready to go out or anything, right?"

If a facial expression—a glare, no less—could be heard across a phone line, then that's exactly what Stacy would be picking up from her otherwise silent brother.

She moves the conversation ahead, knowing she won't get a response beyond the perceived eye roll from Xavier. "Listen," she says, "I just got some texts with some *very* interesting information from Zamuda of all people."

On the line, Stacy hears her brother shifting in his gaming chair. "Oh really?" he says. "I'm listening…"

OUTSIDE OF THE Keppler house, the one currently occupied by the sole remaining male heir of the family, the security cameras suddenly blink off to become empty black eyes capturing and recording nothing at all. With that sudden technological change complete, a stone-thick pale fist knocks against the front door. The thick wooden slab rattles on the solid steel hinges Xavier had installed for additional security.

Knock! Knock!

LEANING AGAINST THE wall in the hallway outside her bedroom, Stacy whispers to her brother. "You know how they found Cass on the floor of the shed behind Ruth's house? There was blood everywhere, and the initial report chalked it up to her falling and landing onto some secret stash of booze she kept out there? Thing is, the analysis came back on the blood samples they gathered at the scene, and, well, it turns out—"

"The blood. Not all of it belongs to Cass. That's what you were gonna say, isn't it?"

Knock! Knock! Knock!

Now the pounding on Xavier's front door is loud enough that it gets picked up on Stacy's end of the line. She ignores it, just like Xavier's ignoring it.

"How do you do it?" she asks, referring to his Holmesian instincts. "Every. Single. Time. They're working on analyzing where the non-human source or sources came from."

DOWN IN HIS basement, Xavier's milking the moment of being right, of impressing his big sister.

"It's a gift, really. Maybe *I* should've been the one to become a detective," he says.

KNOCK! KNOCK! KNOCK! KNOCK!

Finally, the commotion upstairs gets Xavier's attention. He glances to the stairs, eyebrow arching.

"What the hell? Hold up, sis, I think some neighbor kids are doing some old 'knock on the weird guy's door' hazing ritual again. Dunno how the little bastards get past the security system, but, hey, no tech's ever one-hundred-percent reliable…"

XAVIER HANGS UP before Stacy can reply. She's left standing in her hallway, not even sure what she was going to say to him.

CHAPTER 31

PEERING OUT FROM Cass's room, Malek Freeman faces his son standing just outside in the hallway, a dull, vacant look on his face.

"What do you mean I can't come in and see her, father?" Matt asks.

Malek doesn't let the cold, near-robotic intonations of his youngest child get to him. He braces against the doorframe, filling as much of the space as he can.

"Did I do something wrong?" Matt asks.

The wording throws Malek off. It's not how an adult would speak, not in this situation, at least. There's something child-like about the words Matt chooses. It hurt to hear them, since they remind Malek of what was taken from him and from the other members of their family.

Still, he believes he must find a way to watch for the wellbeing of *both* his children. "Matt, Son, I told you already. Your sister, she…she needs her rest. Okay?"

Before Matt can reply, the young man's flanked by Ruth's Mutt-and-Jeff security detail, the bumbling goons that Malek's ex has assigned to be around their boy twenty-four seven. Lewis and Coleman give Malek dirty eyeballs all around. He can only imagine what Ruth's told the dim-witted duo about him. It sure doesn't seem as though it was anything good.

"We got a problem here?" one of the bodyguards asks.

Still holding on to the doorframe and feeling more than a little tired of all the faux drama and posturing, Malek pushes himself forward, driving the trio away from Cass's room. "I dunno," he says. "Y'all tell me."

While the rent-a-cops exchange looks like *what the hell did we get into here?* Matt keeps his eyes focused ahead. Staring at his father, but also seeming to stare *through* his old man.

"Nuh—no, no, sir. No problem here," Lewis or Coleman says. At the very least, their stuttered excuses provide the trigger needed to get Matt moving away from the room.

"Goodbye then, Father," he says. "Give my regards to Cassidy."

The bodyguards follow. Malek's left alone, though not entirely alone. He's happy to at least have Cass with him, one way or another.

THE DOUBLE DOORS to Studio A-1 at XNS headquarters are shut tight. No one's getting in or out without the proper clearance and vetting. That's the idea, at least. The glass-encased light-up "LIVE" sign above the doors sits dull, unlit. Which makes sense. After all, there's plenty of time for that later when the lights, cameras, microphones, and the rapt attention of millions will all be directed toward Ruth and her Matty. The people meeting behind those thick studio doors are focused on the future, on what lies ahead. On what *will* happen rather than what *is* happening now.

"So what do you think, Commissioner?" Ruth asks from the other side of the doors. "Will your men be able to adequately secure the studio for my interview with Matty?"

"Lieutenant Commissioner, ma'am," Zamuda answers, also from the other side of those doors. "I gotta be honest with you…"

Inside the in-progress set-build, Zamuda rubs a hand across the back of his neck, choosing his words as carefully as he can. "My professional opinion is that this whole interview is a bad idea to begin with. Your son's…you've…you've gone through this traumatic experience....these traumatic *experiences*, even. And now you're gonna put yourself back through..."

While he's talking, trying to find the right words, Ruth crosses the studio space and walks up a short trio of steps to the soundstage where her special will be broadcast live. The crew has set up a desk with two padded, pillow-clad chairs on either side of it. Ruth will sit on one of the chairs, and her son will be on the other. For the moment, though, Ruth addresses Zamuda from on high, her words echoing off the studio's walls as she speaks.

"Oh, I'm sorry, *Lieutenant* Commissioner. Was I asking for your professional psychiatric opinion? Or was I asking for your professional input as a law enforcement official? Asking, I'll add, as a mother who knows her child and what he may or may not be up to better than anyone else on this whole freakin' planet."

She takes a quick moment to catch her breath, but Ruth's not quite done yet. "I'll remind you again to consider this assignment I've arranged for your department and how it might be your last shot at redemption in the eyes of the public. All because I am in a forgiving mood. Forgiving for some of you, but *not* for all."

Zamuda opens his mouth like he's going to say something, to argue.

Ruth's still not having it. "Your job, the job of all your men and women in uniform, is to keep my son safe. Not to ask stupid questions. Understood?"

"Sure thing, sure." Zamuda doesn't let Ruth see the hurt on his face. He turns his back to the stage, to her, and gets down to business, assessing potential threats. His fingers get a workout as he points and counts off different zones in the studio space, mapping out a security strategy for the upcoming broadcast.

"We'll post armed guards at all entrances. And some interspersed in the audience. And more backstage with you before filming starts. Metal detectors will be used throughout the building, not just at entrances. We'll bring in as much manpower as we have, and then some."

Finally, he turns back and catches a small smug smile on Ruth's face.

"That's much better," she says.

The hairs on the back of Zamuda's neck stand up.

But that's not all.

MOMENTS LATER, OUTSIDE of Studio 1-A, one of the double doors is pushed open, and Ruth sticks her head into the hallway. She calls out to the departing lieutenant commissioner. "Zamuda!"

Hearing his name, he stops short. His cheeks go flush.

"One more thing before you go," Ruth says, baiting her hook.

"Yeah?"

She crooks her finger back toward the studio doors, reeling in the big fish. It's enough to draw Zamuda back to her. He lets her cup a hand over his ear and her mouth, lets her whisper to him.

"Thank you again for keeping some of the specifics of Matt's return under wraps. My accountant assures me the money will be arriving shortly."

She doesn't wait for a reply or any acknowledgment of what she's said. Instead, she steps back from the door and lets it swing shut fast before her. It slams shut in the lieutenant commissioner's face.

AND SO, ZAMUDA stands alone outside those studio doors. The weight of the world's been smacked across his usually happy-go-lucky face.

"God-fucking-dammit," he says.

CHAPTER 32

STACY SITS ON the edge of a worn-in couch cushion. She's alone in the living room this time. There's not even a television blaring nerdy game shows to give the illusion of company. The only light in the room comes from her phone screens—both her usual one and the direct line to Xavier. Unfortunately, neither screen provides her with much insight into the status and well-being of her younger brother.

Of course, that doesn't stop her from activating the screens every five seconds or so. Again and again, she checks to see if there's anything new posted for her. Anything. Especially texts. Any messages at all, really.

It's while she's in the midst of scrolling through old messages between herself and Xavier, trying to see if something might've slipped through the cracks and been marked as read when it very much was *not* read or even seen, that Jeff leans over from the back of the couch and starts massaging her shoulders.

He's got a gentle, nurturing touch. Never pushing too hard, but always hitting just the right spots. Stacy tilts her neck, leaning into the touch. She slowly realizes her fiancé's been talking to her this whole time. Trying to distract her, to ease her mind and fill it up with domestic babble. It's in those moments that Stacy wonders if maybe they shouldn't have waited so long to get married. She wonders if maybe those instincts telling her Jeff would have been a good—no, *great*—father are not too far off the mark. Perhaps in another life, one that wasn't so marked by loss, she could have found time to mourn a life that never was.

"So, I was talking to Craig—from work. You know how he and Nancy have a cottage in the Outer Banks? Well, they said we could have first dibs on it for a week this summer. Just gotta tell 'em when. I—"

Jeff stops mid-sentence and lets go of Stacy. He leans further forward over the back of the couch, angling his body to get a better view of her face. Instead of ignoring him, Stacy turns to meet him halfway, allowing herself to take in his inquisitive gaze.

"Stace, what's wrong?" he asks.

She holds up her phone so Jeff can see the screen and its lack of activity. "I texted Xavier more than four hours ago. He hasn't written me back…"

Jeff stands, his face displays a level of concern that's not equal to Stacy's but is moving damn close in that direction. "Geez, really? He's never so late getting back to you…"

Stacy returns her attention to the phone screen. The lock screen provides a blank canvas on which all her worries and fears are projected.

Suddenly, she discovers Jeff's face is no longer reflected behind hers in the ebony and green glass of the screen. She can't say how long it's been since he spoke to her. Time's slipped away. Now he's in front of her, standing above her and her phone.

"You should go check it out," he tells her. He leans closer, this time to kiss the top of her head. She shudders at the light touch of his lips against her scalp.

Stacy appreciates this blessing, even if she already made the decision to leave, to go check on her baby brother, moments earlier.

XAVIER'S FRONT PORCH—THE front porch of the house where he and Stacy grew up—is bathed in red light. Flashing, strobing crimson is flecked with a more infrequently flashing white. The camera, once perched above the doorframe, hangs lewd and lifeless from its previous moorings. Multicolored wires spill from this broken machinery like intestines.

The ringing alarm provides a discordant soundtrack to this lightshow. A propulsive sound, steady and unwavering. It emits the kind of noise that makes it nearly impossible to think for even just a moment. The combination of blinking lights and blaring alarm produces roadblocks to the parsing of reality and fiction. At least that's Stacy's impression of her immediate experience outside her brother's house—*her family's home.*

Stacy has no rational explanation for how the house's reinforced front door has been ripped off its hinges and thrown onto her brother's lawn. The massive wooden slab's been discarded like a child's plaything.

She stands in the open doorway, letting the red light wash over her, letting it make her skin tone look like raw meat stripped bare of any covering. She allows the siren screams of the alarm to fill her head.

A disembodied robotic voice draws her deeper inside the house.

"Perimeter breach. Perimeter breach. Front door."

Matter-of-fact. Doing the job it's programmed to do. No judgment, no investment.

"Perimeter breach. Perimeter breach. Front door."

THE FLASHING LIGHTS and alarm screeching, the robotic voice pronouncing doom—these elements accompany Stacy inside the house and remain her companions as she descends the staircase to the basement. Moving off that bottom step, the toe of her sneaker dips into a dark puddle, wet and sticky on the floor. She's too disoriented by the light-and-sound show to realize that what she's stepping in is her brother's blood. At least, she doesn't realize it at first.

Then, the sticky substance flows across her shoe, clinging to cloth and leather alike. The scent of copper fills her nose, producing a strong enough sensation to make her gag.

But Stacy swallows back her bile, ignoring the harsh aftertaste of stomach acid. She's content to let her shoe remain bloody, doesn't move it out of the puddle. Just leaves it in place, marking her presence.

Overwhelmed by this new horror, Stacy drops onto her hands and knees, splashing more of her brother's blood on her clothes and person. She knows there's a risk of contaminating the crime scene, but there are some things—like family—that outweigh such logical concerns. She crawls slow and steady toward her brother.

Her brother's *body*.

"Xavier?"

She calls his name like they're still kids playing hide-and-seek in the family basement. Calling for him like she's grown tired of playing and wants the game to be over. Wants them both to go back upstairs to their parents, to find them waiting with open arms.

"Xavier? C'mon, dammit. You're supposed to be the one who stays safe. The one who hides and doesn't get found..."

But Stacy can clearly see her brother and how he's stretched and mangled before her on the basement floor. She doesn't need to find him. He's there. He's found.

He's never going to answer her.

She pulls her phone out, presses a button, holds it to her ear. She waits.

"C'mon, c'mon," she says, "Zamuda, please pick up."

Red lights still strobe over her head. The alarm shrieks its shrill chorus in a never-ending loop. Stacy presses the phone harder to her ear. With her free hand, she pulls at her hair.

Whatever Stacy wants to say next gets caught in her throat. She squeezes the phone tighter, trying not to let it fall onto her brother or into the blood pooling all around him. Finished with her hair, her hand now picks at the skin on her face. She scratches her cheek, scraping the bottom portion of an eyelid.

Forcing herself to stop staring at her brother's body, Stacy takes in the rest of the basement. She finds the formerly crowded space emptied of all technology present mere hours before. No keyboards or mouses, no special jerry-rigged phone, no monitor wall connecting Xavier to the world beyond his home. Everything's gone. Scanners, printers. Everything.

The wall where the monitors hung is stripped bare. Whoever broke into Xavier's home, and broke him, clearly did some redecorating.

Red blood, smeared across the wall, dries black. Slashes and swirls, curved lines and angles. It dribbles down each individual letter. Still too fresh to properly stay in place, but easy enough to read.

It's a message for Stacy. A warning.

STAY AWAY.

PART 4

SPECIAL

CHAPTER 33

WEEKS LATER, AFTER Stacy's world was destroyed in one horrific—and still unsolved—act of violence, the slim bouquet of white lilies resting atop Xavier's coffin is her sole personal touch, the single deviation from the funereal plans her brother laid out in explicit detail for those who'd survive him. The priest leading the graveside service, a seventy-something Asian man, has a front row seat for Xavier's willful strangeness as he stumbles through the dead man's handwritten eulogy and shares his final words with those gathered to send him on his way.

"And so, we gather today under the eyes of God, who the deceased has requested I remind you does not exist…Really?"

Stacy's too tired to laugh at the priest's exasperation, too exhausted to smile, too worn down and depleted to properly acknowledge how her brother's playful, teasing spirit carries on even past his own death.

She figures it's enough, more than enough, for her to be there and dressed the part of the grieving family member. Today, she wears a short-sleeved black dress, a black beret atop her head, and sunglasses—round and hopefully emotionally impenetrable. Jeff, with his black suit, red tie, and pressed white shirt, stands close. His arm is soon around her shoulder. She's happy he's there as an essential accessory to help her cross the finish line after an extended series of terrible days.

"We can only hope, as Xavier Keppler's remains join those of his dearly departed mother and father, that—"

Stacy lets her sunglasses slip down her nose, allowing herself to take in the pale blue of the sky overhead.

"—he's found peace in the kingdom of Heaven. Which again, per the wishes of the deceased, I must remind all in attendance does *not* exist."

The priest sighs.

He stands at the head of Xavier's casket, which waits on risers, ready to be lowered into the open ground once the service ends. The handles are dull brass. Stacy catches her reflection, smudged and distorted in their metallic surface.

There's no one at the funeral except her, Jeff, and the priest. It's exactly the way Xavier would've wanted it. But it hurts Stacy more than she can put into words. Even while letting her fiancé hold her, she can't help but feel alone.

"And so, we end as all things must..."

The priest holds his hand over Xavier's casket, letting rich, black dirt sprinkle from his hands and onto the vessel of eternal rest.

"Ashes to ashes...and dust to dust..."

STACY SEES ZAMUDA, huffing and puffing worse than any Bad Wolf, big or otherwise, show up too late for the graveside service. By the time he's reached Xavier's resting place, the attendees are departing. He calls to Stacy and Jeff as they walk arm in arm.

"Stace? Hey! Hold up, okay?"

Sparing her former partner a look back, Stacy finds Zamuda hunched over, hands on his knees, sweat stains running down his dress shirt. He's trying to catch his breath. When he looks up again, Stacy's still adding distance between them.

"Dammit, Stacy! I just...I just wanna tell you I'm sorry... sorry for what happened to your brother."

It's not enough, Stacy thinks. All the time passed since she found her brother's body and the message left for her, all the time since her childhood home became a crime scene, and

Zamuda decided professional distance was necessary from his former colleague, his friend. All of it has caused barriers to rise. These last-minute efforts at reconciliation? *They're not enough.*

Stacy and Jeff continue to a gravel parking circle where Jeff's car waits for them. By the time Zamuda catches up, Stacy's in the passenger seat. Buckled up, head straight, and eyes forward.

Zamuda moves to that side of the car, but Jeff's faster. He intercepts the lieutenant commissioner, blocking him from Stacy on the passenger side. "I'm sorry," he says, "but I don't think she's in the mood for talking with *anyone* from the department."

It's clear that "anyone from the department" stings, and Zamuda's not the type to keep that hurt under wraps. Still, he tries his best to swallow it back. "Uh huh," he replies.

Stacy's sunglasses hide the fact her eyes are drifting to the side. Her window's rolled down slightly so she can hear what her old partner's got to say. The pain on his visage is clear. He's raw and exposed here.

A long pause follows. Jeff looks at Zamuda, searching for the right thing to say next. Eventually, nothing more comes than a simple "I'm sorry" before he moves around the car and returns to the driver's side.

"Yeah, yeah, seems more and more people are feeling sorry around here," Zamuda says, dipping into soliloquy. "But pretty soon, ain't gonna be anyone around to accept their apologies…"

Whatever else he has to say is lost under the noise of the engine starting and the black tires rolling across gravel.

SOMEHOW, SOMEWAY, THE drive to the front gates of the cemetery feels longer than the trip to the gravesite. The continued silence from Stacy after her brother's burial and the awkward, chilly reception she gave her former partner is certainly not helping things. Regardless, Jeff tries to navigate some choppy, extremely hazardous conversational waters. Because that's the sort of thing a guy like Jeff does.

He tries.

"I mean, I get it, you know?" he says. "But don't you think you should've at least talked to him?"

Stacy doesn't seem to be listening. Her finger taps the glass of the passenger window, pointing to the side of the gravel drive running the length of the cemetery.

"Could you pull over?" she asks her fiancé. "I'd like to get out and walk for a bit."

Not really believing what he's hearing, but pulling to the side anyway, Jeff has had *just* about enough.

"Wait…what? Are you serious?" he asks.

Stacy looks away from the window long enough to nod her confirmation.

Jeff lets the car drift to the side of the road. They've just made it past the front gates of the cemetery. Once Jeff parks, Stacy opens the door on her side of the car. She steps out onto a patch of grass and weeds. She adjusts her dress while trying to avoid any sticker burr hangers-on from the overgrowth.

She shuts the door behind her, but Jeff rolls down the passenger side window in response. "Can you please get back in the car?" he asks her.

There's another long pause. This time, it's Stacy who breaks the silence. "I appreciate you speaking up for me back there. You know, you and Zamuda—you two aren't really that different…" she says. "You both just wanted to keep me safe."

She moves closer to her fiancé's car. She leans in through the rolled-down window, like a neighbor looking to pass the time gossiping over a shared fence. "But now, Jeff…Now it's me who needs to work on keeping *other* people safe."

Jeff's hand shoots across the console. His body strains against the seatbelt he's still wearing. He grabs for Stacy, but comes back empty with nothing to show for his efforts.

"Stacy, please…"

She steps back from the car, returning to the roadside overgrowth.

He tries again. Louder, more insistent. Letting his fear and urgency color his words. "*Stacy!* Stacy, please…"

But she's already walking away.

CHAPTER 34

"OUR NEXT GUEST is a fellow member of our XNS team. Her must-watch and very personal new special is premiering *live* later this evening—an event that is certain to be a can't-miss. Please welcome…Ruth Freeman!"

Cue the self-congratulatory applause from the two XNS morning-show hosts. There's the one who's just given Ruth her introduction. He's Sam Ford.

Sam Ford looks like a guy who'd be named Sam Ford.

News anchor extraordinaire Debi Megyn's on the scene as well, pulling double duty away from the news desk and showing a more relaxed, folksy yet still expensive look to the rabid media-consumers out there.

The crew and staff behind the camera join in the applause. Hands slap hands in rolling waves of appreciation. On one side of the studio set, a curtain parts, and woman-of-the-hour Ruth Freeman makes her grand entrance across the soundstage.

The news network's morning show, filmed in a smaller studio in the XNS building, is so brightly lit that the over-stuffed cushioned furniture—a loveseat-sized couch for the guest and two chairs set catty-corner to the couch where the hosts perch waiting for the chance to fawn and soft-ball—is quite visible. Even exposed as it is, the furniture is…*fine*. Nothing secondhand, but nothing fancy either. Its fabric feels more than a little worn in places. That's the first thing Ruth notices as she sits, pressing her back into the cushions.

SOMEONE AT THE hospital's got the TV tuned to XNS in Cass's hospital room. Ruth is on the screen. As the door closes behind him, Malek hears his wife exchanging dull pleasantries with the hosts. However, Malek's got far more important things on his mind. Life-and-death things.

"I'm sorry, doc, but *what?* Yesterday…yesterday y'all were telling us she was fine…I mean, she wasn't gonna change. So, what—"

The youngish doctor doesn't appear phased by the pained expression on Malek's face. Whatever the kid's learned in med school, bedside manner was not an area of specialization. He's quick to cut the older man off and get down to business, however brutal and untenable the news he's about to share may be.

"Mr. Freeman, I understand that is what you were *originally* told. But in trauma situations, where you have a patient suffering from the amount of brain damage your daughter's experienced, things can change…fast. Now, I'm not exactly sure what happened overnight, but whatever it was…your daughter's condition is deteriorating rapidly. I understand that this may be difficult to consider, especially given the circumstances, but Cassidy does have you listed on her DNR forms. As a result, we need to talk about…"

The doctor's words become so much hissing static between Malek's ears.

NOW, BACK IN the morning-show studio, Ruth, the woman of the hour, sits on the interviewee couch fielding questions from both sides.

"This special tonight—your mother-and-son interview. How do you feel about sharing such a personal moment with an audience estimated to be in the millions?" Sam floats his underhand pitch of a question across the proverbial plate.

Ruth's answer comes just as easy, with her head positioned perfectly and her eyes focused on the right camera. "What an excellent question, Sam! Obviously, before I joined the XNS team, there were already so many people who'd been just so supportive of me and Matty and our family as we waited and prayed for and worked toward his return. So, really, I look at this special as being less about *us* and more about sharing my son's return with the people who were there for us. My family is *their* family. Then, now, and forever."

HUSBAND AND DAUGHTER, the two unmentioned members of Ruth Freeman's family, are together now. Yet, somehow, both are also alone.

Malek stands by the head of Cass's hospital bed. There's no scent of sweat, nor blood, nor even the chemical residue of medication lingering over the room. Now, when Malek breathes in, he tastes nothing. There's a persistent nothingness matching his daughter's diminishing form.

All the wires, the monitors, everything that was once attached to the young woman has been removed. All that's left is her half-shaved head, bare and scabbed over. Her eyes are closed, her lips parted. She's barely exhaling. Her weakened frame remains covered by a thin hospital gown and blanket. But it's already like she's not even there.

Malek reaches a hand out, running his fingertips along the sutures from her emergency brain surgery. "I'm sorry, baby girl," he says. "I'm so, so goddamn sorry."

Then, he pulls his hand back, fast, like he's touched a live-wire. When he speaks, he hears himself rushing, trying to get through the hard parts before he breaks down again. "You can go now…okay? Okay?"

The sensor on her finger is the sole bit of medical equipment still attached to Cass. The long white cord connects to a patient monitor on the other side of her bed. The on-screen line is slow to rise and fall, but it's there.

For the moment.

beep beep beep beep beeeeep

Moments later, Malek slides down the door outside his daughter's hospital room and knocks the back of his head against its slick wooden surface. Then, his hands shoot up to his face. Covering his features, he loses himself in sobs.

Back in the room, the heart rate monitor finally flatlines.

beeeeeeeeeeeeeeeeeeeeeeeeeeeeep

NOW IT'S DEBI'S turn to ask questions. Ruth may have all the attention, all the press, all the spotlight, but Debi Megyn *is* Debi Megyn. and she will not concede to second place.

"Ruth, if I could, I wanted to see if you had any comment regarding Xavier Keppler's murder …"

The half-asked question takes Ruth by surprise. It flusters her, and that shows on her face—on camera, even. "I don't know, I…"

Debi, perhaps envisioning future news Emmys, presses the attack. "He was Stacy Keppler's brother. You know, the retired detective sergeant who was assigned to your son's abduction case? But now it seems that this Mr. Keppler is deceased. He's dead, that paparazzo outside the hospital, and I mean, obviously your daughter, who was—"

Ruth's smiling again, trying to wrest back control of her emotions. But her nostrils flare, as if she'll breathe fire and set the studio and the talking heads on either side of her ablaze. Before she can respond, though, affable Sam tries to defuse the spiraling situation.

"I, uh, I think what Debi's trying to say is that people are just wondering about the safety around—"

"I think I can ask my own questions, Sam," Debi says, interrupting her co-host.

"Oh, *can you*, Debi?"

Ruth stares into the camera. Her bottom lip quivers as the hosts on either side of her bicker.

Ruth's no longer smiling.

The show's announcer chimes in—a disembodied voice echoing through the studio.

"We'll be back with Jasper the Piano-Playing Pug after these messages from our sponsors!"

CHAPTER 35

BACK AT HOME, dressed in a stretched-out J.Crew sweatshirt, powder blue leggings, and ankle socks rolled over at their tops, wiping sleep from her eyes, Stacy finds a sticky note on the monitor that sits on the desk she shares with Jeff. The tiny yellow square clings to the black of the powered-down screen.

She plucks the note free and brings it close to read. It's in Jeff's scratchy handwriting, which means she has to squint to decipher some of the letters. In the end, she reads:

Stace,

Giving you some space (Ha! a rhyme).
Please stay safe.

Love,
Jeff

Stacy holds on to the note as she navigates their nearly empty home. Moving from room to room, she switches off lights as she leaves one space and turns them on in the next. The light fixture above the kitchen island bathes that room in all-encompassing white light. Stacy blinks under its power, and, thinking better of having it on, switches the light off once again.

She treads across the smooth surface of their kitchen floor, headed for the refrigerator. She opens its door and stares inside. There's not much to choose from. Some of the take-out boxes appear swollen and exude a slight odor, suggesting that, if they're not past their sell-by-date, they're damn close. The same goes for the half gallon of milk with a quarter drank from it, whose remaining liquid is colored light blue like a developing bruise.

Stacy's usually the one who buys the milk and usually the one who cleans out the fridge. She sighs, knowing she has herself to blame—at least partially. She shuts the door and leaves the kitchen empty-handed.

She reenters the home office. She's got more reading material waiting for her there. Something more substantial than Jeff's Post-it. There's a certain unaddressed envelope recovered from her dead brother's house.

Both house and letter belong to her now.

The letter calls to her, demanding attention and possible action.

She pulls out the wheeled office chair from under the desk. Sitting in it, reaching across the desk to free the letter from where she tucked it away earlier, Stacy prepares herself for the next steps.

Step one: Read the letter.

That's easy enough once she starts. She flips through, page after page, imagining her brother doing the same thing. But when her mind wanders to Xavier reading the letter and trying to use its content to draw out whoever or whatever killed him, things start to get harder for Stacy.

Step two: Continue reading the letter.

Eventually, she decides a change of reading location is just what the doctor ordered. She moves to the living-room couch. The TV's off, and Jeff is still gone, still giving her space. For the moment, it's just Stacy and the letter—the chronicle of what happened to Matt Freeman, according to his dead sister.

Approaching the end of her reading, she stops to consider how she and Matt Freeman now have dead siblings in common. The text message she received from Malek Freeman lingers on her cellphone. She only glances at the portion that came up on-screen as a pop-up when the text arrived: "Cass is gone."

Step three: Read the letter *again*. But *really* read it close this time.

Stacy stops halfway through the second read through. There's still no one in the house, so she's talking to herself when she says, "There's just…there's no *way* she could have written all…"

Step four: Find something to compare what you're reading against.

Soon, Stacy's off the couch and on her knees, paperwork fanned out before her. There's an old filing cabinet in the back of the bedroom closet. Its drawers are open and the accordion file folders inside are strewn across the floor, emptied. Notes and Christmas cards, letters and postcards, little pieces of ephemera Cass Freeman sent to Stacy over the years. Stacy's held on to all of these miscellaneous communications. Now, she wonders if she held on to them for this exact moment.

"Here it is…"

She holds one of Cass's earlier letters, something written to Stacy during the girl's high school years, against *the* letter. The one sent to Xavier's house in spite of the fact that Stacy gave Cass a post office box she was supposed to use—a safer, more private way to keep in touch without risk of the messages being found or having suspicions raised with the girl's mother.

More proof, she thinks, *that this letter isn't written by Cass. Or at the very least wasn't delivered by her…*

Step five: Check the fridge again.

Nothing to do with the investigation, Stacy's just struck by the sudden urge to find something, *anything*, to eat. Yet somehow the fridge's contents have lessened in both number and in desirability. She runs a hand through her unwashed hair and wipes new sleep-crust from her eyes.

Step six: Turn on the computer.

Back in the home office, Stacy invokes her brother before pressing the power switch on her computer.

"Xavier," she says, "I know you didn't believe in an afterlife; but I still hope you're up there, or wherever, laughing your ass off at how long it's taking your sister to finally turn on this machine…"

The computer cycles up, and Stacy navigates her web browser to one of her brother's beloved conspiracy sites. She brings up a wiki entry about the Gray Men, one Xavier's even contributed edits to. Seeing one of his old screennames brings a smile to Stacy's face, but it's the kind of smile that hurts like hell.

Step seven:—

DING DONG!

DING DONG!

Her doorbell's chimes shake Stacy from her cocoon of focus. She spins the computer chair around and stands, feeling the blood rushing through her extremities when she does so. There's an accompanying head rush as well.

"Oh shoot! Just a second!" she calls to whoever waits on the other side of the front door.

SOME GUY STANDS back from the home of Keppler-Stacy, studying the brick-and-wood façade of the one-story dwelling. His eyes are wide and hold an expression close to curiosity.

Some Guy moves to the side of the house, letting himself get lost in the shadows between Stacy's domicile and her neighbor's home.

MOVING WITH LEGS on pins and needles, Stacy takes the letter with her to the front door. One of the pages escapes her grasp, flutters to the floor.

"Aww, c'mon!" Stacy grumbles.

DING DONG.

Again, the doorbell.

The letter, whether it's actually from Cass Freeman or not, feels too important, too *substantial* to Stacy's growing investigation for it to be allowed to fall from her grasp. As a result, she's soon on the floor again, gathering the errant page.

DING—

"Please don't ring the bell again!" she calls. "I said I'd be right there."

Finished recovering the page, Stacy's fingers soon curl around the handle for a too-brief moment before she throws caution to the wind and pulls the door open wide, ready to welcome in whoever's been doing all the pounding from the outside.

Once the door's opened, Stacy's immediately swallowing back any exasperated words she may have wanted to share.

Because of the girl.

She's about ten years old or so, based on Stacy's quick assessment of her height, the roundness of her features, her wardrobe, and the wide-eyed yet intelligent expression on her face.

Around the age Cass was when we first met.

But she pushes aside that thought, that reaction, refusing to let it color this new interaction. After all, this girl is on her porch, not in an interview room. She isn't sitting in a dull-gray, metal folding chair, her feet unable to reach the floor. There's no camera over their shoulders, watching and listening.

This girl's brown hair is pulled into pigtails, one slightly larger than the other. Like she either did them herself or whoever did them for her was in a hurry.

The stack of oversized paper clutched to the girl's chest, covering her overalls and frilly-necked t-shirt, speak to the kind of business this girl might have and why it's brought her to Stacy's front door.

"Oh," Stacy says, pausing to regroup and avoid the lambasting she'd planned. "Oh, hi sweetie. What can I do for you?"

There's no hesitation, no masking of her purpose. The girl answers with her whole heart.

Just like…No. No, don't think of her. They're not the same.

"Thank you, ma'am. I'm, uh, I'm…I'm looking for my dog."

The photo images bleeding through the backsides of the papers come into stark relief.

The girl presses on, delivering her practiced speech.

"His…his name is Whitley, and he's a really, really, really good dog. But he's been missing for a while and he hasn't come home again. My folks don't think he's gonna come back. But I keep looking and asking people to help. I'm out in your neighborhood today. Here, uh, would you take one of my flyers?"

It's not as if the girl has to ask. Stacy's already got her hand out. She's already accepting one of these mini posters with its Comic Sans font and a smudged printed photo of the mutt at the bottom. A parent's cell phone number, or maybe even a house line, is listed.

MISSING DOG

A description of the absent canine follows. Stacy scans the page again. Partially to see if there's any way she can help, partially because she can't stand the idea of eye contact with the girl at this moment.

She stops when she reviews the address section of the flyer.

"Bobtail Drive?"

The street name emerges as a question, and Stacy looks up at the girl for an answer.

The girl nods. Then, she waits, seemingly wise beyond her years. Like she understands that patience is required as the old detective puts some pieces together.

"That's been a busy part of town lately, hasn't it?"

Again, the nodding, that silent confirmation. *Police, news, the Freemans, other secrets…* Stacy finds it easy to mentally rattle off everything and everyone tied to Bobtail Drive and to her case that's not really *her* case. It's more of a feeling, more of a series of unfortunate events through which she's trying to redeem the reputations of those lost and, if she's being totally honest, of herself as well.

"You're from there and your folks let you travel this far from home? After what happened to…"

The girl doesn't nod. She stares at Stacy, unbent and unbroken. "Ms. Freeman says all of us children are safe and should be safe forever. She says it's the ones who take the children or let children like her son be taken who should worry. She says he came home…and the people who took him won't go anywhere ever again."

Stacy's got no response to these words. She can only hold her hand out, indicating that she'd like a second poster.

The girl smiles slightly as she hands over another flyer. But sadness remains quite visible in her eyes. Now that she's attuned to it, Stacy can hear it linger in the girl's speech.

"I told your husband that Whitley likes to run away sometimes and get into the neighbors' backyards. But not like this," she says. "Never for this long."

The girl hasn't left the porch yet. She hasn't descended the steps, hasn't returned to the neutral territory of the sidewalk.

She stands there with her pile of posters showing her long-lost, almost certainly dead dog on them, and it's Stacy who ends up beating a hasty retreat. "Aww, geez," she says. "I'll look, okay? Okay? I just…a dog? I gotta just—"

Stacy feels like a coward, allowing the door to slam closed in her face and cut her off from the melancholy girl on her front porch.

With the door closed and Stacy leaning against it from inside the house, she lets her heavy, panting breaths wrench her shoulders up and down and down and up. She waits through several too-long, too-agonizing moments until she hears sneaker-clad feet scuffing the porch steps, marking the girl's departure. Only then does Stacy speak again.

"Poor little thing. That dog's probably dead."

Then, she's off like a bullet fired from her service weapon. She beelines from the front door to the bedroom. Moving deeper into her closet, she ignores the musk of unwashed sheets marred by sleepless nights and days and all points in-between. She ventures to her side of the closet and shoves aside a series of dresses, the majority of which have the price and sizing tags retained. Even a nearly forgotten wedding dress, purchased with eager early anticipation for her pending nuptials to Jeff, gets moved aside. One more something in the way.

"Nothing *but* dead since *he* came back," Stacy says. "Cass was right. She was right from the start. This *is* what he wants."

With the forlorn dresses cleared away, Stacy crouches at a reinforced metal safe hidden away from prying eyes. Hidden even from Jeff.

She works its combination lock, twirling the numbered circle round and round and round. Pausing between digits, she strives to recall the correct sequence. "Almost got it…"

Then, it opens, and Stacy reaches inside. "I'm not gonna let him take any more," she says.

And she means it. She means it with every fiber of her being.

WHEN STACY RETURNS to her front porch, she's alone. Her hair is washed. Her whole body, even. The cool air feels good against her slightly damp skin and clothing. She wears the moisture as a shield against the encroaching humidity. She takes a cautious step down, like she's leaving the safety and sanctity of home. Her hand grips the railing.

After a quick second of contact, she pulls her hand back. To an outside observer, it might appear as though she's felt some shock, something lingering on the railing that connected her with whoever may have stood outside her home moments before. But that's not the case at all. If anything, it's a coincidence. A fluke.

She's not even feeling all that present in the moment. Instead, she's thinking back to the girl on her porch, the one with the missing, almost certainly dead dog. She's remembering something the girl said, something that's not adding up after further consideration.

"I told your husband that he likes to run away…"

The sudden crunch of a footfall somewhere off to the side of the house sends Stacy hurtling headfirst back into the here and now. Holding the railing again, she peers to the side, trying to get a sightline around the house.

"Jeff! That you?"

No answer. But Stacy's not letting this go. She descends the porch steps, moving to level ground. Off the concrete walkway, she maneuvers through the grass, hurtling to the side of the house.

Except there's nothing to see or hear there.

Not even a boot print. Not even a whisper on the wind.

MOMENTS LATER, BACK in the bathroom, Stacy studies herself in the toothpaste-splattered mirror. Her old blue-and-black police patrol uniform is a little tight now. But it fits better than she expected. She's tied her black tie tight and symmetrical, cinched at the neck like a hangman's noose.

"Not bad for twenty-some years..." she says.

The patrol officer's cap sits snug on her head, her silver gray hair tucked under the brim so that not a lock is visible. The old aviator shades Jeff gifted her because of an in-joke where he got Cagney and Lacey confused with Starsky and Hutch provide the final puzzle piece to Stacy's reimagined self—her disguise.

While she's dressed in this manner—assuming no one's paying too close attention—it's easy to imagine Stacy being mistaken for *one of the guys*. Just another cop in what will be a room, a building, full of cops. It hasn't even been a full three months since Stacy retired. She doesn't have time to consider how dressing in this patrol officer's uniform is like she's throwing herself into the past. Not tonight.

"Okay, time to work," she says, giving herself one last pep talk.

CHAPTER 36

RUTH SITS AND waits for her stylist, Brenda, to finish putting her TV-face on. Brenda lived in the same neighborhood as the Freemans back when she was Mrs. Brenda instead of Ms. Brenda. She'd never worked a day in her life before her divorce, but Ruth recalled how she always looked flawless at neighborhood get togethers and PTA fundraiser galas.

Once Ruth got wind of her old neighbor's separation and subsequent change in social stature, she insisted the higher-ups at XNS bring Brenda onboard to handle her hair and makeup. The network heads pushed back for a brief spell, but only until Ruth shared the offers she'd received from CNN, Fox, and even E! Entertainment Television, who were looking to expand their human interest programming.

They were smart enough to realize when they had a golden goose.

There's part of Ruth that wishes more people would remember her for things like her generosity to poor, poor Brenda. As her made-up face and styled hair develop under the other woman's stewardship, Ruth engages in the expected chitchat common between stars and those who help them shine. "Oh, Brenda, I should *hope* there are a lot of cops here," she says, responding to an earlier quip about *boys in blue*. "They *owe* me—owe my family—that much, at least."

She catches sight of her own eyes bugging slightly in their

sockets, the twitching flare of her nostrils. Ruth reins it back as Brenda replies: "Yes, of course, Ms. Freeman."

Ruth doesn't have the energy to correct the woman for failing to call her *Mrs.* Freeman. She's not even certain she wants to be called that anymore. Still hasn't quite decided what she wants to do with Malek—a man who she knows deep down in her heart has long outlived his usefulness to her.

Feeling quite finished with the conversation in general, Ruth closes her eyes, allowing Brenda's makeup brush to dance across her face. When she opens her eyes again, she begins practicing her opening monologue for the special, feeling out the words.

"Just as there is no greater pain for a mother than the loss of a child, so too is the joy of reunion amplified…What do you think? Too cheesy, or…oh."

A new face appears in the mirror. There he is, leaning down so his face is fully captured in the silvered surface: Matt.

Her baby boy.

Ruth grabs the arms of the makeup chair and turns herself, and it, around. Already taller than her, Matt towers over his seated mother. He looks down at her, and there's a confusion visible behind his eyes. Ruth feels her heart beating rapid-fire in her chest at the sight of her son's distress.

"Matt, honey? Everything okay in your dressing room, baby? Because I told them to—"

He leans toward her fast. Faster than expected.

She grips the arms of the chair and plants her feet on the ground to keep from tipping backwards.

"Mom," Matt says. That's all. Nothing more seems set to follow that single word.

For a moment, the briefest of moments, Ruth wonders if Brenda hasn't gone and used too much hairspray on her and that the Matt standing before her is nothing more than an illusion.

"Matt?"

No spoken answer comes. There's only Matt bending down, leaning closer to his mother. His lips pursed and eyes closed.

He kisses the top of her head, bringing back accents of vanilla and citrus, and inhales as he returns to an upright standing position.

For once, Ruth's the one at a loss for words.

"Oh" is the best she can manage.

He's already leaving her side. Already backing away from the makeup chair and vanity mirror. Ruth sweats from the glare of the bright bulbs around the mirror frame. The perfumed scents amplify in the heat, making her feel like she's wearing a cake on her head.

Brenda's back, ready to work. Like she never left. For all Ruth knows, maybe that's true. "Is your son okay, Ruth? He seems kinda…I dunno…off."

Ruth waits until the makeup artist has reapplied her eyeshadow and liner. It's not until her work's done that Ruth makes eye contact with Brenda's reflection in the makeup mirror and addresses her in a slow, measured, and ever so menacing tone. "Get. Out. Fucking. *Now.*"

Once the dressing room clears, Ruth turns around again and finds Matt with his back to her. His forehead rests against the wall in a corner of the room.

More than anything, she wishes she had a single clue what her baby boy's thinking.

A COUPLE HOURS later, it's almost time for the show. Ruth and Matt have both finished with hair, makeup, and wardrobe. Ruth's checked in with her producers and gone over the program for the evening's special. All that's left is to smile for the camera, talk to the people at home, and show the world that her son is back and he is fine. He's still her baby boy, just as he was before he was taken.

Mother and son sit in high-backed cushioned chairs. Special ordered, just for the evening's programming. They're the kind Ruth had in her living room those nineteen or so years previous. The originals were destroyed. Too much brown liquor was spilled on the cushions by the other child, Cassidy. The bad one. The one who stayed, but should've been the one who was taken. Dead now.

Ruth forces any thoughts of the young woman out of her head. This night is about her—her and her son.

The seats of the new chairs touch at an angle. Another of Ruth's decisions. If she can't hold her son, if she can't have his hand in hers while they're on-air, then this particular arrangement will provide that desired sense of closeness. A round-topped display table sits behind them. Framed photos are arranged across its surface. Pictures of Matt, the way Ruth remembers him best. Her smiling, loving, laughing little boy.

The man sitting beside her, shifting nervously against the seatback of his chair like he can't get comfortable, like he's unfamiliar with the concept of comfort, bears only the faintest traces of the boy Ruth lost.

She looks out at the blank, expectant faces of the studio audience members. Curiosity, wonder, and perhaps a few stray traces of fear manifest in the rows and rows of people seated for the show. The thin earpiece attached behind Ruth's ear crackles to life. She hears Gregg's voice, speaking from the control room and telling her what she already knows.

"Okay, Ruth," he says, "we're live in five, four, three…"

JEFF'S BACK AT the house. Now he's the one alone on the living room couch. Stacy's nowhere to be found. The glow of their television set washes out Jeff's features. Opening graphics and a deep-voiced narration outlining the events of Matt Freeman's abduction and miraculous return mark the start of Ruth Freeman's night of special programming.

Jeff wants to pretend he doesn't care. After all, he's seen first-hand how torn up his fiancée's been over these recent inexplicable events. Finally free of her dangerous work on the police force, yet pulled back into it out of some obligation to this family, this case—the one that seemingly got away—it pains Jeff to see Stacy so stressed, so tortured. He'd like to pretend that if he ignores it, it will all go away.

But he knows that's a lie. It's a sensational story, something impossible to ignore. And he's sure the same holds true for the woman he loves.

"I can't believe Stacy's missing this," he says.

SOME MEMBERS OF the Herenton Police sit interspersed throughout the studio audience. Ruth recognizes a few faces from her previous interactions with the department. Not just from the many years spent searching for her son, but as past guests of and consultants on her show, part of the investigations and fieldwork done on behalf of others who'd suffered like her, those tortured by too many *what if*s. So many other missing people—children, adults, the elderly, loved ones, forgotten ones. Ruth's seen and talked about enough missing, *taken*, individuals to fill a whole other phantom country.

The United States of the Disappeared.

Knowing full well what dangers lurk in the shadows, Ruth now feels some level of power, some degree of control returning as she looks at all of the undercover cops surrounding her and her son.

Hell, for all Ruth knows, some of the audience members she *doesn't* recognize might also be cops. Plus there are the uniformed officers on the job outside the studio and out of camera view. She asked Zamuda for more female officers. Now she notices a mother and what looks to be a "teen" daughter standing to the side, whispering to each other. Ruth can't help but wonder who they *really* are. But she refuses to let herself go down that particular rabbit hole. After all, she's got a show to host.

"And now, ladies and gentlemen, it's my turn to officially reintroduce to the world…my son, Matthew Harold Freeman."

OVER AT THE funeral home, the head mortician finishes incinerating one of the latest bodies to grace his establishment. All of this young woman, her scars and blank expression and shaved head, have been quickly reduced to a keepsake box of gray ash. Later, when he's finished, the mortician will slap the preprinted "CASSIDY FREEMAN" label on the box of ashes and forget all about the girl.

But for now, he's watching a little portable TV set on one of the slabs where cold dead bodies will wait to be made beautiful for their final close-ups. Funny enough, he recognizes the woman on-screen. And not just from seeing her on TV all the time.

He's sure the TV woman came in earlier that day, accompanying the now-cremated girl's body from the hospital *and* asking him if he could work quickly and discreetly.

"Ma'am," he'd said, "when you work with the dead, speed and discretion are the best tools to have."

And now she's practically glowing through his tiny portable TV screen.

"Can you tell me something about the man who came…who rescued you? Take your time, though. I…I know how hard it must be…"

She's good, he thinks. *Damn good.*

SOME GUY WATCHES the faces of Mother Freeman-Ruth and the Hybrid Freeman-Matt from the darkness. Stacked machines taken from the home of the deceased Keppler-Xavier are now plugged into power beyond the comprehension of the backwards species that believes themselves to be in control of this planet Earth and all the stars that surround it.

Some Guy follows the Hybrid Freeman-Matt's face from one screen to the next, his eyes twitching fast enough to catch a different word or two on one screen, then on the other, and so on.

"I'm—

not—

sure.
It's all—
so confusing."

RUTH COULDN'T BE happier with how the evening's broadcast is going. She looks out from the stage, past the lights, to the crew, getting a quick glimpse at their work of filming, recording, and broadcasting this interview with her son. Her only living child. Each shot is captured just as she'd envisioned, just as she'd outlined to Gregg and the special's other producers.

A close-up of Matt lets the audience, watching wherever they may be, really feel for her beloved son, really connect with him.

"Ever since I came home, all I've wanted is to share what happened to me with *you*. With the world," he says.

Knowing the camera is on her now, Ruth gives the audience her most beatific smile. The poor mother in mourning, suffering for many years but never *ever* giving up hope that her child would be returned to her. She lives and breathes this role.

Matt continues: "I don't want to feel like I'm different now. Different from who you remember. But I guess…maybe I am."

The money shot follows: Ruth's hand stretching out, reaching for her son. "It's okay, Matty," she says. Then, leaning closer, she asks him one more question. "Just tell me, the one thing I want to know is, did you ever wonder: *Where's Mommy?*"

A derisive snort comes from the audience, loud and sneering. That's not at all what Ruth wanted. With just one noise, this audience member has ruined everything. They've sabotaged Ruth's pageantry of grief and redemption.

Now, they're making it worse. A uniformed officer standing in the middle of the audience with aviator shades and smooth, seemingly soft cheeks approaches the stage with their service weapon drawn.

And they're speaking, too. "Enough. This is all…*enough*."

Ruth recognizes the voice.

WHITLEY'S HUMAN GIRL peers out from behind her parent's couch while pretending to enjoy playing with her Barbies. She has to pretend because all she can think about is her lost dog out there somewhere, anywhere. Nobody seems to know where—at least no one she's talked to yet. If Whitley's human girl had her way, she'd still be out there, visiting everyone in town and giving them a copy of the flyer.

She notices a stray Barbie head deposited onto Whitley's bed and brushes it to the floor. Then, she pops her head back above the couch to check out the TV, because the voice that just interrupted Ms. Freeman sounds so familiar.

On the screen, Ms. Freeman's trying her best to keep her show going, acting as if no one's said anything at all.

"Wh-when the Patays had you, did…did you…Hold on. What's the meaning of this?" Ms. Freeman doesn't sound too happy. Not too happy at all.

XNS'S USUAL SUSPECTS of on-air personalities and staff members not involved in the evening's broadcast have gathered in one of the big conference rooms where they've got access to a live feed—the same one coming into the control booth in the studio, direct from the studio cameras. Making, sharing, producing the news is part of the job for every person in this room.

So, naturally, they're the first to notice when things go wrong.

"Um, I, uh, I think something's wrong …" Debi Megyn says.

Rick hasn't been paying close attention, focusing instead on flirting with one of the new interns from UVA. He tries brushing off Debi's comment like it's no big deal. "Uh yeah, I mean the whole thing feels exploitative as hell. If you ask me…"

But Morning Show Sam is next to speak, cutting Rick short, grabbing his chin, and turning it toward the screen. "No, asshole," Sam says. "*Look.*"

BLACK-ARMBAND-CLAD MEMBERS OF the paparazzi commune outside the XNS building. It's as close as the network and the police allow them to be for the evening's entertainment. Still, every man and woman there knows the real action will come after the show when everyone's leaving. They've staked out all possible exits and even a few places that might serviceably double as hidden exit points. Each paparazzo believes they will be the one to snap a pic of the Freemans' returned son.

They watch the broadcast via the network's streaming feed on their cell phones. The quality's decent enough, even if the picture freezes every now and then. At least the audio comes through crisp and clear.

From what they can gather, apparently one of the uniformed police officers has interrupted the evening's proceedings and pulled their gun. A woman's voice, shaky but growing in power, addresses the mother and son, who are still in their seated positions on the stage.

"My brother. Your sister. The Patays. The people at that honky-tonk. Where does it end, Matthew?"

MALEK FREEMAN'S EYES sting from the ammonia in the cleaning products he's been using all afternoon and into the evening. His hands are dry and starting to blister. But he's happy with the work he's done, cleaning his daughter's apartment. The floor and walls almost sparkle, with the layers of dirt and spilled booze chipped away at last. Overstuffed garbage bags sit, row after row, from the walls to the middle of most rooms in the apartment.

Malek is certain he'll blame the ammonia when the tears finally come. It won't be the pain of losing his child. *No.* It won't be regret. He won't let that happen.

He's folding laundry now. A pile of Cass's clothes fresh from the dryer. Clothes she'll never have to wear. Will never *get* to wear.

There's no working TV in Cass's apartment. It's been pulled off the wall, thrown hard to the floor, likely during one of her past binges. Once Malek finishes with the clothes, he'll turn his attention to sweeping up the shattered screen glass, using another trash bag for the busted set.

ZAMUDA HANGS BACK behind the curtains at XNS, uncertain whether he needs to stick his head (and neck) out just yet. After all, the last thing he wants for himself, or for the department, is to trigger a panic on live television. Panic…or something even worse.

That's why he's got his radio out, silencing its static hiss to whisper questions in a harsh, trying-his-best-not-to-sound-worried voice.

"What the hell?" he asks. "What's that uni doing out there, and…is that a…is that a *gun*?"

The next voice he hears is familiar, and not at all one he expected to hear.

But perhaps maybe it should've been.

"I think this needs to end, here and now," Stacy says from the studio audience.

Zamuda's known his former partner long enough to be absolutely certain that she means every syllable of what she says.

CHAPTER 37

AS SHE MOVES unimpeded through the studio audience and toward the stage where Ruth and Matt Freeman are seated, Stacy's well aware of how easy everything's been up to this point. She's tossed the uniform cap and aviators, allowing her face and hair to be shown in their natural state. In a way, it's her act of defiance. She's letting Matt know exactly who's coming for him.

From the corner of her eye, Stacy catches one of the camera operators shifting their bulky rig as slowly and carefully as they can. She knows the camera's lens will soon focus on her. If she's going to act, if she's going to do what she came here to do, then her window of opportunity is likely to close soon.

"Whoever—*whatever*—you are, Cassidy was right. You're *not* Matt Freeman. Now, I want you to tell the world the truth."

Gasps, shouts, and other cries follow in a rippling wave from the audience. All of it is white noise as far as Stacy's concerned. Just distractions from her objective.

On the stage at last, she aims her old service revolver at the so-called Matt Freeman's head. Ruth grasps both armrests on her chair, her body lifting slightly off the seat cushion. She looks as though she's ready to make a move as well.

But Stacy's aware of all potential dangers surrounding her. She came prepared.

"Moseley! Timberlake!" she shouts, calling to some of her former colleagues she recognized in the audience and who are likely to try and play hero. "All of you stand down, okay?"

Ruth Freeman does not look happy with any of this.

"Wait a minute. Now, just wait a goddamn minute," she says. Then, she adds a quick aside to her production team: "And don't you *dare* cut away from this in the booth."

That bit of business handled, Ruth directs the full brunt of her anger at Stacy and the gun in Stacy's hand. "You miserable bitch," she says. "What did we ever do to you? Why can't you leave us alone to be happy?"

Harsh words, yes. But Stacy's still got the gun. She takes one, two quick steps, moving closer to Matt.

"Why don't you ask your *son*?" she says.

"Everyone, stand the *fuck* down," Zamuda shouts, taking the opportunity to make his presence known from backstage. He steps from behind the set's curtains. He keeps his distance but maintains eye contact with Stacy.

"Stace…what are you doing here?" he asks.

Before Stacy can answer, Ruth takes the opportunity to stand and make sure her opinion is heard on the matter. "Don't stand down! Shoot her! Shoot her *now*!" There's a palpable rage radiating off the woman, her cheeks reddening and her makeup cracking under the lights.

If she wanted to get Stacy's attention, if she wanted to draw the former detective's ire away from her son, then Ruth's outburst is a success. Stacy pivots, keeping her feet planted in her stance but shifting her arm so the gun's trained on the show's host instead of the guest.

Stacy's words come firmly, deliberately. "Did I ever tell you how I reached detective so quickly, Ruth?" she asks. "All those times, checking on Matt's case—did that ever come up?"

There's no answer from Ruth. Only seething.

So, Stacy continues. "I'll save you any guesswork. It's because I was in the top of my class in, well, *everything*. Not something I advertised or bragged about. Not something the fellas I graduated with felt like pointing out either, imagine that. But it's the truth."

Matt Freeman's voice provides an unexpected interruption. "And yet you still couldn't find a lost, scared little boy. Isn't that right, detective?"

Her gun still trained on Ruth, Stacy flicks her eyes to the other chair. Matt pushes himself up to a standing position. Just like his mother. His eyes zero in on Stacy, like he's locking her in a tractor beam. There's none of the light, wavering-voiced innocence Stacy encountered back at City Hall when he originally "returned." There's a cold inhumanity to his speech instead.

"You left me alone," he says, "with the *monsters*. You failed me."

Ruth reaches for her son. But Matt avoids contact.

"No, Mother," he says. "Let me go."

"Matt, baby, please. She's not—she's nothing." Ruth's pleas drop to nearly a whisper.

Stacy remains steadfast, determined to adapt to this sudden interruption and stick to her mission of exposing the truth—whatever that might be—about Matt Freeman, or whatever being stands before her now. She makes another scan of the studio, reassessing her situation. She catches sight of Zamuda, his eyes focused past the stage, out to the audience.

"Nothing," Matt says, like he's savoring the taste of the word on his tongue. "Yes, all *nothing*."

Looking into the audience, Stacy sees several approaching officers stop short and stand down at Zamuda's signal.

"Do you all know what *nothing* feels like?" Matt asks.

The question draws Stacy's attention back. She feel her grip loosening on her revolver. Second thoughts and doubts take over. "Please, just—"

But whatever she's about to say is cut short, same as the distance between her and Matt Freeman. He moves fast, too fast. The space of feet reduced to inches in split seconds. He towers over Stacy, looking down at her gun as if it were a child's plaything. Not even a cap gun, but a pointed finger. No threat at all.

"It feels like *everything*," he says.

Stacy readjusts her grip. She lowers the weapon so the snub-nosed barrel is aimed at his chest.

"So, why don't you go ahead and shoot me?" he asks her.

The studio lights reveal a flush of red rising from Stacy's neck to her cheeks and forehead. She's having a harder and harder time nailing down the right words.

"I...I..."

But before she can finish her answer, Taser wires shoot out and their hooks are driven through the fabric of Stacy's old uniform shirt. They dig into her skin. Once connected to Stacy, the electric current travels fast through the wires.

Stacy's only got time for a half-hearted "Huh?" before she feels the shock.

Her whole body jerks forward, arms flying above her head. She screams, feeling the searing heat starting in her lower back and spreading everywhere. Her gun falls with a bang—but not a *bang*—against the stage. Stacy drops seconds later. Wires connect to her back like marionette strings. Electricity flows through the Taser wires and into her prone form.

She convulses as Matt Freeman remains standing above her, looking down with the blank, expressionless face that's become so familiar to Stacy. It's this face that's replaced the videotape-captured image of the small boy's ice-cream-smeared grin.

Moaning, trying to fight against the pain, Stacy presses her palms against the stage and pushes herself up.

As if she can stand. As if she can still finish what she came here to do.

Then, the hooks of two more wires break her skin, and a new shock adds to the efforts of the first. Moaning, grunting, screaming from the steady onslaught of pain. All she wants is to pass out.

Oblivion would be a relief.

CHAPTER 38

JEFF HOPPED OFF the couch as soon as he heard Stacy's voice on the broadcast. Now he's sunk down to his knees in front of their set, pressing his face to the glass of the screen.

"Jesus! Stacy!" he cries.

Of course, he knows it won't do anything. He knows his words can't save her.

RUTH'S BODYGUARDS, LEWIS and Coleman, stand over the fallen Stacy Keppler, unsure of what their next move should be. Lewis holds both Tasers, and Coleman's got his Desert Eagle out, the massive handgun trained on the still-twitching woman—the woman who's *still* trying to fight against the multiple shocks coursing through her body.

"Stay down! Stay the *fuck* down!" Coleman shouts. Just like they yell in the movies.

Lewis, wanting in on the action, tries to add his part. "Don't make us—"

But he's cut short by the rampaging Lieutenant Commissioner Zamuda, bounding to the front of the stage with his own service weapon drawn. He aims at Ruth's behemoths. "Nobody's doing a goddamn thing," he says. "Put your weapons *down!*"

WHEN THE FIRST shocks coursed through Stacy's body and she fell onto the stage, Ruth found herself scrambling backward, then sitting hard against the chair in which she'd been interviewing her son minutes prior. She's still sitting there, taking in the angry confrontation between her men and Zamuda. Her fingernails dig into the chair, pricking twin holes in the fabric on either arm.

She's watching, waiting.

Lewis turns to his boss, pulling Ruth more directly into the action. "Boss?"

But Ruth's not looking at her brick wall of a bodyguard. Her focus is on Stacy Keppler, who's finally still, an unmoving pile on the stage.

And, of course, Ruth is also watching her son, stealing glances his way now and then.

Before Ruth can say anything, however, Zamuda's yelling again. "Don't ask her, Bluto! I'm the one in charge here."

Another voice rises from the stage floor. Stacy is apparently not as incapacitated as Ruth believed. The former sergeant's words emerge in mushed-up, garbled, half-formed syllables. "Hupp muhhh…"

Ruth can just imagine how *that's* going to play on-air: her private security threatening to kill a police officer. Even a *former* police officer. A *woman*. After taking this in and processing as fast as she can, Ruth barks an order of her own from her chair. "He's right," she says. "Stand down. Now!"

Soon, she's on her feet again. She steps over Stacy and heads for her Matt. "I don't care what you do now," she says, willing herself to believe that. "I just want to hold my son."

Mother and child embrace. With Matt's arms around her, squeezing tight, he speaks to her again. "Mommy."

Ruth hopes the mics pick it up. She hopes the cameras are focused on them and that the people watching at home get to hear what her precious baby boy just called her.

"Mommy's here, baby," she says. "Mommy's here."

THE EVENING HASN'T gone at all the way Zamuda expected it would. He certainly didn't show up to XNS Studios thinking he'd soon lead his former partner and friend away in handcuffs by the broadcast's abrupt conclusion.

But that's what's happening. He's waved the other officers away, sending them to do crowd control. To wrangle witnesses—and God knows there were plenty of them—and collect statements. He wants to take care of Stacy, wants to make sure no one (especially Ruth's goons) has a chance to fuck with her any further.

He's finally got Stacy off the stage and is now looking for the quickest route to an exit. He needs some way to get her out of the building and over to the closest precinct holding cell without raising too much of a ruckus. He'd prefer there be no ruckus at all, as a matter of fact.

Zamuda's trying to play things by the book but also understands that he's locked in a situation where the book might just need to be thrown the hell away.

"Easy there," he tells Stacy. "One step at a time."

When he looks up to assess how many more steps they might need to take, he notices one of the bulky studio cameras has pivoted, nearly doing a one-eighty to track the pair's departure. "Holy, sh—I can't believe we're still live," the cameraman quips from behind the machine.

Zamuda stops short. He leaves Stacy standing, wobbling slightly on her feet for a moment. "Say what now?" Zamuda asks as he approaches the camera.

Of course, he's not exactly in the market for whatever answers the camera jockey might provide. Instead, Zamuda presses his palm against the camera lens and shoves the whole apparatus back, hard as he can.

"How 'bout you get this fucking thing outta my face, huh? Is *that* live enough for ya?"

CHAPTER 39

STACY DOESN'T SMILE when they take her front-facing mugshot at the precinct. She doesn't make much of an expression, period. All of her energy, coming back ever so slightly after getting the living daylights Tased out of her, is directed at listening to one of the TVs playing in a corner of the bullpen. It's on XNS. Because of course it is. What else would folks be watching?

"XNS wishes to apologize for the language and scenes of violent, disturbing content that aired live earlier this even—"

"Turn!"

The command from the officer working the camera is meant for Stacy.

She follows the direction, letting them capture her side profile.

"The situation at XNS Studios has been resolved and the suspect is in police custody."

That's me, Stacy thinks. *They're talking about me.*

It's strange, there's a moment that follows where she can think of nothing else except that she's glad her mom and dad aren't alive to see this. But she *does* wish her brother was around for it.

Xavier would've absolutely loved it.

THEY'VE GOT STACY in a holding cell all to herself, kept apart from the usual drunks, domestic disputes, and riffraff. She supposes she should appreciate this special treatment. But for the moment, she's finding it difficult to give a single goddamn about anything. She stares ahead, focusing through the bars of her cell, out to the gray concrete that's been painted a slightly different darker shade of gray. She can recall plenty of times when she's stood on the other side of such bars.

But she doesn't want to think about those times. She doesn't want to think about what happened at XNS. She doesn't want to think about the battered, broken body of her brother, or his blood that was used to write a warning she could not, *would not*, heed. She especially doesn't want to think about Cass Freeman, the scared little girl *or* the scared young woman. She doesn't want to think about how fear must've held Cass in its iron-clad grip for so many, many years. Defining her, limiting her, and ultimately destroying her.

Sitting on a hard-backed bench in her cell, Stacy finds that it's difficult to control what you're thinking about in such circumstances.

She raises her hands, both appendages still trembling slightly from the lingering effects of the shocks, and covers her eyes.

LATER, STARING THROUGH the evenly spaced bars of her cell, Stacy's sporting bloodshot eyes and puffy, crimson-purple circles underneath those eyes where she's rubbed and rubbed to rid herself of every last teardrop.

"Jesus, Stace. I mean, if you wanted to call off getting hitched to Jeff, there *are* other ways."

Zamuda's attempt at a joke falls flat before it's finished leaving his mouth. Stacy can almost hear his regret as he steps forward to her cell.

Still staring straight ahead, trying not to focus on any one thing in particular, Stacy can't help but continue playing detective. For one thing, she notes looks of concern and fear, two extreme emotions, battling it out on her former partner's face.

"Sorry, just…that was a shit joke," Zamuda grumbles.

Stacy doesn't give anything back though.

"How you holding up?" her old partner asks, trying again.

No. Still nothing.

"You got a lotta folks mad here, Stace. Mayor, Governor, not to mention the network. They're demanding we send you to lockup. But don't worry, I'm out here trying to buy some time to—"

"What?" Stacy interrupts, but refuses to look at her old partner, refuses to give him that bit of herself. "Still need time to work out a cover story with your girlfriend Ruth?"

Her words cut Zamuda to the quick. He steps back from the cell, shaking his head.

"Whoa, whoa, whoa. Wait a minute…What?"

But Stacy's having none of his blustering protests.

"You're a terrible liar, Z. It's why so many people like you," she says. "Just tell me—how long have you been sleeping with her?"

Zamuda doesn't have any more words of protest to offer. Instead, he settles for stuttering, stammering half-syllables. Flecks of spit fly from his tongue and lips, coming out so fast that his mouth must soon run dry.

Finally, one word, one self-damning word, emerges in a rasp.

"How?" he asks.

"I'm a detective," Stacy answers. "It's who I am."

Then, a moment later, twisting the knife: "Plus that woman wears a hell of a strong perfume. And lately…so have you."

There's more evidence—names half-erased in old files, unaccounted for hours in both Zamuda's and Ruth's schedules—but the perfume is enough. Stacy lowers her eyes, pushes back against the wall of the cell. She allows what she's said to sink in.

When it does, there's nothing more he can say to her. As he turns his back to her, he releases a sigh that draws his shoulders forward, making him hunch slightly on his approach to the exit.

"Goodbye, Stacy," Zamuda says.

A uniformed guard waits by the door. This young officer's pulled the most unexpected of assignments, but he's got the look of an eager beaver about him. Like he's someone desperate to please his boss. The young guard pipes up as Zamuda nears.

"Anything else special needed for this prisoner, LTC?" he asks.

From her cell, Stacy takes in her former partner's response.

It's nothing more than a shrug of the shoulders and a murmured answer: "Nah, do whatever needs doing. I got more important business to take care of."

CHAPTER 40

EVEN BEFORE EVERYTHING that happened to her and her family, Ruth Freeman never had much in the way of a sense of humor. Now, however, she wishes she could laugh in the face of this absurdity that's clinging to her and her loved ones, even following them home. But she can't see the lighter side of what's happened and continues to happen to her and those she loves. That's what has led to her wandering the dimly lit hallways of her home. This house was where she'd once dreamed of building a family alongside her husband, Malek—gone now, *God only knows where.*

Ruth stops outside the open door to the shared family bathroom. Lights are on. Someone is standing by the bathroom sink, facing the mirror.

It's Matty. Her son. Of course it is. As far as Ruth can see, they're the only two left from the dream of domestic bliss she once had. That vision was first shattered nineteen years previous when Matt was taken.

But he's not taken any more. He's here now. With me.

Matt keeps his back to the open door, turned from his mother's watchful eyes. But that doesn't mean his face is lost to her. She can see everything, as his visage is reflected in the round oval of the bathroom mirror.

Something's wrong. When Ruth takes in her son's reflection, she doesn't find the boy she lost, or even the young man who returned to her.

This Matt's eyes glow, changing colors—yellow, black, and red. His jaw extends, hangs low and loose to reveal extra rows of teeth like a shark's. A wormlike tongue, too large even for the extra space provided, lolls obscenely. He raises a hand, but his fingers are too long, capped with sharp nails the shape and thickness of carving knives. He clicks and clacks these claws together. Over and over again. It takes a moment for Ruth to realize there's a rhythm, a pattern. Like Morse code, but…different. Strange. Alien.

Is this my little boy?

The question scares Ruth far more than any part of the damn ex-Detective Keppler's interference ever could.

Then, as if she spoke the query aloud and was overheard, bones pop and snap, his spinal column lengthens and turns, skin stretches, and Matt faces his mother, his head twisted around while his body remains facing forward.

His new, too-large mouth stretches into an obscene smile.

"Hello, Mother. Would you like to come in?" he asks.

Ruth wills herself to bring forth a smile of her own. She utters a quick prayer inside her head, beseeching whatever powers might look over her and her family that her hesitation to smile will not be noticed. *I'll do better this time. I'll fight harder for my boy. I'll be his mother. Please, please, just don't take him away from me again. Let me keep being his mommy, please.*

"Oh, no, sweetheart," she says. "I just wanted to check on you."

She keeps smiling. Keeps her eyes open. Looks at her son and his stretched-out features, at his body parts twisted around the wrong way. She won't look at the wallpaper behind the sink, at the potpourri and candles on the toilet tank, or at the decorative towels hung just so.

No, she only has eyes for her son.

"Of course," Matt says. "Love you."

From the hallway, Ruth grabs the burnished brass knob of the bathroom door and pulls it shut. "Love you," she says back. But it's only a whisper.

Behind her, swirling blue and white lights from police cars provide an all too familiar illumination to her front yard and driveway. There's chirrup and squawk of sirens, either coming to rest or starting up their cries—Ruth's always had a hard time telling one noise from the other. Even after all this time.

At least she's not surprised to see them coming. The way she and Matt snuck away from XNS, the glare the lieutenant commissioner shot her way as they fled…Ruth's been waiting for this moment.

And now here it is.

THE POLICE CRUISERS congregate in front of Ruth's house like a pack of hungry dogs, salivating for the table scraps thrown among their throng. Black and white with piercing blue eyes, these vehicles make for squat, heavy hunters. They shield the men and women that Ruth knows wait inside.

Only Zamuda's got the nerve to get out of his vehicle, walk across the yard, and stand on the bottom step of the front porch. As Ruth stands in the open doorway, looking at the man who she's been fucking off and on for years—and more *on* for the past few weeks—she supposes she can begrudge her would-be policeman lover a few points for bravery. He's facing the challenge head on.

She lets him speak first, lets him stumble and stutter his way through the delivery of lines he clearly rehearsed in the police cruiser on the way over.

"Listen, I, uh, we…we think it'd be best if your son…if he comes with us. For the night, I mean. Honestly, we don't know who else the, uh, who Stacy might've been in contact with… who she might be working with…"

Ruth doesn't answer. And apparently her lack of a response sends a smoke signal up that the lieutenant commissioner takes notice of.

"Hey, uh, everything okay, Ruth?" he asks her.

"What? Oh, *oh*, yes, yes, of course," Ruth lies.

She glances back into the house. The light shining through the crack at the bottom of the bathroom door seems to hum when she stares at it for a moment too long. Like the light itself is alive, broadcasting its signal into the world.

Unsure of how much time she's just spent staring at the light, Ruth forces herself to turn away, to face Zamuda once again.

"Ah, yes. I kind of figured this would be the case. My son was just…he's okay, mind you…he was just getting ready. You know how that can go, yes?"

But she *doesn't* know if Zamuda understands. She's not sure if she *wants* him to understand. She spies his hand going up, signaling something to the officers waiting in their vehicles.

"Uh huh," he says, "well, let's just go and see if he needs any help, okay?"

It's the fastest Ruth's ever seen Zamuda move, outside of some jackrabbit humping in one of the XNS supply closets. But with a sudden quickness, he's up on the porch and pushing past Ruth, heading inside her house. She grabs his sleeve when he passes, trying to slow him down.

"Wait, don't just—"

But her warnings are drowned out by Zamuda's calls directed at the closed bathroom door where Matt is. Matt with his head turned the wrong way. Matt with his inhuman face and sinister features.

"Matt! Matt Freeman!"

Zamuda pounds a fist against the bathroom door.

WHUMP WHUMP WHUMP

Then, he stops.

Waits.

Finally, he speaks again: "Alright, son. Whaddaya say you come out, okay? We just wanna take you somewhere where we know you'll be safe. Where we can protect you."

Ruth tenses. She waits for a monster to show. She squeezes her eyes shut. Breathing in, breathing out.

Until, finally, she hears the teeny click of the knob turning. And then, the door is open.

And there's Matt. *Her* Matt. The way she remembers him and the way she'd always dreamed he would be when he finally returned to her.

Her precious child smiles. A normal, healthy, happy smile. The way it's supposed to be.

"Why, of course, Lieutenant Commissioner," Matt says. "I'm sure that as long as I'm with you, I'll stay *perfectly* safe."

More than anything, Ruth wants to believe that.

No, she thinks, *not more than anything*. In that moment, she understands that there's plenty of doubt within her, a deep-seated feeling that no one can keep her Matty safe.

No one except for me.

PART 5

CONFESSION / CONFRONTATION

CHAPTER 41

THE LOUD CREAKING of unoiled hinges wakes Stacy from her unpleasant scattershot slumber. She recognizes the sound—the opening of the old door leading to a short hallway of holding cells where she's spent the evening. They've already processed all the overnight ne'er-do-wells and cleaned out the other cells in the hall. So, whoever's walking through that door, Stacy figures they're coming to see her.

Her body still aching all over, she forces herself to sit up on the metal bench that's also serving as her bed. However, that's the extent of what she's willing to do. She won't crane her neck, won't let her eyes go wide as she tries to find out who's heading toward her.

She does recognize the voice of the guard on duty, some younger officer playing the part of escort for her visitor. The kid—barely twenty-four, which is definitely a kid as far as Stacy's concerned—probably spent the evening bored out of his skull, likely disappointed his prisoner wasn't the madwoman everyone saw on TV. He volunteered plenty about himself though. His age, his name (Giurintano), and his favorite color (purple, surprisingly). Stacy gave him nothing in return.

Office Giurintano does the talking during the short walk to Stacy's cell; his words are punctuated by the squeak of two pairs of shoes against the smooth painted floor.

"Technically, we're not supposed to let anyone from the public back here. But I figure, given the circumstances…"

"I appreciate it, son." The other's voice is familiar to Stacy, but she can't quite place it yet.

She waits until she senses the visitor's shadow falling over her. Only then does she lift her eyes from the cell floor and take in the sight of Malek Freeman standing on the other side of the bars. It's hard to get a read on his expression.

"Hello, Officer…Ms. Keppler, Stacy," he says, finally settling on what he's going to call her.

Stacy's relieved, feeling like there are so many worse names for her that he might've chosen.

As Officer Giurintano steps away, giving Malek and Stacy their moment, the Freeman family patriarch takes another step closer to the cell. His hands wraps around two of the bars. If Stacy wanted, she could rush forward, scratch him, tear at his flesh, bite him. But she remains seated. Waiting.

"I was sorry to hear about what happened with your brother. I was…"

Stacy wasn't expecting to hear about her family. She was sure he'd want to talk about Ruth, about Matt, maybe even Cass. Hearing him mention Xavier, even in this circumspect manner, comes as a shock.

She knows there are more surprises ahead when she spots tears running down Malek's cheeks.

"Him, Cass…" He trails off again.

Stacy can feel the pain shared between her and the man outside her cell. She can't help but admire the way Malek pushes forward, forcing those necessary but devastating words out.

"I appreciate the hell out of everything you did for Cass…for all of us…back then. I'm sorry I didn't say that more. Sorry I let Ruth drive so much of…so much of everything."

Even while she's staring at the cell floor, trying to keep her own emotions in check, Stacy notes the way Malek glances back to the end of the hallway, sees him checking on Officer Giurintano. A subtle move, but Stacy's old habits of observation, of body language detection, are as sharp as ever.

"I came here today," Malek says, "because I had one last thing to tell you. One last thing to hopefully tie everything together, give you the final pieces of the truth—as crazy as it may be. I only hope you can do something with it."

More feet shuffle outside her cell, drawing Stacy's attention upward. Malek stands with his face practically pressed against the bars. His words come in a harsh whisper. "I'm sorry. Sorry I sent that 'letter' and made it look like Cass sent it. Sorry I dropped it at your brother's address. I found it in her things after…after…Well, I thought doing so would throw *them* off the scent."

Stacy won't look away now. Not for anything.

"I was wrong," Malek tells her.

Feeling the pain in her joints, the aches rushing up her spine, Stacy plants her feet on the floor and stands, stretching while she does so. This time she's the one taking steps toward the cell bars. Moving closer and closer.

"Tell me *everything*," she says.

With the bars between them, Malek nods at the request. "Okay," he answers, "I will. But just know, Detective, this information, it won't bring your brother back. Won't bring back Cassidy either. Hell, it won't even bring Matty back. Not the Matty we lost all those years ago. They're gone. All of them…gone."

Stacy replies in a low whisper, her hand cupped around her lips in case any stray surveillance cameras might be watching them with dispassionate mechanical eyes. "You think I don't know that already?" she asks.

Soon, she's wondering if Malek's memory is flowing backward like hers. She wonders if he's also reflecting on that awkward reunion at City Hall. Maybe he is, given the way he answers her—the details he provides.

"I think I suspected long before I knew, you know? But Ruth, she kept Matt under lock and key for those first few weeks after we got him back. Even kept him away from me—his father. So, I didn't have a chance to start confirming suspicions until that time at City Hall when you met us, actually."

Bingo.

Malek continues, "Watching him with you...something clicked. Whatever came back to us, it *wasn't* my son."

Stacy's heart breaks all over again, observing the undeniable devastation on Malek's features. She wonders if he also still sees the boy with the ice-cream-smeared face the same way she does whenever she closes her eyes.

But before she can follow that particular thread, she catches a shift in Malek's expression. Not sadness any longer, no. Something darker.

Fear.

Horror.

"I started following Matt. Watching him. Hoping to find a sign, some tell, a screwup. Something I could point to and say, 'Ah ha!' God help me, he was supposed to be my son. And I just..."

Stacy lets her hand touch Malek's, passing along whatever strength she can spare so that he can finish this confession.

"That night when Cass...She was *so loud*. So wasted and distracting. Made it easy for me to go unnoticed. Didn't take long for that...that *monster* wearing Matt's skin to show its true colors," he says.

Before going on, Malek takes a deep breath, swallowing a sob back into his chest.

"That night he...he attacked Cass. I was there, in the backyard, peeking in from behind the shed. He'd already massacred one of our neighbor's dogs, like, just for the hell of it. Then, he did the same to his sister. I...I watched it. I did *nothing*."

Stacy feels her own breaths coming in short, staccato pants. She recalls the girl with the missing dog, recalls the non-human DNA found at the scene where Cass was found. Again, she's struck by the notion that the pieces of this puzzle add up, but not in a way that supports a totally human, completely rational view of the world.

Meanwhile, Malek continues: "Matt, whatever that thing is, it walked out of the shed with Cass's blood on, and...just walked out like nothing happened. And I stayed, crouched in the grass on the other side of the shed, just weeping. Helpless."

Stacy feels the pressure of Malek's fingers hooking onto hers. It hurts a little, but she knows full well that it pales in comparison to the pain Malek's carrying on the other side of the bars.

"What could I have done? What would *you* have done?" he asks. Then, before she can answer, he adds, "I failed both my babies."

Damning himself with those words, Malek tightens his hold, pressing his body up against the bars even more.

"But now, I'm done failing them," he says.

Stacy's confused by his sudden force, unsure of what's happening or what her part in it is supposed to be. "Hey, what are you—"

But Malek cuts her off, his loud sobbing switching to a harsh, insistent whisper. "Just play along," he says, "and I'll get you out of here. I'll get you out so you can finish this. Now, *grab me!*"

Shouting that last part, Malek turns back, and continues yelling at the top of his lungs to Office Giurintano. "Help! Help! This crazy bitch…she got me, man!"

If Malek wasn't right in front of her, pantomiming this pretend attack, Stacy's certain she'd see an eager Giurintano pull out his walkie-talkie and smash his thumb against the side button to bring the device squawking to life. She *does* hear his panting voice, calling out, "Whoa! Whoa! Uh, requesting… requesting backup in holding cells. Over."

But Stacy never grabs Malek—it's the other way around. So, once he's done holding on to her, it's easy for him to stumble back from the cell. For a former athlete turned into a man seemingly broken by anger, fear, and mourning, those few feet back to where Giurintano stands, distracted by his walkie-talkie, are easy enough for Malek to cover.

And just like that, he's got one trunk-thick arm wrapped around the guard's neck, applying a chokehold.

"Now," he says, "open the door to her cell, or I *will* break your goddamned neck."

Stacy remains standing, her body against the bars. She can't get a clear view of the confrontation between Malek and the young officer. Her ears are ringing. She breathes in, then out, stuck waiting for what's to come.

Then, an electronic and mechanical-sounding yawn echoes down the corridor. A buzzing alarm bell sounds. Stacy hops back from the cell door, allowing the bars to roll to the side on their track.

Soon, there's nothing stopping her from taking one, two steps forward and walking out of her cell.

By the entrance to the hall, Malek's got Giurintano restrained. He calls to Stacy: "You know, I suspect this young man's backup will probably be here soon."

And, as though he's summoned them, the door to the holding cell corridor crashes open, the clang of metal on concrete echoing like a second-struck alarm bell. Red lights blink and flash in rapid succession overhead as more uniformed officers pour in to see just what the hell is going on. The first one through the door, some mean-looking overeager son-of-a-bitch type, pulls up short and his fellows bunch around him.

Whatever they expected, it clearly wasn't Malek Freeman holding one of their fellow officers in a chokehold.

"Hello, sirs," Malek says, the pleasant tone of his voice an obvious put-on. "I believe *this* belongs to you."

Then, with a strength pulled from whatever deep well trauma has provided, Malek grabs Officer Giurintano by his belt loops and hurls him into the encroaching cadre of officers, knocking everyone off balance, stopping their progress.

However, the men don't fall like bowling pins, nor anything else so Keystone Cops. All Malek's throw really does is activate the officers, switching their temper from dumbfounded curiosity to a thirst for vengeance. Batons come out, the sliding *shkk* of the metallic wands extending to their full length echoing off the concrete walls. Hungry, feral eyes lock on the middle-aged man who just harmed one of their own and embarrassed the rest of them.

With these wolves descending, Malek turns to Stacy and offers a one-word command: "Run!"

The mean-looking overeager son-of-a-bitch officer who was first on the scene serves as the speaker for his pack. "I don't care who you are...or whose *daddy* you are. You made a big mistake...*boy*."

Stacy slips past at the other side of the hall, avoiding the officers. It's like she's not even there, like she doesn't even matter to them. She makes it to the open door and glances back for a moment. The look that Malek returns sends a clear signal: She needs to go, needs to run, needs to stop whatever sinister plot was started those nineteen years prior when his son was taken.

It's a lot for a single look to convey, especially one glimpsed so briefly. Because shortly after it's given, the first baton crashes down onto the top of his head, and Malek's eyes roll back white.

Stacy's out the door and running.

CHAPTER 42

RUTH RUBS AT her temple, her eyes squeezed shut. Pain makes itself obvious on her face. Though, even she's not sure if it's of the emotional or physical variety. Her champagne-colored blouse hangs loose and unbuttoned off her shoulders as she sits at the end of the bed. The periwinkle cups of her bra provide the sole bits of color in her ensemble, the rest of which consists of a black leather skirt and long near-sheer nylons. Once her blouse is buttoned, she'll no longer be just Ruth Freeman. She'll be *Ruth Freeman*. With all the responsibility, all the problems that being the public-figure version of herself entails.

But, for the moment, she's content to indulge in some complaining. "Owww," she says. "My head is *still* killing me."

Sitting against her pillows, clad in nothing but his boxer shorts—tiny red hearts on white cloth—Zamuda responds with some gentle teasing. "Are you sure *that's* what's killing you?" he asks with a smirk.

But Ruth is having none of it. "Oh, shut up," she says.

She follows with a turn, then quickly crawls up the bed to where Zamuda's resting against the headboard. She nuzzles at the space between his shoulders and neck, smelling him, inhaling the mingled scents of sweat and coffee and mustache wax, plus her own sex radiating from his person. She kisses his neck and takes a playful nip at his scruffy, unshaven cheek.

"Come here," she says, watching as his eyes wander to her periwinkle-cupped breasts, delighting in the rise she senses within his boxers.

However, before she goes further, Zamuda's got his hands on her shoulders, pushing her back as gently as his big bear paws can manage. "No, no, no. I know where this leads," he says. The image of him comforting Ruth after her son was taken away, this time by his officers, and offering to stay with her for the evening, is likely still fresh in his mind. It was so easy to throw herself against him, to appear to melt into him, so that he would be with her.

Leaving her pouting, or at least attempting to, Zamuda swings his legs around to hang from the side of the bed. Taking a deep breath in, then a slow one out, planting his feet on the carpet, he says, "And I got work to do, too."

Ruth's up and by his side. Zamuda blinks fast at her sudden, too-close presence and barely swallows back a cry of alarm.

She whispers in his ear, "Where is my son? Where is Matt?"

Zamuda grabs her wrist, pushes her back. There's no smile on his face now.

"No, dammit. That's enough," he says.

He stomps around her bedroom, gathering clothes, continuing to voice his displeasure. "I already told you, we're following advice from our department's Bureau contacts here. They advised keeping you separated for both of y'all's safety, in case there's another attempt by—"

As he straightens from bending over to pick his gray slacks up off the floor, Ruth's hand rushes forward. Her slap is fast, and lands hard enough to jar his head to the side.

Ruth intends to make certain her words hurt him even more.

"Well, what the hell good are you anyway?" she asks. "You're the one who let her get so close to him and me in the first place. You soft piece of shit."

MOMENTS LATER, RUTH'S given up the tough-bitch routine and instead stands on her front porch, calling out to Zamuda, pleading, begging. But he's out the door and on her walkway, heading for his car.

"Wait! Please…please wait. I'm sorry. I swear, I'm sorry. It's just, I get…I get so upset when I think about my son. Please. Please. *Please.* I *need* to know where he is."

Her words don't fall on entirely deaf ears. Just before reaching his vehicle, Zamuda turns to face the Freeman house again. But he doesn't share the good news Ruth is hoping for.

"Goodbye, Ruth," he says. "I'll keep your kid safe."

She stays on the porch, lost for words. In her head, she calculates whether she can run across the concrete in time to grab Zamuda, to beg and plead, hit or strike.

He's opening the driver's-side door when he calls out to her again. "When this is over, I think some counseling's in order. For your *whole* family."

Before she can return a blustery protest, he's in the car. Door shut, engine on, foot on the gas, leaving her behind.

RUTH CAN BARELY make out the taillights of Zamuda's car, rolling down to turn at the end of her street. She's back to business though. Her face is a mask of calm determination again. She holds her phone against her ear.

"Lewis? Fine, Coleman, whoever you are. Like I can even tell you assholes apart. Do you got him?" she asks.

Her bodyguards' blue pickup truck—acquired for this purpose—pulls out from its spot down the block, engine growling with overcompensating machismo.

They follow the path Zamuda's took moments earlier. "Stay on him," she says. "I wanna know where Matty is."

Ruth stays on the line, watching the truck's taillights. But her mind's elsewhere. Her mind is back on a summer's day close to twenty years prior. Her little boy with ice cream around his mouth and its cone clasped between both of his hands. But then, the memory transforms, the image shimmering, as if she's viewing it through a heat haze: The boy's now got bulging, insectoid eyes, a slavering jaw with too many teeth and a too-long tongue, the ice cream cone is crushed between oversized hands where long yellow claws replace fingernails.

Ruth wills herself to love this new vision of her Matt as much as or more than she does the previous incarnation. She bites her lip, thinking of her boy transformed, urging love to overtake her. To sustain her. She bites down until she draws blood.

Then, seemingly happy with the results, she adds, "Matty needs his mommy."

But the phone line's already dead, with Coleman having already hung up on his boss long before.

CHAPTER 43

JEFF WISHES HE'D had a chance to visit Xavier's house—the house where his fiancée grew up, even—while his brother-in-law was alive. *Heck, I wish I'd gotten to actually be his brother-in-law,* he thinks. Now, the Keppler house is reduced to fascinating territory for exploration rather than a haven of connection. The upper floors remain a hodgepodge of Americana, wallpapered bathrooms, linoleum on the kitchen floor, and fuzzy tennis-ball green furniture. With Xavier's security features offline following his murder, Jeff can walk through the home and feel as if he's been afforded a glimpse straight back through time and into Stacy's youth.

In contrast, the walk down the creaking basement stairs offers no sense of nostalgia, no vision of his significant other's past rendered in sepia tones. Instead, the basement's bare-bones quality compels Jeff to grab the railing and hold tight as he descends into a darkness lit only by a flickering red light on what appears to be a broken carbon monoxide detector hanging from the ceiling.

Jeff's running monologue provides him as much of a safety net as his tight grip on the wooden railing. "So, Jeff, pal, what do we do after spending hours under police interrogation following your fiancée taking hostages on live TV, huh? Mind you, this is after hours of freaking question by the F.B. flippin' I…"

The yellow hazard tape that stretches across the bottom of the stairs now hangs limp and lifeless, forgotten by the police officers who put it there. Jeff grabs it, pulling away the one pop of color in the otherwise off-white, bland, and boring basement space. He tosses it back behind himself, then steps down into the basement proper.

"Oh, I dunno, Jeff," he continues, "maybe next you should come by your fiancee's dead brother's house and poke around a bit. Especially seeing as there's no way you can stomach being at your own house right now—"

He stops when Stacy steps from the shadows. Her finger is at her lips, shushing away any panicked cry that might follow from her love.

"Shhhhhh."

Jeff's mouth opens, but no sound comes out. He stretches his arms out to his sides, palms slapping against the narrow walls at the bottom of the staircase. The twin strikes echo through the stripped-bare basement.

Finally, the words come. "Stacy, what the fu—"

She cuts him off again, placing her finger to his lips this time. "I said 'shhhh.'"

Before he can reply, she pulls him into an embrace. She holds him tight. With her arms still wrapped around him, squeezing tighter, Jeff manages to get out a single word.

"Dammit," he says.

Stacy looks up at him, resting her cheek on his chest. "Yeah," she says, "this isn't the retirement I envisioned either."

Despite wanting nothing more than to hold his fiancée, Jeff lets her go, stepping free of her embrace. "Where...why...did you *break out of jail?*" he asks her.

Stacy nods, but her eyes are wandering, searching the basement. "Mmmhmm," she says.

She leaves Jeff standing by the staircase and walks to the center of the room, to the spot where that carbon monoxide detector dangles from its wiring. He watches her gets on tiptoes, reaching for it, reaching for it...

Once the white disc is in her grasp, Stacy pulls down hard, disconnecting the wires and freeing the device from the ceiling. Her momentum carries it to the floor as she releases her hold. The molded plastic shatters, sending shards skating across the floor.

Before Jeff can get closer and see what's so damned important about a carbon monoxide detector, Stacy's on her hands and knees, picking through the debris.

"Ah, Xavier, you clever sonuvagun. Here it is," she says.

As if *that's* supposed to explain everything.

THE *IT* THAT Stacy is referring to is a small wristwatch-like gadget with a digital screen, something like a homebrew Apple Watch. Standing at his fiancée's side, Jeff studies the watch with a raised eyebrow and the accompanying skepticism it implies.

"Stace, c'mon. Don't you think we should maybe…I dunno… call a lawyer for you?"

But her focus is on the device in her hands, the one that was hidden away in the busted carbon monoxide detector. She touches the screen, swiping at it, twisting nobs on the side. She approaches the tech like someone familiar with it but who hasn't had much of a chance to use it just yet.

"Do you know what the best thing is about having a brother who is—or who *was*—a paranoid but tech-savvy shut-in?" she asks.

Realizing the question's meant for him, Jeff reacts the only way he can think of: with utter confusion.

"Huh? What?"

With her free hand, Stacy grabs his chin and gently pulls him to screen level with the device.

The screen is now illuminated, having been dormant and charging within the carbon monoxide detector shell for who knows how long.

"I never got down here to check before. Couldn't bring myself to come back here," Stacy says. "But now…if Xavier was able to do what I hope he did…this might be the last chance I have to expose the truth."

Suddenly, the initially blurry image on the device's tiny screen turns into a map. Jeff's eyes go wide at the revelation. They go wider when he sees a tiny dot of red moving along the map.

"He makes you gadgets like this," she says, answering her own question, "and makes you promise to try them if he should ever die under…questionable circumstances."

Jeff's no dummy. He's already putting together the missing pieces. "The dot. It's moving through…that's town, isn't it? It's a…"

Stacy waits, still smiling. Watching her fiancé figure things out.

"Your brother, he…he put a tracker on the guy who…on whoever attacked him. Whoever killed him."

Stacy nods again. "Mhmmm."

Jeff's chin is lit up crimson from the reflected tracker dot. "So… you can follow this and…find the bastard who killed Xavier?"

"Mmmhmm," she says. "Find 'em and find out who they truly work for. Now that this is activated, whatever he tagged the bastard with is turned on as well. It means I've got a shot."

THERE'S A FINALITY to the embrace shared on Xavier's front porch that neither Stacy nor Jeff are willing to admit to or confront. Body pressed to body, the beating of one heart overlaps with the beating of another. Finally, Jeff lets her go.

He looks at his fiancée, sees her bruised and tired. The tracker is strapped to her wrist. He watches her descend the front porch steps and then turn to stare back at him for a long, tender moment.

"You're a good woman, Stacy Keppler," Jeff says with a half-smile on his lips.

Her own smile stretches across her face. Cheeks go red as she blushes. "You're not so bad yourself," she says.

And then, with what might be her final words to the man who loves her, she says, "Thank you."

CHAPTER 44

RUTH POINTS TO the graffitied door in the middle of the second-floor landing of the eXcelsior Motel—its name styled just like that on the neon sign that illuminates the cracked asphalt of the parking lot with its seedy fruit-juice red glow. The disdain of her gesture threatens to overwhelm her words.

"You're sure this is the place?" she asks.

Coleman and Lewis, flanking their boss, both nod in confirmation.

Perhaps sensing their boss's need for more information, Coleman says, "Yeah, of course. We watched the, uh, Zamuda get winded taking these stairs coming from his car over there."

Ruth stares down at the parking lot, scanning the vehicles in the fading paint of their slots until she locates Zamuda's, further corroborating her bodyguards' intel. Satisfied, she nods and returns her attention to the motel room door around which they're gathered. She side-steps and gives Coleman a nudge toward the multi-colored, paint-dripped entrance.

"How lucky for you," she whispers. "Now, go ahead and knock. Tell whoever answers that you're here for a shift change."

Coleman's eyebrows spring up at that last command. But when Ruth stares back with impatience growing on her countenance, there's only one thing for him to say in response.

"Wait…you're serious? *Really?*"

But, arms crossed over her chest, brow furrowed, Ruth's having absolutely none of this insubordination. She communicates as such to both Coleman and Lewis.

"I don't pay either of you to ask questions. Okay? Now *do it.*"

There's no argument. Coleman knows better. Both bodyguards know better. Coleman shrugs, signaling Ruth's victory. Then, he reaches out and lets his knuckles rap against the graffitied door. Two quick, strong strikes, trying to match what he thinks the knocks of a cop on stakeout might sound like.

Knock. Knock.

Before anyone answers from the other side, Coleman pitches his voice up an octave or two, adding a whiny twinge to his pronunciations.

"Hey, uh, we're here to relieve you. Uh, sir?"

He steps aside, pulling Ruth with him. Lewis does the same on the other side of the exterior frame. Everyone moves out of the sight line of the door's peephole.

INSIDE THE ROOM, Zamuda cups his hands over the peephole and squints, trying to see who just knocked before announcing they'd arrived for shift change. Unfortunately, he's having a hell of a hard time seeing through the hole. However, he's not surprised that he can't. He's always had a bitch of a time focusing through the little glass magnifying circles.

Plus, he's *tired.* The whole day, the whole night before, hell the whole month, nearly—it's been one drain after another for himself and for the department.

Not to mention for Stacy. The one whose reputation, career, her whole life is getting dragged through the mud because of one mother's vendetta. One mother, and maybe also her son.

He shoves those last thoughts aside. He can't think about Stacy at this moment. He's already got some of his men, the ones he could spare, canvassing the neighborhood around the precinct and around Stacy's neighborhood as well. He hopes they find her, if only so he can be certain she's safe. He wishes she understood that was why he tried keeping her in the holding cell.

It was supposed to protect her.

Now she's gone, and Malek Freeman's apparently taken her place in holding and…

Enough.

If only to push away those intrusive thoughts about his former partner, Zamuda slides the latch away and twists the lock. He turns the knob and pulls the door open. He doesn't even look back to check on the other officers in the room.

Or on their guest of honor.

"Shift change already? Feels like I just got…"

THE MOTEL ROOM door is open now, and the look of realization crash-landing on Zamuda's face is unmistakable. As he pulls the door open, Ruth steps in front of him and is joined quickly by her flanking bodyguards. The trio fills the doorway from outside.

Eyes wide, then darting side to side, his mind working a mile a minute, Zamuda attempts to match them on his side of the doorway, tries to stop Ruth and company from seeing what's behind him in the room.

Finally, Zamuda gets his shit together enough to speak. "What the…no, *no*. Ruth, *c'mon*, I told you to leave this alone."

Suddenly a thin, sinewy arm snakes forward through a gap that even Zamuda's large frame can't cover. The hand attached to that arm reaches for Ruth, and her eyes light upon seeing it.

Her son's voice follows. "Mama! You came for me."

Zamuda places his hands up on either side of the doorway to brace himself, with his feet firmly planted on the room's pilling carpet. Even with Ruth trying to push past, trying to reach her son, Zamuda is intent on making it clear that he's not about to give up an inch.

He shakes his head at Ruth.

"Uh uh," he says. "You three need to leave *now*."

Ruth's not having it. She presses against his bulk, not the way she did the night before, but with angry intensity. A spiteful rage is directed full force at the man keeping her from her child.

"Dammit, Zamuda. You can't keep me from my son."

Matt leans in from behind the lieutenant commissioner, his face appearing in the doorway, drawing Ruth's attention.

"Mama, please!" he cries.

HEARING THIS PLEA, Ruth feels transported. She's no longer facing the tall, powerful, haunted young man who returned to her. Instead, she's looking at her little boy once again. Lost and scared, being kept from her—from his mommy.

She reaches for him again, offering reassurances. "I'm trying, baby. I'm trying!"

Zamuda lowers his hands from the doorframe, places one of them on Ruth's chest. Again, there's nothing intimate here, nothing sexual. He puts his hands on her and gives a shove. Quick, hard. Enough to send her stumbling back.

"Get away," he says, his voice a tired, exasperated growl.

Ruth digs her heels into the walkway floor to stop her backward slide, her face reddening. "You…you…"

Here's another rare instance where the media darling can't find the right words to say, but her expression speaks a million and a half things.

None of them good.

WITH HIS HANDS off the doorframe, Zamuda creates a wider opening for Matt Freeman to reach through. Catching the young man lunging for his mother, Zamuda throws his hands back up, drives his hips behind him to knock Matt away from the door and his angry mother.

No, not just angry. She's gone crazy. Rabid. All for her boy.

Blocked physically, Matt lets his words loose instead.

"He hurt me, Mama," he says. "He was one of the ones who hurt me when *they* took me. The police knew where I was and they hurt me. Lied to you and hurt me bad."

Zamuda's head snaps back, shocked by these accusations. "Hold on…"

"He knew where I was the whole time and he let them hurt me. He hurt me, too. And he never let you know."

"What the hell'd you just say?" Zamuda's ready to turn around and knock the shit out of this weird punk of a kid, not really giving a damn who he is or what he's been through. Nostrils flare. Hands close into fists.

But then, Ruth calls to him.

"Zamuda?"

His name is the next to last thing he hears, followed by the crack of the world exploding around him.

ZAMUDA'S BLANK, DUMB expression is terrifying enough for those looking into the motel room from outside. But it's made worse by the growing hole in the man's forehead. Blood and brain matter, skin and skull fragments, all sluice from the spot where the bullet from the gun that Ruth fired drove through his skull with explosive force.

The walking dead man's lips move for a split second, as though he'd started to say something before the trigger was pulled and now his body's going through the motions, trying to finish.

"Muh…"

It's not much. A syllable slathered in fresh blood, drowning in red.

Lewis stares at the wounded man.

Beside him, Ruth's eyeing the gun held tight in her hands. The ache of the gun's recoil travels up and down both arms. Like everyone else nearby, she's finding it's nearly impossible to distinguish any sounds outside of the echoing *-ang ang ang ang* from the weapon's discharge.

On her other side, Coleman appears shocked. So shocked he hasn't glanced down to see that his boss snatched his weapon from his holster and fired it at the lieutenant commissioner at point-blank range.

Then, it's as if time catches up with them all. Zamuda's legs give out from under him. He crumples to the ground, his bulk stretching across the doorway, leaving him half outside and half inside the room. As he finishes dying, mother and son find themselves face-to-face once more.

Ruth reaches for Matt. Matt reaches for Ruth.

"My baby," Ruth says, "come to Mama."

Matt squeezes her tight, whispering into her disheveled hair. "You saved me. I think you even saved yourself."

He leans down and plants a kiss on his mother's forehead. Then, he steps back, moving deeper into the motel room and beckoning for his mother to follow. "Mom, why don't you come in and rest?"

RUTH JUST KILLED a man. A policeman. Her lover.

He's lying at her feet, oozing vital fluids from the hole she made in his head. But she's already stepped past him moments earlier, venturing into the motel room where they've been holding her son, where they tried to keep him from her. Ruth finds herself losing time. *Or having lost time?* Holes form in her moment-to-moment experience.

She hears her precious boy telling her, "I have work I need to do. Work I *want* to do." She can't remember when he says this though. She can only focus on how cute it sounds for a little boy—for *her* little boy—to talk about doing *work*.

Inside the motel room, someone's left the TV on. Its electric glow pulls Ruth deeper into the room.

"Of course, dear, don't go far," she says, the way she'd call to her Matt on the playground whenever he wanted to run and scream and laugh, and all she wanted was to hold him close, to never let go.

A monster's face is reflected in the television's screen. Shifting shadows stretch too long over the young man's features. *Where'd those come from?*

Ruth closes her eyes. Losing count of how long it's been, she opens them as fast as she can.

"Oh, don't worry, you'll still be able to hear me if you need to," her boy says, the sweet innocent voice of his childhood emerging from the face of the monster.

Ruth ignores the monster, focuses on the voice.

"That's nice, dear," she says. Shutting out the screams and shouts, she chooses to ignore all these other people around her and her boy, all those voices trying to make themselves heard. None of them matter. All these people are nothing compared to Ruth and her son.

The monster leaves, crunching, crushing footsteps marking its departure. Ruth can focus on the television again.

"Oh, there I am," she says.

On-screen, XNS runs an advertisement for her show. Her hair, her makeup, her Invisaligned teeth. All look spectacular. Before he was taken, Matty would've told her she looked like a princess.

TRANSFORMED BY TECHNOLOGIES and biomechanical surgical methods beyond the capabilities of any sentient beings on Earth, Matt Freeman soon stands atop a pile of corpses. Grafted-on claws burst from the pads of his fingers, clicking and clacking against the painted rail in a victory shout of sorts, stripping away color with every scrape. His clothes are torn, ragged, like he's the monster-man in a black-and-white chiller flick. Drool squirts past his extended jaw and too-long teeth, splattering the severed arms and legs of the uniformed police officers he's run through.

He lifts a foot, allowing talons to burst through the white leather of his new Keds before bringing them smashing down against the shattered back of one of his mother's bodyguards.

Whichever one it is, his counterpart's been equally torn apart, split down the middle, each half thrown in a different direction along the upper walkway.

This is the first time Matt's gotten to let loose with his enhanced body. Gotten to revel in the new possibilities that *they* gifted him. The time before, the time with his sister, that was just a taste, something to tide him over. But it was too soon, too far away from the moment of truth—the reason why they brought him back in the first place—so he had to hold back, only show a little of his new, true self.

That's no longer the case. Now he can sense the countdown is soon to commence. He's proven himself viable. Part human, part…something else.

If they're watching—and he *knows* they are—they will understand that the many years spent on taking him, changing him, completing the long—*impossibly long for human space travel*—journey home to see how this hybrid species would fare, it was all worth it.

I will make them proud.

RUTH PRESSES HER face to the cool, slightly vibrating screen of the motel room TV. Eyes opened wide, she sees herself on the screen. *Is that the same commercial? Has no time passed at all?*

She doesn't know. So, she repeats what she said before.

"There I am," she says.

"Mom?"

Matt's voice breaks the spell. She pulls back from the TV, turns to the still-open doorway of the motel room. Ignoring the pungent stench of blood and guts and death, she finds her son amid a scene of chaos. He looks the way that he's supposed to look. Not like a monster. He's covered in blood, but he looks like a human.

Of course, a human.

"It's time to go," Matt says.

"Of course, dear," she says, answering her son.

Ruth imagines herself, old, white-haired, trembling, living in some home with bingo and bedpans and pills in plastic containers. Her boy, a grown man, accomplished, confident, maybe with a family of his own, would come to see her at the end to tell her it's all okay. Everything would be okay, all thanks to her. She was a good mother, and that will have made all the difference.

It's a nice dream, she thinks.

"Of course, dear," she says, uncertain if she's repeating herself or not.

Matt takes her hand and they walk out of the room, along the walkway, down the stairs.

Finally, the parking lot.

"Can you drive?" Matt asks. "I never learned."

Ruth nods, already pulling out her keys. "Yes, dear," she says.

One click and a beep later, her car unlocks.

Ruth speaks again. "Matt?"

He clears his throat, signaling that he's listening.

Such a good boy.

"Mama loves you," she says before opening the driver's-side door.

"I know you do," he says, opening the passenger's-side door and ducking into her vehicle.

Ruth sits behind the wheel, ready to take her child wherever he wants, *wherever he needs*, to go.

"So, where are we heading?" she asks.

She puts the car in reverse, concentrating on making a swift exit from the motel parking lot, racing away from any approaching sirens.

Still, she can sense Matt smiling next to her as he answers: "Oh, we just need to see Some Guy…"

CHAPTER 45

STACY'S IN JEFF'S car, driving slowly. Creeping past block after block. She finds it necessary, especially as she has to keep checking the passenger seat where Xavier's home-made tracking device displays the steady blinking light on its screen.

The light hardly seems to move the dark.

"Well, whoever they are, they don't seem to be moving much," Stacy says.

Her words have no audience though. Jeff's home, Xavier's gone, and Zamuda…

She heard the police band on earlier. Something about a motel room, a *massacre*.

For dispatch to use that word…

There's no one left for Stacy to talk to. All she can do is drive, following that red, blinking dot. She hopes she can track down whoever or whatever killed her brother and, maybe, hopefully, get some answers worthy of the sacrifices being made all around her.

CHAPTER 46

"DO YOU REMEMBER when you and Cass used to play bubble pirates in the bathtub?" Ruth asks her son.

She readjusts her sweat-slicked hands on the steering wheel, trying to keep control of the vehicle. Just a mother out for a drive with her son.

"No," Matt says. A one-word answer with nothing else following.

Ruth's bottom lip trembles. She feels an urge coming on, an unmistakable compulsion to correct, to instruct, to *parent*.

But before she can, Matt's reaching over toward her.

"There he is!" he shouts.

Too late, Ruth realizes her son isn't lunging for her, but for the steering wheel. He grabs it, pulling sharply to the side. Her grip isn't strong enough to counteract his power. She doesn't even have time to lift her foot off the gas. Her eyes move to the windshield, peering through the glass at what her son has just seen.

Someone's walking toward them. Some Guy. *Some Guy, isn't that what Matty said?*

"Baby, what are you…"

Before she finishes, Ruth comprehends that there's not enough time to slow down—not in actions or words. Even if she hits the brakes, even if she takes her foot off the gas or manages to regain control of the steering wheel, the strange-looking giant man clad in spandex and Ruth's car are locked in for an inevitable collision.

She screams some cliché, something like "Oh my God, we're gonna hit him!"

As the distance separating machine and man turns into inches, she can't help but wince inside, thinking, *God, are those really gonna be my last words?*

And then: It all happens.

The front of her car crashes against the bulk of the man, this Some Guy.

Is this the same Some Guy who rescued Matt? Or the one from that bar? Or the one Cass and Keppler's whackjob brother would go on about? Is it all the same Some Guy? How could that be?

Whoever he is, the struck man should be flying. He should be thrown into the air like a ragdoll, flying across the street like a fired bullet. But he's not moving, he's standing firm. Even with the whine and shriek of the car's metal hood and frame bending, twisting, crunching inward, Some Guy stands still, feet planted on the asphalt.

Meanwhile, the windshield glass shatters inward, slicing Ruth's arms as she throws them across her face for whatever meager protection they offer. It sounds like they're driving through a thunderstorm. The glass falls like dangerous raindrops, and a thunderous roar is provided by the vehicle lifted off the ground, its front end heading down, back bumper going up and up and up.

Ruth squints her eyes to avoid any further damage from the glass. She watches through a narrow slit as the car tumbles up and over the man who *still* remains on his feet. Then, the car drops back to earth.

It lands upside down, the jarring impact rattling the skulls of mother and son. The roof dents inward, nearly colliding with the top of Ruth's head. A little harder and it would have struck her, perhaps breaking her neck.

Now, her ears won't stop ringing. She feels the hurt from multiple impacts, a pain so great it's like her bones, even her teeth, are aching.

Eyelids flutter. Ruth knows she must stay awake. She knows she can't stay in the car. There are so many things she knows.

Too many things.

HER EYES OPEN to find the nightmare still in progress. She's upside-down in her smashed and broken car. Trembling hands reach across her sore belly to unlatch her seat belt. The silver tab comes loose and so does Ruth, falling awkwardly onto the dented ceiling of her car. Desperate to escape, overwhelmed by the compactness of the space she's in, her head turns to face the driver's-side window.

Its glass has been smashed out by the impact, same as the windshield. Moving, one hand leading, the other following, then the rest of her body after that, Ruth army-crawls through the narrow exit outlined with jagged glass. Beads snag and tear her skin, but she keeps moving. There are gashes along her hairline; thin trickles of blood turn into raging rivers of crimson with each exertion. Her eyelids are sticky and tacky with gore, the copper taste of blood heavy on her tongue. But she keeps going.

Finally, her palms touch hot asphalt, and a new searing pain jolts through her. She launches upward, rising to her feet perhaps more quickly and definitively than she would've liked. She makes a noise, something between an exhausted yawn and a vicious shriek—an animalistic bloodstained emission.

Then, she sees him. Some Guy, still standing several feet ahead of her ruined vehicle. He's finally moving somewhat, looking behind his spot on the road, seeming to survey the destruction. In contrast to the vehicle and Ruth, Some Guy appears unscathed. As he absorbs the wreckage he's helped cause, his blank expression reveals nothing of the inner workings of his mind.

Matt's sudden burst of laughter is a sharp, unpleasant thing. An ear-splitting peal of chuckles and giggles cuts through the ringing in Ruth's ears, bypassing the thrum of blood flowing within her body. The high-pitched childlike tones are not a match at all for the young man whose face, like his mother's, is now coated in jammy blood, with glass sticking out from his skin like needles in a pincushion.

Ruth ducks down to peer inside her car only to find her child still buckled into his seat. He's continuing to laugh, showing no signs of stopping. He laughs like it's all a game or a carnival ride. It's easy to imagine her baby boy grabbing her hands, holding her chin, getting up close and begging her: "Again, Mommy, again!"

It's too much. Ruth closes her eyes again.

NOW, RUTH STANDS on the side of the road, well away from the smoking ruin of her car. She can't remember when she moved, when she got out of the way of the broken vehicle and the other man—that *Some Guy*—who is somehow unbroken, almost unfazed entirely.

Matt stands next to his mother.

At least he's not laughing anymore.

No laughter, no tears, nothing comes from her baby. Only his hands, curved into crescent-moon shapes, tightening around her neck, his thumbs pressing hard at her throat. Squeezing tighter. Tighter. The tip of his tongue sticks out from between pursed lips, showing how much concentration is going into his handiwork.

Feeling the blood flowing more heavily from her previously acquired wounds, feeling the pressure of her son's fingers, the heat of his ragged breaths on her face, Ruth tries to speak, tries to plead for her life.

"Muh Muh Matty, puhlease ssstppp."

She catches a glimpse of something in her boy's eyes, a flash of cruelty and unchecked viciousness, something telling her there's no stopping, no reasoning with this man, this monster. Her child.

But then, she gets a reprieve—in the form of Some Guy.

Having apparently made his move while Ruth and Matt were distracted, Some Guy now stands before them. With one hand, he reaches down and pulls the son from the mother. Then, he grabs Ruth and hauls her back to her feet.

His face remains flat, expressionless, as he issues a one-word warning. "Stop."

Speaking to Matt, he adds, "You were supposed to come alone, Hybrid Freeman-Matt."

Matt's long, pink, alien tongue slips past his lips, lapping up stray flecks of blood on his face. "You saw how she fought me, tried to stop my attack," he says, locking his eyes on his freakish would-be bodyguard. "My human mother is strong. You can bear witness for us, help me convince *them* that she is worthy of salvation and transformation. There is much she could contribute mentally and physically to aid in the harvest."

Some Guy gives no answer.

Matt's jaw drops, his eyes bugging out as the alien-implanted orbs push back his human-born ones. His voice emerges with a more guttural tone, accompanied by the clicking of nails turned into claws. "Let me put it this way. She *will* come, too. Or I will destroy you. You and all the rest of your underdeveloped half-species."

Some Guy remains still for a moment. Then, he nods. "You are both coming with me now."

He releases them, and it's all Ruth can do to stay on her feet. What she wants to do is collapse into a shivering pile of fear-filled flesh. It's hard not to feel as if she's finally awakened to the same nightmare that so many others around her have been suffering through.

No longer holding the Freemans, Some Guy's fingers pinch something attached to the bottom hem of his tank top.

Ruth finds enough of her voice to ask questions: "Matt? Who is this? What's he talking about?"

Her questions go unanswered. There's a far-off look in her son's eyes, as if his soul has departed, is journeying somewhere in another world.

Some Guy's no more of a help when it comes to providing context. He holds the shiny metal disc in his massive fingers, then squashes it between those digits. Flickering sparks spray out in the aftermath of the disc's destruction.

Some sort of technology is all Ruth can figure. The massive mountain of a man, or whatever Some Guy is, treats it with such nonchalance. Like he's pulling a flea from a dog. Like he knew it was there all along and was only waiting for the right moment to get rid of it.

"She'll be here soon. We must be in position for the next phase."

More words Ruth doesn't understand. Or that she *does* understand, but not all the way. It's a mist-shrouded context covered by a fog that she can't quite cut through.

Then, still giving nothing away by his expression, Some Guy strides forward, heading somewhere—wherever *in position* is meant to be.

Next, his eyes still distant, focused on worlds apart from Earth, Matt follows Some Guy.

And then there's Ruth, rushing to keep up with her boy. Staying as close to her son as she can because she's already lost him once and she refuses to let it ever *ever* happen again.

CHAPTER 47

"GOOD GOD, LOOK at the size of him. How…how did no one notice him before? Like, *really* notice him? Xavier…Cass…I'm so, so sorry."

After pulling over when she first spotted this Some Guy walking in the middle of the road and then hearing the squealing tires of the car she knows belongs to Ruth Freeman, Stacy carries on a one-sided conversation, speaking to no one but herself.

Of course, she recognizes the absurdity in what she's saying. Just the same as she knows that what she's witnessed is an impossible thing. She watched a human being get struck head-on by a car, and somehow the vehicle came out as the one worse for wear.

That's something that should not be.

Later, once the trio's departed, Some Guy leading the procession of son and mother away from the accident scene, Stacy observes from a safe distance as the tides of reality come crashing down on this moment to reveal the absurdity and impossibility undergirding everything that's just come to pass.

Pedestrians emerge from around street corners, shopkeepers and apartment-dwellers poke their heads out from their respective sanctuaries, as if they'd all somehow had the most urgent business to attend to moments prior and only now are able to confront what's happened on *their* street.

The black skid marks and cracked cement of the sidewalk, the smoke pouring from the ruined car, the broken glass with sinking sunlight glinting off it—all signs show that *something* has happened here.

Yet, Stacy's the only one who saw it directly. She can't figure out how that could be. Unless, of course, someone wanted her to see.

Needed me to see.

She rolls down her window to listen, taking in the words of the dreamers roused from their deep slumbers.

"Hey, hey, there's been an accident here!"

"Anyone see the driver? Anyone see…anyone?"

"What the hell happened?"

These others, they're going to be left feeling as though someone's snipped out a few precious moments from their comprehension of reality. Stacy can't help but wonder if they're actually the lucky ones. But there's no time to dwell on that.

She puts her car back into drive and slow-rolls past the growing crowd surrounding Ruth's ruined vehicle. She heads off in the same direction that she saw Some Guy, Matt, and Ruth all traveling. More than ever, she's uncertain what she'll find at the end of the trail. But she's also unwilling and unable to turn back now.

CHAPTER 48

THE EMPTY LOT ahead of her is the last place Ruth would've guessed was their destination. Then again, there isn't much that's gone according to her plans, especially since that *bitch* Stacy Keppler interrupted her moment of healing and redemption with her beautiful boy Matt live on-air.

And he is still beautiful. Don't think too hard or too long about what you've seen since. He's your beautiful baby. That's all.

Meanwhile, the lot is a picture-perfect portrait of abandonment and degradation. Crumbling brick-and-cement foundations of some wrecked but never cleared buildings, broken glass, nails, smashed liquor bottles. Cigarette butts stamped in such a way that they collectively form swirling patterns if you squint just right. Crabgrass and weeds sprout from the hardpacked, gravel-covered ground as Nature stubbornly fights to regain what was always hers. Ruth can respect that. She knows a mother will always fight to keep what she's made.

Of course, what Ruth really doesn't understand is *why* they are now standing in front of this forsaken industrial lot. And she can't grasp why Some Guy's just made the pronouncement: "We are here."

Here? Where's here? What is here? There's nothing here.

She finds her voice again and asks, "Here?"

She first looks to her son.

Matt's answer is one word, that same word echoing back to her: "Here."

Some Guy, still giving nothing away, repeats that word. "Here."

Ruth takes a step back from her unlikely companions. She turns her back to the lot, its emptiness growing more and more unsettling to her the more time she spends staring at it. It's as if there's more to the emptiness beyond what her eyes can see, some optical effect rendering her ill and disturbed physically, mentally, and perhaps, yes, even spiritually.

Shuddering, Ruth takes a first timid step away from the site. But she stops short and turns back to Matt to try and offer her child an explanation, an assurance that she's not leaving him alone. She would never, *ever* leave him alone.

Not ever again.

"I have to…This is too much. I have to go," she says.

Her eyes drift across the street. There's a car parked over there. One Ruth is sure looks familiar. But she's too tired, too worn down, to pinpoint exactly where she's seen it before.

But no, Matty…

Mother's intuition kicking in, Ruth turns back to find her son reaching for her. His hand is smooth and soft, untouched by trouble, the way she always hoped he would be. *So soft, so innocent.*

Matt's other hand is held by Some Guy, the odd stranger— *or strange creature*—who seems to have a connection, a bond, with Ruth's son. He pulls the young man deeper into the empty lot, dragging him closer to the unsettling nothingness.

"Mother, you can't leave me," Matt says. "Not now. Not when we've come so far."

And there they are. The exact words that will break Ruth's heart.

"They want you back. Returned to them. Come," Some Guy says to Matt.

As if he doesn't understand what's happening here between me and my son. Between Matt and his mommy. Mommy and Matty…

Moving through the scattered debris, the majority of it centered in the emptiness of the lot, Ruth picks up that there's a shimmer effect covering the ruins. It's like the outline of something that doesn't match the scene spread out before them. As if there's a halo over the smashed bricks and ground-down glass-bottle dust and the condoms long since emptied of their spilled seeds, everything desiccated under glare of the sun.

Some Guy and Matt move ahead, boots and shoes crunching across gravel. Until, finally, they come to the place where the shimmer glows brightest, where there's nothing to be seen head-on, but rather an unpleasant gut-churning feeling is *experienced*, like something monstrous and depraved that's just visible out of the corner of one's eye.

Some Guy and Matt step forward into this nebulousness together.

And then, they're gone. The shimmering halo, the unsettling slice of decayed urban landscape, sucks them in and swallows them whole.

Panic hits Ruth immediately. No ramp up, no slow boil. The heat's been on her too long already, and now she finally comprehends the doom in whose company she's found herself.

"Oh my God, Matt! I'm coming…"

Her cry is cut short as she too steps through the shimmer. When she's gone, there's nothing left but an empty lot.

Nothing special at all.

CHAPTER 49

STACY, HOPING THAT what she's just witnessed from across the street in her car really happened and isn't some hallucination, makes her way through the lot she now knows is *not* as empty as it appears.

No, maybe hoping isn't quite the right word.

Is it *anticipating*? She thinks that might be closer to the truth, if nothing else.

Still, she feels like she's gone blind as she moves cautiously through the lot, putting one foot in front of the other. Unsure exactly where she's supposed to go other than forward. There's a heat radiating off the nothingness spread before her. It makes her wonder if Ruth and Matt and that other one—that Some Guy—felt it as well when they moved through the same debris.

One second they were walking across the lot, and the next...

Stacy glances back at her car, parked across the street. For a moment, she considers a wave back to the vehicle. For another moment, she considers how sad it would be to have her last goodbyes directed at some inanimate, artificial thing.

Instead, she turns and raises her foot, thinking she might be close to that shimmer effect—the same one she spotted pulsing before the trio disappeared.

"Let's hope this works for—"

"—ME TOO."

Stacy starts her sentence with one quickly fading understanding of reality, of the way the world, the universe, and everything all around her is meant to be. But she finishes with that original viewpoint obliterated.

When she stops speaking, she's no longer standing in the empty lot. Her feet squish against the ground as though she's knee-deep in mud. But there's no give to the surface below her. Out of sheer momentum, her legs continue moving forward. One foot in front of the other. But every movement feels heavier than the last. Like there are cement blocks tied to her limbs, restricting and hindering her movements.

Instead of the tan-and-orange dirt of the lot, all peppered with gravel and garbage, the ground—if Stacy can call it that— displays a more uniform silvery gray hue which gives off a rainbow glow when viewed at certain angles.

But even as Stacy is struck by the sudden certainty that her feet will break through this skin-like layer below her, she finds a wiry toughness to the material. A corded layer, like wires on a suspension bridge, keeps the "flesh" in place.

Finally, she has to stop. Her head swirls with a million thoughts, dreams, half-realized memories. Visions from her life. Visions of impossible things, as well. Things she can't or couldn't know. Dark shadows on childhood bedroom walls. Zamuda naked, bleeding from a hole in his forehead, an opening like a third eye. A too-long tongue licking blood and brain matter up from inside.

A city. A world. A place constructed from the same material she walks on now. Part flesh, part technology. A world apart from her own. A world that looks out on a star that isn't the sun—not the one Stacy knows, at least.

It's too much.

Stacy vomits, then wipes the sick away from around her lips before she's fully registered that she's taken ill. A tiredness follows, an ache that pulses through her limbs, throbbing up her neck to pound nails inside and outside her skull. There's a tiny voice speaking in a language that Stacy doesn't understand—until suddenly she does—demanding that she stop. Shut down. Lie down. Give over to the ship—somehow she *knows* it's a ship that she's stumbled onto.

She glances behind, trying to center herself, trying to remember the way she came. Trying to look for that spot across the street where her car is waiting. Crenellated flesh-like walls, wrinkled like gray matter and drawn to a single puckering of flesh and wires, greet her instead. There's less of a shimmer on this side and more a semigloss smear, like petroleum jelly on a camera lens.

Stacy closes her eyes. She focuses on her breathing. In and out. Wherever she's found herself, at least she can breathe. She tries to let that information be a comfort.

If I can breathe, then I can live.

Now, centered again (or as close as she'll come), Stacy remembers one more thing she's brought along that might help her stay alive. She reaches for her holster and pulls out the gun that she snagged before fleeing the precinct. The so-far-unused black metal is a cold comfort.

Gazing around at the fusing of flesh and machine, witnessing technology far beyond anything anyone on Earth has ever seen, Stacy can't help feeling like a cavewoman holding on to a stone wheel before being run down by someone's self-driving electric car. The future's coming in fast, giving no mercy to that which came before.

Stacy closes her eyes, shakes her head. She refuses to let her mind be led down dark corridors. Instead, holding her gun in position, opening her eyes wide to take in as much as she can, as much as she can handle, she continues her search. She's a woman on a mission—recovering her suspect. She's on the right path. She's damn sure of that.

All that remains is to follow this path to the end.

CHAPTER 50

IN THE "EMPTY" lot across from Stacy's car, rocks and bits of glass bounce off the hardpacked ground.

No one's around to see, but if they were, they'd see those scraps, those bits of unfinished, ruined, or abandoned structures, the accessories, the geologic features, all colliding with each other. Liquefying, melting, turning from one state to the next and back again. Sometimes emitting a glow, white-hot, like the light from a high-powered search lamp, then dulling to a darker black than the night sky. A refraction, each piece reveals an empty lot piled high with garbage and debris in miniature until it shatters or explodes or otherwise splits apart into more pieces showing more landscapes in Russian-nesting-doll succession.

No one's there, but if they were, they'd hear a groaning roar, like some great beast waking from slumber, paired with a mechanical hum, such as that of an engine brought to life, followed by a shaking, as if the area around the lot, covering the lot, were shifting, moving to accommodate the beast rising under the cover of a glamour that keeps its true form out of sight.

No one's there, but if they were, they'd feel the intensity of skin-pinkening, blistering heat, melting those particulate bits bouncing and shifting beforehand. The ground—the *real* ground below—glows orange and red as flickering flames spool out from underneath, made by something still unseen, unobserved, unfathomable. Infernal yellow fingertips crawling, pulling in more oxygen.

This is power beyond measure.

RUTH NEVER HAD time for science fiction, for spaceships and laser guns or fantastical far-off futures. The only future she's hoped for, wished for, and fought for involved her son returning to her. She's now living in that future, and so her vision's grown unclear when it comes to what will happen next. As a result of her disinterest in the speculative, Ruth's mind must search feverishly to find the right words to describe where she's found herself.

First, there was the passage through the glimmering illusion of the empty lot. Then, their emergence into this unnatural place. This structure that is vast beyond comprehension.

There was nothing there. Ruth knows that. Her eyes told her as such. But now, now there *is* something, something huge, that she's just finished walking through. Some Guy and Matt show no signs of stopping, of waiting for her to catch up. She focuses on them, especially on her boy, and ignores the techno-organic walls and floor and ceiling, the whole of the structure, pulsing, throbbing, like a living, breathing being.

Command deck. That's the term she lands on for where they end up. Like the production booth back at XNS Studios. Here, strange formations, bulbous growths emerging from the floor, are topped with bioluminescent ridges that seem to hum under the direction of Some Guy's fast-moving, deliberate hand motions. There's a shift in the tempo of the ship's "breathing." The ceiling above them puckers, and the *shlik shlik shlik* of something long and serpentine unravels over their heads. Then, the *straps*—because that's what Ruth decided they're called—emerge.

She watches her son and Some Guy standing in position, letting the squirming straps clench around their chests, their legs, pulling them into wider stances. She waits for hers to do the same.

For a moment, nothing happens. She looks to Matt, his name half-formed on her lips. He nods at Some Guy, and the big man reaches for the glowing ridges, swiping his fingers across the spiny protrusions until Ruth is grasped and held in place like the two others.

"We are prepared for departure," Some Guy says. "Now, for you, Keppler-Stacy…"

That is a name that Ruth didn't expect to hear. It's a name she almost allowed herself to forget, something shoved to the side to make room for all the new information and inexplicable experiences.

But, of course, the detective is here. *Of course she is.*

Ruth won't let her ruin this though. She simply will *not* allow that to happen.

CHAPTER 51

THE SHIP'S WALLS vibrate, amplifying the low rumble of Some Guy's voice. The doubling effect makes it seem as if he's got Stacy—still wandering the winding corridors of this impossibly large, cloaked alien vessel—completely surrounded. Like he's on top of her, even, pressing his bulk against her body. Smothering her with skin she imagines as cool and clammy, spongelike to the touch.

"We know you are on board," he says.

Stacy's got no clever comeback primed on the tip of her tongue. Nothing like the action-movie heroes and heroines whose adventures she and Jeff might watch on a typical Saturday evening, splitting a Cabernet. She's got no Jeff now.

Her nostrils flare as she smells fear-sweat dripping from her pits and forehead. The onset of panic is amplified when the cords, segmented like on a giant earthworm's body, lewd in their veiny pinkness, extend from the ceiling. These blind creatures flap and slap under the glowing lights of the interior.

But all of them reaching, grabbing for Stacy, are still capable of moving in one direction.

Once they've got me, it's over.

Stacy doesn't know—or won't admit to herself—what *it* refers to here. But that doesn't matter. Survival becomes her watchword, and she tries to sprint away from the lashing cord-like appendages.

Except now is when the floor, something she expected to be spongy from the beginning, like how she imagines Some Guy's skin must feel, gives under the pressure of her tread. Sucking her down into the ship and holding her in place, it's as though the ship's gravity has been increased tenfold, twentyfold.

Stacy's arms are pulled behind her. She feels one of the slithering cords reach behind her and extract the service weapon she'd taken from her precinct escape. A whirring sound follows as that particular extension retracts into the ceiling, taking Stacy's weapon with it. Then, the other cords hoist her up so she's on tiptoes with her shoes still cinched by the techno-organic flooring. It's as if she's been strung up, crucified.

She hasn't been to church in a decade or more, yet she spits when the visual of her crucifixion comes to mind. She mutters a quick prayer to avoid any accusations of blasphemy that might be levied against her by whatever higher powers are out in the universe.

They're here, she thinks. *The higher powers are here. I'm with them now.*

Some Guy speaks through the walls again, his intonations vibrating her limbs and even her head.

"Please, do not resist. This is a necessary step to prepare your body for liftoff."

Rattled by the crescendo of chaos, Stacy grabs hold of whatever sounds familiar. Like *liftoff*. She remembers watching shuttle launches, replays of Moon landings, witnessing humankind seeking to go beyond the atmosphere of Earth and touch stars and satellites.

Understanding they're in the middle of a liftoff helps Stacy. It gives her a better sense of what's happened before, a clearer vision of what's taking place right in this exact moment, and an impression of what her immediate future holds.

For someone like Stacy, her eyes, ears, and mind open wider to possibilities beyond planet Earth. She grasps what the whispering, chittering, rhythmic *chik* and *chak* of alien claws echoing off the ship's walls are meant to be.

Of course, she realizes, *it's a countdown. Counting all of us on board down until it's time for liftoff.*

"Stop, no! Let me go!"

She cries out because it feels like something that should be done. But even as she screams, the words sound hollow in her ears.

"Five, four…"

Stacy wants to close her eyes. Yet she's struck by the unshakeable sense that tiny, microscopic filaments, not unlike the larger cords around her waist and limbs, have slithered across her face and pinned her eyelids open. But she's unsure if that's the truth or just something she's imagining.

"Three, two…"

She's unsure of many things. *Too many things.* Unsure of how afraid she should be. Unsure of how afraid she *is.*

"One."

PART 6

HOME

CHAPTER 52

THE RED LIGHTS glow from an electric read-out panel. The panel, looking like something out of a Cold War-era spy film, has just popped up from a secret compartment below the wooden surface of an oval-shaped desk. A very particular oval-shaped desk where countless great and not-so-great and some perfectly forgettable leaders have sat. The whole secret-compartment setup is like something out of a Cold War-era spy film but *very real*. And these red lights have the President of the United States scared shitless.

The old man's face goes slack and his lip quivers as he reads the words generated by the panel's digital output. Green-tinted letters blend with the red warning lights, somehow reminding him of boyhood Christmases.

Out on the family farm, they'd bundle up with cocoa-filled mugs and sing carols and hymns under the stars. Or maybe that was just something he saw one time on *The Waltons*. Life, TV—it all blends together sometimes for him, as he likes to joke with his aides and members of his Cabinet. He pretends he doesn't see the looks they give him whenever he gets lost and confused like that.

But now? Now, he's not sure what to say or what to do. If what he's reading from the screen is true, there may not even be anything worth saying or doing.

As he likes to say, he's "the goddamn leader of the free world." But what's a world when it's suddenly thrust into a universal context? What's a world with intelligent life when it's no longer a unique proposition?

He suddenly feels very small, very insignificant. It's been a long, *long* time since he's felt that way.

"You mean they're real?" he asks. "And I'm just finding this out…"

JOHN MANDRAKE STANDS in the doorway to the Oval Office, watching his boss's resolve and self-assuredness melt away. Expressions of confusion, befuddlement, and terror cross the old man's face—more than usual, even. All those years in the Bureau, then in the private sector, then back in government— but this time in an advisory capacity, a so-called "hand of the king"—and Mandrake can only remember one other time when he's seen someone so overwhelmed, so out of their element.

What was that podunk police sergeant lady's name? What was that town in Virginia proper, the one with the missing boy? They'd brought Mandrake down to rally the troops, to help guide the investigation, because the cops there had no idea what they were doing. That woman…He felt kind of bad when he had to show her up. But those so-called leads had just been…nonsense. Fantasies. At least, that's how he remembers it.

But this isn't some small-town lady cop, this is the President of the United States…

Then, Mandrake remembers the job at hand, remembers why he came to the Oval Office in the first place. He realizes that if the images that just somehow appeared on the government satellite are real, then he might owe a big apology to that Virginia cop.

But first things first…

Mandrake clears his throat, trying to get the chief executive's attention. "Mister President," he says, "we need to move you and your family to the bunker…now."

An awkward moment follows. Mandrake worries he might have to physically remove the old man from his chair and drag him to the underground bunker.

Then, the President makes eye contact, and it's like Mandrake's let down his dad, his grandpa, his Little League coach, and every other male role model he ever had, all at once, for good or ill.

"So, we're hiding?" the President asks. "Guess they must think this is the end, huh?"

Mandrake has no desire to bullshit, no urge to obfuscate. Instead, he shrugs his shoulders. Because that's his truth.

He doesn't know.

He really doesn't know.

He doesn't know a goddamned thing.

The wheels of the desk chair squeak as they're pushed across the rug under that most famous of desks. The President hobbles to his feet. "Yeah, yeah, of course," the old man says. "Jesus."

Mandrake knows better and thinks the President should as well. After all, it's not Jesus who's coming. Not if one follows the signs and portents from the heavens...

THE HERENTON POLICE have had a hell of a week. Scratch that—a hell of a couple days. A live on-air hostage-taking, a motel-room massacre, one of their own gone rogue and escaped from a holding cell, a town hero arrested and roughed up by some angry men on the force. The trickle-down stress has rolled onto everyone's shoulders in the department.

That's certainly true for Dispatcher Tarnisha Whitehall, who chipped one of her acrylics getting ready for work in the morning and who *still* hasn't heard back from her cousin Ray-Ray about whether he'll be able to pick up her kids in the afternoon since her shift at the 911 call center is slated to go past the time when the daycare closes.

Tarnisha's already had two warnings from her supervisor Sergeant Ellis for requesting to clock out early, and she's not looking to find out what happens when a third strike comes her way.

And that's all from before she gets to the ever-ringing phone lines at her workstation. They just haven't stopped ringing. She and everyone else on the switchboard takes one call after another. It gets so Tarnisha can't help but wonder if a full moon's coming, perhaps Mercury's in retrograde, or there's some other cosmic imbalance that's working black magic over her and everyone else in the city.

"You're telling me…sir…you're saying all the paint on some buildings down around this empty lot…it's all *melting off*?"

It's calls like this that make Tarnisha want to tear her weave out, hang up, walk out the door, and just keep walking. On and on, never looking back.

OF COURSE, IF Tarnisha *were* to take that walk, if she *were* to head in the right direction, and if she *were* to stop for a moment and look—*really look*—then she'd see the same thing the frightened maintenance worker's calling about from his work phone.

The white and gray paint covering the old brick buildings is all peeling away, bubbling on the walls of the structures around the empty lot. A noise accompanies it, a roaring sound, and an intense heat that drives him back from the site he previously considered abandoned, insignificant, and inconsequential.

Now, he can barely keep his eyes on the site. Not only that, but he can hardly stand on his own two feet. His skin goes pink and blisters in certain spots, all from his proximity to this change. He can't help but wonder how much hotter it will get before his flesh melts from his bones, just the same as the paint that's stripped off the walls.

Somewhere close by, sirens scream and tires squeal.

They're coming, he thinks.

JEFF IS SURE he saw his phone light up with a new call. At least he's convinced himself it happened. He holds the rectangle to his ear, pressing hard enough to send a little ache back through the canal, the resulting pain sharp between his eyes and down the low slope of his nose.

"Oh my God, Stacy..."

It's like he's uttering a desperate prayer. She's not on the line. No one's there at all.

But that doesn't stop Jeff from calling out to her.

"Stacy, *Stacy*, is that you? Where in the world are you?"

THE CLOAKING DEVICE is disabled and the vessel hangs above the city of Herenton, Virginia, revealed to anyone who might care to look up. Fires erupts in waves of yellow, red, orange, and white. The bottom of the ship pulses with explosive, infernal colors, flowing out in wave after wave.

It appears as if the ship and those flying it have captured the heart of a miniature sun and are now blowing it up over and over again. The reactions and eruptions build, one on top of the other.

As a result, the vessel rockets skyward. Flames lick heavily down the streets, worm their way into the buildings. The inferno catches any unfortunate souls in its path in a white-hot, bone-incinerating embrace.

Up and up, the ship travels. Through cloud cover, through the ozone layer, breaking free of the planet's gravitational pull.

Further and further on, until the planet Earth is a fading memory. A blue dot. Then, smaller. Smaller still.

Then, gone.

THESE ARE TINY samples, pieces of a whole, all adding up to the end of the world.

CHAPTER 53

STILL BOUND BY the pulsing gray and pink cords that dangle from the alien ship's ceiling, Stacy hangs helplessly as the floor beneath her appears to shift forward. Whether it's the floor moving or the ceiling above her changing, that doesn't much matter to Stacy. The end result's the same. She's conveyed through the labyrinthine halls of the ship like raw material on an assembly line.

Thrust forward with whiplash-inducing force, Stacy cries out in pain. She blinks, adjusting to the sudden intensity of light in the glowing room in which her progress is finally halted.

A quick look around lets her know she's not alone. After minutes, hours even, spent searching and then tracking them at a distance, she's now face-to-face with the trio of Ruth, Matt, and Some Guy.

It's Matt who acknowledges Stacy's presence first. Giving her a smirking once-over, he says, "Welcome, welcome, Detective Keppler. Welcome to the end of the world as you know it."

Stacy doesn't have time to think things through. No time for a clever comeback, either. Even as the cord-like appendages press against her wrists, stomach, and ankles, she wriggles and writhes against them, trying to break free.

"Let me go!" she shouts, unsure of who the demand is intended for.

Pausing for the briefest of moments as her struggles net her no relief, Stacy's eyes narrow. She focuses on the young man whose return she fought and worked so hard for. When his eyes flash black and yellow at her, showing how he's given over to the alien side of whatever it is he's been made into by whatever forces have forged a ship like the one they're all traveling through space on, Stacy can't help but feel sick to her stomach.

There's no trace of a soul behind the insectoid eyes. No shred of humanity or compassion left. There's only a cold, calculating intellect—something beyond humankind. But even as those alien eyes regard Stacy, the rest of Matt Freeman stays in human form, or at least in a close facsimile. His mouth whispers, soft and petulant, making demands of and questioning the blank-faced Some Guy.

"Can we let her go?" Matt asks, pointing at the techno-organic restraints, his tone making it clear the question isn't a matter of mercy but for the sake of making Stacy's torment more personalized, of giving it a one-on-one, bespoke approach. "I mean, what can she do to us at this point?" he asks.

But if he expects an immediate or definitive answer from Some Guy, Matt is soon let down.

"I cannot make that decision," Some Guy says.

The youngest Freeman crosses his arms over his chest, his insectoid eyes making for a stark contrast with his very human, very immature pouting act. "Fine," he says, "I'll do it myself. Let her go!"

The ship's response to Matt's command is immediate and merciless. The cords unwind from Stacy's body. For a brief second, she appears to float above the floor, held in place by sheer will and whatever strange physics govern the vessel's interior.

Then, she drops hard. Feet slam against the floor as she lands in a half-crouch. A knee strikes her chin and she bites through her bottom lip. Blood oozes from this semi-self-inflicted wound.

Stacy coughs up blood onto the floor of the spaceship. Her eyes are drawn to the way the segmented floor pieces appear to suck up her bodily fluids, the way the pulsing lights on the floor change their hue as they self-clean, removing the mess she's made.

Stacy wipes the back of her hand across her mouth, sending more blood droplets to the floor. She lifts her eyes and finds Matt standing over her. The awkwardness he displayed on their first meeting after his return, whether an act or not, is stripped away. It's clear that this place, this moment, is where he is most comfortable. This may not be what he was born for, but it is what he was made to do.

"I suspect the harvest of Earth's already begun. Too bad we couldn't all be there for it. Selecting the strongest, the most powerful, the most ruthless, all to become like me. Did you know that is how the Gray Men spread? How they thrive? It's okay if you don't, Detective. I'd never dream of holding that against you."

Then, with a long theatrical sigh, almost childlike in its delivery, Matt adds, "But now, duty calls…"

Still coughing, spitting, trying to clear her mouth of the blood that's accumulated there, Stacy rises to her feet. Matt remains towering over her. His body language betrays no signs of fear. But when Stacy's finally standing, she lunges forward, on the attack all at once.

"Well, well, well," he says, "back on your feet alread—"

Except, it's not the boy/man/monster/whatever he might be that Stacy's got her sights set on.

It's his mother. It's Ruth.

Stacy's hands fall against the other woman's shoulders and she shakes her, pushing Ruth back as hard as she can, then drawing her forward to repeat the process all over again.

"Why?" she asks, the question emerging in a rage-filled scream.

More questions follow, delivered in that same manner. "How could you let this happen? Was it worth it? Was it?"

The whole time Stacy's attacking, Ruth won't look the other woman in the eye. She's grown more passive, more defeated, than Stacy ever remembers the headstrong, proud, and defiant

Ruth ever being, even in her lowest moments during the years of Matt's abduction. But before Stacy can do any more damage, a heavy hand grabs her by her neck.

She gasps. The pressure, the power she feels against her skin, something pressing inward slightly, it's like nothing she's felt before.

"Get off of me!" she croaks.

Some Guy replies in a dull monotone, unshaken by the chaos around him: "No."

Then, he lifts Stacy up off the floor of the spaceship. He holds her there, and Stacy doesn't even struggle. Feeling the freakish, inhuman strength of the being holding her, she understands that there's no point in resistance.

Meanwhile, Matt steps behind his mother. His long arms wrap around *her*, and he draws Ruth into his embrace. The son holds the mother, offering her comfort, whispering messages of love and adoration.

"Mother played her role in this. Just as we all did."

Ruth keeps silent.

SENSING THAT SHE must now wait patiently and look for the next opening, if there is one to be found, Stacy takes her time to scan the command deck. Along with the structures that must serve as controls, guidance equipment, or whatever this other lifeform's equivalent may be, there are blister-like giant bubbles emerging from the walls around the foursome. Opaque oval pods press forward from within these bubbles.

There are enough of the pods emerging from the walls that any remaining available space in the room shrinks significantly. Just as with Some Guy's hand abound her neck, Stacy gets the sense of a noose tightening. Except it's not just around her alone. It's coming for them all.

Matt continues. Even at this moment of extreme life-threatening danger, Stacy can't help but note how much the son has grown to be like the mother. Craving the spotlight, fully embracing being the center of attention, the person with all the answers.

"Some Guy was grown for his role. And I…I was changed, made ready for mine. Those who are judged worthy, they will be harvested. Changed to be like them. Like I was. The Gray Men started long before, working in fits and starts. Until me. I was the first hybrid released into the wild, and look how I've demonstrated how worthy we are to join them, to become like them as we add our best and brightest and most fit to their ranks."

As he speaks, the thick opaque film across one of the egg-shaped pods begins to slide open. The sound of the material sloughing away lands somewhere between the rusty creaking of old machinery and an animal's dying groans.

"They're conquerors, infiltrators," Matt says, his eyes locked on the opening pod. "You'd think our fellow human beings would appreciate that. Find common ground."

He points to Some Guy. "Once they learned they couldn't just grow their own versions of us, not exactly, then they decided to make *us* more like them. That's what I am. Like *them*."

The pod stands fully open, yellow and black gases spilling forth from the container. Stacy finally shifts in Some Guy's grasp, bringing her arms up and clapping her hands over her nose and mouth to keep from breathing in too much of whatever noxious substances are spilling forth from the pod. Her eyes widen as a long-limbed, gray-skinned creature puts its bony hands at the sides of the open shell and then places its legs—one, two—onto the spaceship floor.

"Let me tell you," Matt continues, unfazed, even *pleased*, by the new arrival, "it feels *good* to be like them."

The Gray Man steps from the pod, and its clawed feet crunch through the ship's flooring. The techno-organic matter gives way at the touch of one of the beings for whom it was made. Breaking and reforming, breaking again, reforming again, the ship changes with each of the creature's staggering steps.

It's just like Cass said.

Stacy is amazed to see the gray skin, the elevated forehead, the jaws overpacked with too many teeth, the long and spindly limbs with clicking-clacking claws at the ends of its fingertips. And the black eyes. Of course, the black eyes. The Gray Man's nude form is wet, shiny, as electrified goo falls from it with each stuttering step it takes away from the pod.

The Gray Man moves its claws, scratching, rubbing, and tapping them together—the way Cass described their system of communication. Then it stops just as suddenly. Its moves its head from side to side, those black eyes taking in the presence of Earthlings and near-Earthlings on the ship's command deck.

The creature then switches tacks. It opens its mouth as if to speak. But the noise that emerges, it's not speech. *Of course,* Stacy thinks, *why would it be? Why would I expect words, English even?*

The "speech," such as it is, comes as a long, drawn-out hiss instead.

Matt's obviously overjoyed by this development. Smiling, even as his human jaw extends and the alien teeth hidden inside him press forward from the gummy pockets where they've been secreted away.

"They're here," he says, stating the obvious

Ruth's reaction is closer to Stacy's. She turns her face from the Gray Man and presses it to her son's chest. Again, it appears as if their roles are reversed and she's now the one seeking comfort from her son's bosom.

But that's clearly not what he wants for her. "No, no, Mother," he says. "I want you to see, too. I want you to see what I have become—in part, at least. I want you see what I've been dreaming. That you will become as well."

Matt steps back from Ruth, releasing her from his embrace. There's no hesitation in his movements, no second-guessing. He steps around her, striding with purpose, heading for the Gray Man.

"It's okay. She won't bite," he says.

With every step, Matt tosses away another piece of his humanity. Skin stretching, limbs lengthening, claws and teeth popping out where claws and teeth should not be, the pinkish hue of his flesh dimming to a dark gray. And those unforgettable eyes of his go black, reborn as twin abysses. By the time Matt's reached the Gray Man, Stacy finds him far closer in appearance to the alien than to his birth mother. Ruth must see this too, as she suddenly looks so small, so fragile.

The Gray Man's long limbs wrap around Matt's body. And he—it, whatever Matt may have been made into—appears to relish this embrace.

"This was my teacher, my protector, my parent while I was… away. She taught me everything. Prepared me for the harvest of Earth. For the Reaping of the Worthy."

Suddenly, Stacy hears a phlegmy growl from across the shrinking space that stands free of the other emerging pods. She turns from Matt and his Gray Man keeper, and there is Ruth again.

Ruth's eyes go wide. Her nostrils flare. Stacy doesn't have to be psychic, has no need to read minds, to understand what's happening here. Ruth Freeman is finally waking up. This emerging Ruth is more like the one that Stacy remembers. The one who'd go through hell to get her boy back. The one who'd fight all comers to keep her baby safe and get him back in her arms.

"Wait. *What* did you say it was?" Her words are phrased as a question, but it's clear enough that Ruth's not interested in any answer. Besides, Stacy's sure the other woman heard what Matt said, what he called the creature, just as clearly as she did.

A primal scream bursts from Ruth, a shriek liable to shred vocal chords. As her cry quickly fades to a rasp, the spurned mother launches herself at the Gray Man. She pushes her son aside, adrenaline imbuing her with strength beyond human limits. She strikes the alien with slaps and punches, unleashing a flurry of blows.

Stacy hears the crack of Ruth's knuckles against the creature's damp skin. There's a brief pause, but only long enough for Ruth to reach for a holster strapped against her upper thigh and pull out what Stacy eyeballs as a Desert Eagle, a large gun for anyone, but especially for Ruth.

Of course, Ruth's too far gone, too consumed by rage and hate and fear to fire her weapon. Instead, she wields it as a cudgel. Landing blow after blow on the creature's head. Knocking out sharp and jagged teeth, sending green and black blood splashing to the floor.

"You alien bitch!" she rasps. "Get off my son!"

There's a moment when the attacks become so constant, so persistent, so intense that Stacy starts to believe the other woman might actually win. She starts to believe that her nemesis Ruth Freeman really could single-handedly destroy a being from another world.

But reality crashes down on everyone. Swiftly. Definitively.

Ruth's in the midst of screaming, though her voice is barely above a whisper. "He's mine! Mine! Mine! Mi—"

Then, the Gray Man wraps its elongated digits around her wrists and picks her up like a new plaything.

Using only one of its monstrous hands, the Gray Man squeezes both of Ruth's wrists together and holds her aloft, letting her feet dangle and kick as she tries in vain to regain purchase on the floor. As the creature's head tilts, neon green drool spills from the sides of its mouth. Stacy notices how the creature's black eyes appear to search for answers in Matt's own ebon-tinged orbs.

For his part, Matt Freeman moves toward his mother and the alien both. "Mother, no. Why…why are you doing this?" he asks.

For the first time, Stacy hears something close to the shame and disappointment that came from Matt's sister during those long years when she was alone with their mother and Matt was apparently up in the stars, learning to think and be like some being from another world, some *thing* that should be impossible.

He places a hand to his mother's cheek.

Stacy flexes in Some Guy's grasp, testing for weakness. She's surprised to find he's no longer holding her that tight. Wriggling free faster than she expected, Stacy drops, and there's a brief second of panic, a moment when she swallows back a yelp. After all, she figures it's better to be like Some Guy, given her current situation. She figures she too can play the role of silent observer, waiting for the next opportunity to move.

Meanwhile, oily tears roll out from Matt Freeman's blackened eyes.

"I asked them to spare you," he says. "That's why you're here now. I told them you were…one of the good ones. Told them how you'd fought for me, killed for me. I did that all to show you'd be worthy, Mother."

Down on her hands and knees, trying to stay small, trying to remain unnoticed by the participants in the family and extra-terrestrial drama unfolding before her, Stacy scans the ship's floor. She's looking for the gun she suspects Ruth must have dropped when the Gray Man grabbed her.

"Just being on this ship will be enough," Matt continues. "They've got these tiny machines, you're already breathing them in. They're changing you. Making you like me. Like them. Of course, the final surgeries happen back on the homeworld."

Stacy doesn't have time to consider whether those same machines are now inside her lungs, her body, transforming her from the inside out as well. She's moving slowly, one cautious hand sliding forward, then the rest of her following its lead. The spaceship floor pulses at her touch, changing color and consistency to a dusky carbon steel, matching the discarded weapon. In response to the change, Stacy inches along, trying to find Ruth's Desert Eagle by touch alone.

Hoping against hope that it's within reach.

She looks up for a moment, checking to make sure none of the others are tracking her movements. Some Guy might be, but it's impossible for Stacy to be sure. There's a passiveness to his features, a dullness behind the eyes. It's like he's been turned off, powered down. She doesn't believe she'll have anything to worry about from him.

At least not at this particular moment.

Instead, she looks to the mother, the son, and the Gray Man from another world. They make for a most unlikely trinity.

Ruth's voice comes at a tremble.

"Matty," she says, "I don't *want* to be like you."

Stacy's hand closes around the hilt of the Desert Eagle as Ruth speaks her final words. The sudden contact with the weapon sends a shock, a jolt of intense relief, fear, and uncertainty all rolled into one, coursing through Stacy's body.

But that sensation is counteracted almost at once.

Because the Gray Man takes its free hand, its claws curved like a raptor's talons, and slashes through the midsection of the woman it holds above spaceship floor. The sound of claws through flesh is wet and slick, reminding Stacy of soaked and sudsy laundry spilling from a broken washing machine.

Except instead of shirts and socks and towels all stuck together in a grayish-white blob, it's blood and guts and all the rest of Ruth's insides suddenly brought to the outside. They all fall from her body. The crack of those claws through gristle and meat, severing bones until the bottom half of the mother drops to the ground and all that's left is the top half in the Gray Man's control, dribbling gore into the segmented floor that's greedy for a mess of this type to clean—those are sounds Stacy will never be able to shake from her mind. Not for as long as she is alive.

CHAPTER 54

STACY KNOWS TWO things. One: She's in over her head. Cosmically over her head. She just witnessed a woman being torn apart by an alien creature. Some gray-skinned, ashen-featured monster, looking like a rejected design from a bad sci-fi horror flick. Except it's very real. It's right in front of her. And it's not alone. It's joined by a test-tube-grown approximation of a human being. Like a person made from Play-Doh and imbued with life. Pale and unblemished pseudo-skin, impossibly strong. But also… just *Some Guy*.

And then, there's the boy.

No, not a boy. Not anymore. But not a man either. Not even all the way human.

The other *was* a boy once upon a time. But then he got lost. More lost than anyone ever suspected. Anyone except for one girl—his sister. A girl who died because no one she loved believed her and because Stacy didn't fight hard enough for her. That's what Stacy thinks, at least. Meanwhile, the lost boy came back more monster than man. Like the boy, the man he would've been is now lost forever.

There's one more thing Stacy knows. She's absolutely sure of it as she runs through the facts as they stand.

Two: Stacy doesn't give a damn how over her head she is, how out of her element she's found herself.

Because now she's got the big fucking gun and she's aiming it at Matt Freeman and his Gray Man.

"Freeze!" she shouts, falling back on her old training.

It's as if the Gray Man is only now at this exact moment noticing Stacy's presence on the spaceship. Its head snaps with a click and buzz toward the sound of Stacy's voice. Its oblong silhouette tilts, its mouth opens wide, and its long tongue lashes forward from oversized jaws.

Before it can make another sound, Stacy's voice comes as cool, calm, and collected as she can manage.

"Don't—" she starts, but must leave her warning unfinished.

Despite Stacy's restrained calm, the Gray Man (*or Woman?*) appears unfazed, determined to kill this other human woman as swiftly and thoroughly as it did Ruth Freeman, whose body is even now being slowly and meticulously absorbed and consumed by the ship's semipermeable flooring. The Gray Man opens its mouth wide and sprays its neon green spittle everywhere.

Stacy keeps a firm grip on the gun, her finger resting on the trigger. She's prepared to pull the trigger at the slightest provocation. Of course, she's never had to deal with a monster in her previous firearms training, so it's all new territory for her.

When the creature lunges for her, its long limbs propel it farther than she might've anticipated. Suddenly, the distance between them is closing fast, and Stacy's forced to do the only thing she can to stay alive.

She pulls the trigger once, then twice. Bullets explode from the barrel, the gun's recoil slamming Stacy back on her heels with each firing.

She cries out, her shouts accompanying each explosive firing. Her own vocalizations are almost loud enough to match the thunder of the gun and the resulting sounds of the wrathful Gray Man as it's struck once, twice at near point-blank range. The cacophony echoes, noises overlapping, one on top of the other, then repeating, resonating through the command deck.

Stacy fights to stay upright. But, as the stress her body's already undergone combines with the recoil of the Desert

Eagle, she finds herself on the losing end of a battle with gravity. Her heels slip from under her, and she lands hard on her ass. The short, sharp shock of pain causes her to yelp.

And, as if synchronized with Stacy's exclamation, the Gray Man's shadow falls across her prone form. Black and green blood spills from twin wounds in the extraterrestrial's center mass. Its momentum carries it forward, clawed hands slashing for Stacy—or perhaps clicking outs its final words. But the Gray Man's already losing power, running out of steam.

Dying.

The Gray Man crashes to the floor, just short of reaching Stacy. It's done moving. Whatever substance courses through its form spills in undulating waves onto the indiscriminately ravenous deck instead.

Stacy's out of words, out of breath. All she can do is continue pointing the gun at the Gray Man's head in case it moves, twitches, exhibits any sign of life whatsoever. Stacy finds she's able to breathe again. The sound made by her panting breaths is only barely surpassed by the mournful cry coming from Matt Freeman after witnessing the destruction of the Gray Man. *His* Gray Man.

"Noooooooo!"

With one threat eliminated, Stacy's immediately under attack from the next. Matt's half-human, half-alien arm shoots forward, and he drags Stacy to her feet. Their contact's brief but impactful. Claws pinch at her shoulder, and then she's flung across the command deck.

She slams against a pod-covered wall. Her body aches from the impact. First, her spine strikes one of the curved pod covers, then she slides to the floor.

Stacy's seeing double. There's a split image of Matt Freeman before her. Part human, part alien, the two halves overlapping, then separating, then coming together again. He moves toward her at a jittering pace, like footage from a film reel missing select frames.

Until finally, the part-man part-monster has Stacy in his clawed grasp once more. He pulls her to her feet again. The deep tan of his human flesh ripples with the gray alien skin implanted under the surface. He screams at her, the noise breaking through her dazed and disoriented state.

"Get up!"

Using his engorged, extra-long tongue as a lash, he slaps it against her face. The warm and sticky sensation makes Stacy whimper as it stings one cheek and then the next.

"Do you have any idea what you've done?" he screams. "And for what? Why?"

His shouted questions are a step too far though. They serve as a final wake-up call. Bruised and bloodied, with rust-red streaks in her gray hair, Stacy stares into the all-black insectoid eyes of Matt Freeman. Defiance radiates from her.

"That was for your sister," she says, letting her eyes drift to the Gray Man's corpse.

Matt's next cry is an incoherent bellow. Still holding Stacy but now turning her so she's facing away from him, squeezing a little harder at her neck, he drags her across the command deck. With his free hand, he makes broad, sweeping gestures. The pods on one wall slide away, and suddenly it's as if the pulsing, humming material from which the ship's walls are constructed has become translucent. Instead of fleshy gray segmented pieces, Stacy looks out to a complete and utter darkness, a seeming infinity of nothingness.

It's an impossibly vast emptiness, enough to make Stacy want to cry. Enough to tempt her to curl up and die.

"Do you see now?" Matt asks. "Earth's gone. We're farther away than anyone from our planet has ever even dreamed of going. There's no one coming to save you."

Stacy gives silent thanks to Matt Freeman in that moment. His arrogant, mocking taunts pull her back from the edge of the abyss. She finds herself focused on the here and now.

"Well, then, I guess I'll have to save myself," she rasps.

Before he can react, Stacy brings her elbow up and drives it back full force into Matt's neck, striking his Adam's apple. Stunned, he loses his grip on her and stumbles backward. Stacy falls the short distance to the floor. She rises to her feet as fast as she can while Matt hacks and coughs, trying to catch his breath.

She spots a doorway up ahead leading out of the command deck. Stacy takes off at as close to a sprint as she can manage at her age and in her battered condition. Some Guy stands in her path, unmoving, unfazed. He makes no attempt to stop her when Stacy elbows past him. He stands there staring at nothing, letting her go past.

CHAPTER 55

WHEN THE HYBRID Freeman-Matt grabs the shoulder of the entity bearing the colloquial designation "Some Guy," the Hybrid expresses his displeasure in harsh, barking tones.

"Stop her!" he shouts. "Why didn't you stop her?"

The answer from the vat-grown entity called Some Guy is immediate, stripped of pretense or obfuscation. He wasn't designed with those traits available while communicating to those of his subspecies. "I do not take commands from you, Hybrid Freeman-Matt. My psychic link is severed with the death of the Parent…"

Some Guy's enhanced eyes, engineered to allow him to see much further and understand much more than any Earthlings might suspect, drift to the ruined body of the creature called a "Gray Man," whose true name Some Guy can never properly pronounce because he was made in the image of Earth's dominant species and not that of his creator's planet. But one look is enough.

Hybrid Freeman-Matt leaves Some Guy's side. He heads for the ship's corridors, following the path taken by the fleeing Human Keppler-Stacy. Ranting, defiant, and still quite human to Some Guy's way of understanding, the Hybrid cries out, declaring his intention for revenge. "Useless! Fine! I'll kill her myself!"

CHAPTER 56

STACY HAS NO idea where she is. Not when it comes to the corridors and rooms on this spaceship from another world. Not in the cosmos as a whole.

She's lost.

Her heart and mind are racing, each going full steam ahead, showing she's got some fight left in her still. She crouches behind some of the ruined wormlike appendages, yanked down from their mooring in the ceiling and stomped, smashed into submission by Stacy in a desperate move to hide herself. The unnatural unspooled lengths of techno-organic matter are piled high enough to offer her some coverage.

Only for a moment though. Only until I catch my breath, and then...

And then...

Stacy looks down at her trembling hand. But it's not the shaking member that makes her gasp. It's the way there appears to be something moving under her skin, her flesh and muscle and bone shifting together as if liquefied, changing before Stacy's eyes.

"Oh my God..." she says.

"No, not Him."

It's Matt. He's found the woman who spent so many years searching for him. He towers over her, seeming to revel in his dominant position.

The Desert Eagle fires, Stacy pulling its trigger.

But her fingers twitch, her hand shakes. So, she fires a second time.

Twin explosions bloom between her and the man-monster. Again.

Her ears ring with such force that Stacy starts to think she'll be able to see the soundwaves hit her skull and bounce off again. But when she goes to pull the trigger a third time, she's met by a solitary and impotent *click.*

The sulfur stench fills Stacy's nostrils as she cries out in defeat and disappointment, "No, no, no…"

As the smoke and other particulate clear away, Stacy discovers that Matt's still standing. Grazed in the shoulder and leg, bleeding slightly from the gunfire, but still very much alive. In appearance, he's almost entirely Gray Man. Muscles bulge beneath his stretched-thin, motley-hued skin. His bulging jaw of needle-sharp teeth makes it almost impossible for his words to be heard or understood. Yet Stacy's certain she gets the gist of his retort.

"*Yes.*"

Stacy gets back on her feet, all the time understanding that Matt is letting her do so. Toying with her.

Still, she pulls the trigger again.

Click.

"Please…" She can't come up with any other words capable of supporting her case or conveying her desperation.

Matt reaches for Stacy with his talons and grabs her by the neck. The razor-sharp edges of his claws pinch the skin and lift the woman off the ground. A thin trickle of blood runs from these fresh wounds on Stacy's neck.

One wrong move, one twitch from Matt, and Stacy's decapitation will be an afterthought. So she stays as still as she can, not ready to give in to death's siren song. Something, some not-yet-depleted reservoir of a will to live, keeps her going.

AFTER CARRYING HER back to the command deck, bringing her back to the screen into the void of deep space, Matt presses Stacy's face against whatever transparent material allows them to view this never-ending vista of starlessness.

"It's beautiful, isn't it? You're seeing something no one else you know back on Earth will get to see. Those chosen for the harvest and changed like I was, they will serve as the next vanguard, preparing the way over years and years for the next reaping."

Stacy remains quiet, staying still as she can be. But she sucks in a quick breath when Matt reverts his face to its more human form, pressing his gaunt cheek to hers. "Think about what we're sharing, Detective."

His lips part, and the blackened alien tongue surgically implanted to replace the one he was born with slithers out. Writhing like a snake, it appears desperate to burrow into Stacy's ear. But that won't happen yet. Not until Matt fires off one last mocking quip.

"After all this time," he says, "you've *finally* found me."

"No!" With a cry, Stacy's hand comes up and slashes down at Matt's repellent tongue. Except it's not *her* hand, not the one she remembers, the one she's had all her life. It's a stretched-out, inhuman mockery of a woman's hand, *her* fingers tipped with the same curved talon-like claws. Like Matt's transformed hands, like the Gray Man's natural appendages. Fast and strong, Stacy's new claws slash through the slick meat of her captor's tongue, severing it near the root.

It's no calculated move on Stacy's part. It's a desperate attempt to stave off destruction. It's a close call. But it works.

Taken by surprise, Matt opens his claws far enough for Stacy to slip through. She hits the floor again. Beside her, the inert lump of Matt Freeman's tongue lands with a wet *smack*. Above her, the returned son, the traitor to Earth, has blood pouring from the ragged wound in his open mouth, baptizing Stacy anew.

She takes a half-second too long watching and misses her chance to move. Even as more black-spotted blood spills from his mouth, Matt recovers enough to use his taloned hand to grab Stacy again, this time wrenching her up by her gray hair. He lifts her up, then slams her down. Fast. Hard. He leaves her no time to think, to act, only time to absorb the sudden impact.

The command deck echoes with the sound of Stacy's nose crunching inward and her teeth breaking. Some of her teeth chip, and others she swallows whole, traveling roughly down her throat. There's a tiny voice in her head, pleading with her to let go now. To give in to the death that Matt Freeman seems so determined to gift her. Her parents are gone, and her brother, the girl she wanted to protect, her partner, probably the whole damn planet. Jeff.

Darkness creeps at the edges of Stacy's consciousness, making a compelling case for eternal rest.

But then, another voice breaks through on the mental wire, loud and sarcastic and forever bound to tease and prod his big sister. It arrives at the split second when she needs it the most. A memory of one of Xavier's many rambling yet always entertaining rants or raves about technology, about the way the world's supposed to work and how it actually works and the strange intersections where those two sides meet.

What was it he said?

"When all else fails, just hit the biggest button you see."

Stacy's bloodshot eyes dart here and there. Her vision cloudy with crimson, she gasps for breaths that her attacker seems determined to deny her. Finally, she locks on to a large protuberant obstruction bursting from one of the growths on the floor of the command deck. Though not an exact match to Stacy's human expectations, it sure as hell looks close enough to a big button for her purposes.

Now, all she's got to do is reach out and touch it.

Of course, that's easier said than done. Matt's pulling her up again, preparing to drive her down into the floor. There's an unstable intensity to his movement. The signs are clear: He means for this to be the killing blow.

But Stacy locks her knees, trying to stand firm, to remain unmoved unless she's the one doing the moving. Towards that goal, she stretches out with hands that appear human once again. She reaches for the button-like growth and the vague, uncertain promise of salvation that it might hold.

But she can't reach it. Not with the hands she was born with, at least. It's too far away.

Stacy moans with bodily pain and mental frustration. After all, she's traveled so far, sacrificed so much.

And now her body seems poised to let her down.

No, no, I won't accept that.

This time, the change is deliberate. This time, Stacy focuses and wills her hand to change. The longer, talon-tipped alien-hybrid appendage reemerges, accompanied by Stacy's scream at the pain of rebirthing a part of herself into this new foreign configuration.

But for all the pain, the change is enough. One graying finger extends and presses down on the "button."

The next thing Stacy knows, the transparent material on the wall that showed them deep space moments before slides away. There's a roar, but it's in Stacy's head, as all sound is sucked out into the void. The pull of the starless infinite takes hold of everything and everyone present on the command deck.

Above Stacy, Matt Freeman stumbles. She uses the opportunity to slam her clawed hands into the flooring. She squeezes, gripping the techno-organic material, trying to keep herself anchored to the floor.

The pull of space's vacuum is much stronger than she could've anticipated, however. She's dragged backward toward the opening, her talons carving long, gouging marks in the floor. But she keeps digging deeper, fighting for every inch. Determined to stay on board.

Taken by surprise, Matt isn't so lucky. He's blown backward, yanked out of the ship and slammed into the inky nothingness of space.

Stacy, still holding on tight to the floor, turns her head toward the opening. She discovers Matt close but also too far away to cause any real harm. His mouth opens wide in a silent scream. Black eyes fill with hate, focused on her and the way she continues holding on, fighting to stay alive.

A new shadow falls across Stacy's face. It takes her half a moment, a return glance to the ship's interior, to realize what's casting the shade. She ducks, pressing her body as flat to the floor as possible.

The remains of Ruth Freeman and the Gray Man, an unnatural jumble of human and alien corpse pieces, come hurtling through the opening. Matt, fully transformed and trying to claw his way through the dark and return to the command deck, has no time to get out of their way. His mothers—human and alien both—slam into him. All three fall backward into the void.

Eyes bulging from his skull, ice crystals forming on a face half-man and half-monster—if Matt has any final words to offer the universe, they go unheard, unacknowledged.

Stacy doesn't get the luxury of watching him float away and die. The pull of space is just as hard on her. She fights to dig her claws in deeper, to keep herself secured.

But she's slipping. She understands this with every fiber of her being.

Crystallized tears of blood spill from eyes beginning to glaze over. Her limbs are stretched beyond endurance. There's a necrotizing process ready to work its way through her limbs. The darkness is closer now. Closer than it's ever been before.

Stacy bows her head. She closes her eyes, giving into the darkness at last.

Then, she lets go, pulling her claws free from the ship's floor, preparing to float into the empty space at her back.

CHAPTER 57

AS HER HEAD fills with the aching pain of nothingness trying to have its way with her, Stacy lets go. But just as suddenly, she's taken by surprise as Some Guy grabs her, pulling her back to the ship and into his embrace.

He's strong. Impossibly so. Powerful enough to hold her close with one arm. With the other, he reaches over and slams his fist down on that big "button" that Stacy pressed not even a full minute beforehand.

The opening closes. The window-like covering returns. Sound follows. The rush of air correcting itself on the command deck allows Stacy to catch her breath. Even so, she feels weak, pushed past her limits, and stretched across the floor. Her back rises and falls with hitching, ragged tremors.

Some Guy looms over her. Silent, waiting.

Finally, Stacy feels good enough to roll onto her back and look up at her savior. Her unexpected rescuer. Her words come in a sharp wheeze. "What the hell just happened?"

Some Guy looks at Stacy with something akin to bemusement on his normally muted, unfazed features.

"You survived," he answers.

Some Guy doesn't offer a hand, and Stacy's glad for it. She pushes up against the ship's pulsing floor with her palms. Coughing blood between aspirated breaths, shaking, she expects she'd have been dead ten times over already if not for the alien presences inside her body, in her cells, those micro-scopic techno-organic entities remaking her for a life in the stars.

It's a poisoned chalice she's had a drink from, and the emotional pain coursing through her isn't as easily healed as her physical wear and tear.

Once she's on her feet and steadied enough, she stands by Some Guy, taking his measure through her blood-clouded eyes. He doesn't shy away from her inspection. It seems clear he has no conception of modesty or shame or any other feeling that might make him human.

"You killed my brother," she says.

She's so fucking tired. *So, so fucking tired.* That's the best she can manage under these circumstances.

"I did." His answer is simple, unembellished.

If there was no follow-up or further explanation, Stacy would still have no cause to believe she was entitled to anything more. Part of her wonders if this acceptance comes from the alien tech, that other part of her…it simply knows where the limits are and knows better than to press on.

Still, she *is* surprised when Some Guy continues.

"I am also the only being capable of piloting this craft. And the only one willing to help you…and them."

His last two words result in Stacy looking around the command deck. Observing the oblong pods jutting out from the walls like sores and blisters. They gleam under a pulsating glow, pregnant with possibility.

One silver-coated pod slides open. Stacy balls her hands into fists. Even with whatever changes are taking place under her surface, she still feels the ache of joint pains, the arthritis that used to flare up every now and then, putting in another appearance for old time's sake. She can't imagine she'll last long against another Gray Man. But she'll be damned if she's going to come this far just to roll over and die.

The pod opens.

Then, *a young human woman* steps onto the command deck. Blonde hair sprayed to Jesus, a cut-up pink sweatshirt and black skirt with lace stockings, Doc Martens. A teenager, to look at her. A human teenager from the good old planet Earth. Maybe from a few decades prior to the present moment. But still...

Her eyes are wide; she's shivering.

Stacy's own eyes go wide. She knows this girl. This is *the* girl. The one her parents went looking for. Her bottom lip trembles. Her knees knock together. Her mind races with the understanding of how close they must have come.

Just like me.

"Jennifer...Jennifer Ervin..."

Stacy's former classmate, preserved as she was when she was taken, nods. But her confusion is clear. The girl's trying to puzzle out where she is and who Stacy is. When she speaks, her voice is scratchy, strident, and harsh from disuse. "Missus... Keppler?"

If only, Stacy thinks, before mouthing a silent "no." The Mrs. Keppler that this time-frozen Jennifer knew is long, long gone.

The next pod opens with a *click* and a *hiss* before Stacy's fully absorbed the identity of the first pod's inhabitant.

The next to emerge is an Indigenous male, twenty-something. Straight black hair down his back. His puffy Charlotte Hornets Starter Jacket adds new color to the kaleidoscopic display beneath the deck lights as they bounce off the turquoise and purple and green. His knuckles are scabbed over like he's been in a fight. But there's a weariness behind his eyes, suggesting that whatever scuffle he was last a part of, it ended long before he stood face to face with Stacy Keppler on an alien spaceship.

Then, another pod opens.

Click, hiss.

It's just a boy. Asian. Sucking his thumb. A cloth diaper is secured with a clothespin around his chunky toddler thighs.

Click, hiss.

Another woman. Leather bomber jacket, ruffled white shirt, jodhpurs. A determined fierceness and flashiness in her eyes, her smile. Like she's wrapped up one adventure and is set to take off on the next. There's something so familiar about her.

Like she's someone famous. Someone who might even be in the history books.

Or maybe that's just the impression Stacy gets, given the scarf around the woman's neck and the leather flying helmet and goggles on her head.

Could it be...is that...her?

Then, another pod's opening.

And another.

And another.

And another.

Click, hiss. Click, hiss. Click, hiss.

As one pod opens and its inhabitant—very clearly from Earth—emerges, that pod slides away, absorbed into the ship's walls. Then, the next one opens, repeating the process. On and on until Stacy is no longer anywhere close to being alone. She's surrounded, crowded on all sides by others just like her. Others lost, confused, taken from their homes. Taken very, *very* far from their homes.

Shocked by the overwhelming sea of humanity in which she now finds herself, almost trancelike—partly from the blood loss, partly from the shock—Stacy's brought back to reality when a blonde girl, one dressed like she's stepped straight from small-town America in the 1980s, steps over and takes Stacy's hand in her own.

And why wouldn't she? After all, Stacy might just be the first person—from Earth—that this young woman's seen in quite a while. "Excuse me, ma'am," the girl says, her voice a whisper, dry and uncertain from long disuse, "where are we?"

Stacy wipes sweat and blood from her face with her free hand. The other one keeps hold of the girl's offered grasp. She squeezes tight, not caring if it hurts both of them a little bit. Stacy knows her words will matter more to the girl—whoever she might be or have been. And Stacy's ready to give those words, without hesitation, without second-guessing.

"You're with me," she says. "And you're safe. I promise you that."

STACY STANDS ON the command deck with Some Guy. Those survivors who can handle the responsibility have set up shifts to monitor their progress as the vat-grown humanoid pilots the spaceship through the cosmos. Stacy's taken more shifts than anyone else. She's grown to appreciate the dark spreading out before their vessel, punctuated with brilliant bursts of light from stars and planets. It's a good time to think, even though she's found no answers or obvious conclusions.

She talks. Partly to herself, just to hear her own voice and remember who she is. Who she's tried to be and who she hoped to become in the next phase of her life. Partly to Some Guy. She hasn't forgiven him for the violence she knows he's committed or the violence she suspects he committed. But she understands that he may be beyond concepts like guilt or responsibility.

If nothing else, this tabula rasa of a life-form has proven to be an excellent sounding-board, rarely offering a response or reciprocal communication of any kind.

"The others are adjusting as well as can be expected to the news of us being light-years away from Earth. Not to mention the very likely possibility that Earth's been destroyed, invaded, harvested, whatever the hell *they* had planned," she says.

She allows silence to hang between them for a moment before she continues. "I suppose that's got something to do with the alien technology or whatever the Freeman kid called it, that stuff that's inside us now, huh?"

Through the transparent window on the command deck, Stacy spies massive shapes on their approach. Some Guy is hooked into the ship, segmented cords having descended from the ceiling and burrowed under his smooth, pale flesh. The dangling appendages connecting the ship to Some Guy pulse and throb with an exchange of energy, fluids, and Stacy can only imagine what else. His hands sweep across the control panels. His expression remains as blank as ever.

He gives nothing away about the path they're on or what further difficulties might lie ahead.

Knowing Some Guy's reticence to share, Stacy's always a little surprised when he does answer in his dull monotone.

"You are correct, Hybrid Keppler-Stacy," he says.

Stacy shivers at being called "Hybrid," but recovers fast enough. Or so she hopes.

"Good, good," she says.

Then, she asks her next question—the one she's held back for as long as she could.

"So, tell me…where are we going?"

She points to a cluster of stars in the distance and to rocky planet-sized shadow shapes nearby.

"Isn't it obvious?" Some Guy asks.

Then, the view screen fills with the cresting top of a planetoid. Massive, solid. Mountainous in parts, red and desertlike, similar to Mars back in the old Milky Way. But interspersed with and threaded by blue and green, swirling white clouds overhead. *Water.*

Life.

Stacy notices the explosions next. Bursting trails of smoke and fire rising from the planet's surface. It takes another moment of study, of concentration, before she can follow one or two of those trails to their source.

Spaceships, looking just like the alien craft they're all aboard, rise upward from the planet's surface.

"Isn't it obvious?" Some Guy repeats. "We're going *home.*"

ACKNOWLEDGMENTS

WOW. SO, IT'S finally here. The path to publication can sometimes feel as difficult as humanity's trek to the stars. I can certainly say that this novel would not have achieved lift-off without a number of key people who deserve and have more than earned whatever kind of brief spotlight I can provide here.

First, my thanks to Rob Carroll of Dark Matter INK. We had discussed me writing something for Dark Matter before, and I really appreciated his patience and insights. Having a publisher who's clear in communications and can tell you exactly what they want is an underrated asset. I'm so happy that *Abducted* happened to check the necessary boxes. And the work he's done has extended far beyond the green light to launch. Rob's cover design and interior formatting speak to his own creativity and Dark Matter INK's commitment to producing beautiful, yet accessible books in the speculative fiction genres.

Of course, great leaders can also be measured by the strength and capability of those who work with them. To that end, I'm greatly appreciative to Rob for putting the enthusiastic and insightful Maddie Leary on Team *Abducted* as my editor. Maddie's work helped push me creatively. She never allowed me to settle for good enough. Her queries and suggestions elevated my output and the finished story as a result.

And then the story is finalized, and the novel (my first) is a real and tangible thing—a dream solidified. Now, to get the word out about it…

Helping to kickstart these efforts, the trio of authors who provided blurbs for this book are deserving of much praise and accolades. Ai Jiang (who also deserves thanks for connecting me with Rob in the first place), Renan Bernardo, Stephen S. Schreffler, and Jendia Gammon: your kind and thoughtful words about this book and the story I've told here are worth their weight in gold. I treasure them.

Finally, I turn my parade of thanks to the more nebulous origins of my writing—both in terms of the early dream aspect and the day-after-day, butt-in-chair, hands-on-keyboard practical execution of said dream. Thanks Mom and Dad for believing in your weird son and encouraging him to make up stories. I know it was a long, long road to get here. But what a view, huh?

Thank you to my family. To Grant, Avery, and Jenna. You are my sun. Everything revolves around you. Without your support and love, I don't think I'd make it as far as I have. *Ad astra per aspera*, right? I hope those stars shine extra bright for you always. Boys, as I told your Mom when we got married: I love you more than I love you.

Oh, and one last bonus thanks. Thank you to the person reading this novel. Thank you for taking a chance on this story. I hope you enjoy spending time with Stacy, Ruth, Xavier, Zamuda, Cassie, Matt, and all the rest. I promise we'll clean up the mess and see ourselves out when we're done.

—Patrick Barb

ABOUT THE AUTHOR

PATRICK BARB is an author of weird, dark, and horrifying tales, currently living (and trying not to freeze to death) in Saint Paul, Minnesota. His published works include his debut sci-fi/horror novel *Abducted*, the dark fiction collections *The Children's Horror* and *Pre-Approved for Haunting*, the novellas *The Nut House, Night of the Witch-Hunter,* and *JK-LOL,* as well as the novelette *Helicopter Parenting in the Age of Drone Warfare.* In addition, he is the editor and publisher of the anthology *And One Day We Will Die: Strange Stories Inspired by the Music of Neutral Milk Hotel,* and runs the monthly interview column "Your Favorite Author's Favorite Author" in *Shortwave Magazine.* His 2023 short story "The Scare Groom" was selected for *Best Horror of the Year Volume 16.* Visit him at patrickbarb.com.

EXPERIENCE *ABDUCTED* IN AUDIO

Scan the QR code below to sample or purchase *Abducted* in audiobook, narrated by Jessica Gurd.